TWIZZLE

William Ambrose

ISBN: 1467965677
ISBN-13: 978-1467965675

DEDICATION

For Phyllis, the biggest Twizzle I ever knew

ACKNOWLEDGMENTS

There are several people without whom this book would never have happened. First I want to thank my wife for being the crusty bread in my life. Thanks to Mel Chezidek who showed that there was even a road to go down. Phyllis Flatt for her unending support and for preventing this book from becoming one long run on sentence. Even her "I hate you" was very supportive. A big thank you to Debbie Schultz for her keen eye, it saved many hours of work, Thanks to all those that I've hunted and fished with. A very special thank you to Stacy Cameron for all her help and patience while doing the artwork for the cover. A heartfelt thank you to our armed forces past and present that protected my right to freely write my story.

Chapter 1

A recent Gallup poll was conducted asking people about their beliefs on guardian angels. Do they exist and what do they look like? There was a wide range of opinions. The answers the pollsters received ran the full spectrum. There were non-believers, who curiously enough took the most time answering the survey when a simple "No" or head nod to dismiss the question would have sufficed. On the other side of the spectrum were the elderly church going ladies. Women with a blue tint to their hair who smelled of lilac perfume their grandchildren bought them for some holiday. Thick ankled women dressed in house coats, who covered their heads with kerchiefs before heading into church which they attended daily. They dipped arthritic fingers in holy water and blessed themselves before entering. Women who, when they prayed, prayed with all their heart and soul. These women needed to believe that there has to be something, something more. Something beyond this earth that hasn't treated them so kindly. Yet these women never prayed for divine intervention, their prayers weren't for winning lotto tickets or cars. These were prayers of thanks for what little had been bestowed upon them. Women who used the phrase "Thank you Jesus" or "Lord thank you" several times daily.

When asked to describe a guardian angel, these pious women were all like minded. There was no hesitation about the answer. Their angels were the Sistine Chapel Angels, with a bit of Cecil B. DeMille's Hollywood leading man thrown in. Tall, broad shouldered, strong jaw line with maybe a Kirk Douglas cleft. We are not talking about some little nymph winged pixie. These guys are the F-16 of God's fighter squadron. All over 6'2" with tight muscles and a panther-like agility. Able to wield the heavily engraved broadsword each wore fastened to their waist in a golden sheath. These are your apex Angels.

Others surveyed believed in more of the Walt Disney version of a guardian angel. Scantily clad, barefoot, pixie. These, for some reason, were always female. Watching her never ending stop and go movement, it's not hard to believe somewhere in her ancient lineage there is hummingbird mixed in the bloodline. These guardian angels seem to always have a soft glow to them as if backlit by a 40 watt bulb. A perfect little nymph that Disney himself would burst with pride over. Though, she's not much in a fight with demons for your soul. Tinker Bell might have a magic wand which can light up the sky over the Magic Kingdom on a Thursday night. However, when push comes to shove over my soul, I want the church ladies' version angels, swinging that broadsword, not a pixie with a sewing needle. If I'm looking for a 4th of July light show, Tinker Bell's my go to girl. For fights with Satan's lapdogs, I'm calling in those winged apex angels.

Some Puerto Rican up in the Bronx, when asked if he believed in guardian angels said, "Hell yeah! One of dems rides the number sis with me in the mornin'. Red beret and all those medals - like he some kinda bato ass soldier or sometin'. Never seen him stop no crime though. Why? You lookin' for him? What he do?"

When the pollster tried to explain what he was researching, the Puerto Rican walked away as if this stranger's allotted time had expired. He then turned and faded into the crowd.

Guardian angels are not God's mercenaries or little fairies. They're just some soul that hasn't quite made it through the pearly gates. They were too busy checking out the new surroundings and not paying attention when they got called by Saint Peter or one of the other gatekeepers. Yes I know, you were taught in school that Saint Peter had the book of souls and personally checked everyone in. That may have worked out ok back in biblical times when there were maybe 100,000 souls a year he was dealing with. Now it's a high volume business. He's doing in three days what he used to do in a year. He isn't getting any younger so he had to get some help. There was even some thought to putting in a second gate, but pimping out a gate that size embedded with pearls is a lost art. They could have gone with cheaper materials, but truthfully, who wants to go through the rhinestone gates.

Rhinestone gates are for the passageway to a Siegfried and Roy spectacular starring albino tigers and tall buxom showgirls, flashing cleavage and smiles as bright as the neon signs out on the Strip. Include an all you can eat buffet that's guaranteed to clog one's arteries. Bachelor parties of young, dumb, drunken 20 year olds with sperm counts higher than their I.Q. Chain-smoking seniors who've lost the last of their Social Security checks to ravenous slot machines and are waiting for the bus back to the condo. That is what lies in wait on the other side of rhinestone gates.

So, to keep busy and remain in Saint Peter's good graces, guardian angels keep an eye on us earthly souls. Most are quite fastidious in their duties. Watching and waiting patiently to step in and alter a person's path to keep them out of harm's way. Everyone has heard or read about someone who, for some

3

unexplainable reason, was in the right place at the right time to save someone. We've all heard stories about some guy who catches the baby who's fallen from a balcony. In interviews he states, "I don't know, I just happened to look up," and, "I didn't even make the baseball team back in school, I could never catch the ball!"

How do mothers know their children are up to some mischief when the house is too quiet? "I have eyes in the back of my head," they claim. A mother's intuition, others call it. It's really just guardian angels stepping in.

There are certain saves that, if Heaven had a newspaper, would be front page material. We'd see little angels on cloud corners barking out, "Here ye, Here ye! Read all about it! Angel saves man from Mountain Lion!" Or, "Car rolls over 6 times on highway, driver unscathed!" However most are just ordinary saves. They occur all around you. You just need to pay attention to see or hear them. A mother yelling at a child, "You could have broken your neck!" Or the golden oldie, "You're damn lucky you didn't poke your sister's eye out with that thing!"

Signs that an angel has stepped in to save the day are, a trembling parent hugging their child so tight the kid can hardly breathe. Another is a parent that is so scared and mad, all at the same time, that they are marching the child down the street. The parent usually has a death grip on the child's arm and walking so fast that the kid only touches the ground every fourth or fifth step. This child is normally sentenced to his room with strict orders that not a single solitary peep should be heard emanating from their room. Another sure fire sign is the sound of a car tire screeching. Well that's not really the sign, it's not hearing the crashing sound right afterwards, and that's the true sign. Though it could be angels just messing with us to keep us on our toes.

There's no doubt about it, guardian angel work is not for the faint of heart. It's a grueling 24/7 job. No holidays as the holidays are their busy season. Imagine this: Little Johnny finally gets his Red Ryder BB gun for Christmas. He's not waiting to go outside and shoot dad's empty beer cans. Not when there is a perfectly good Cocker Spaniel he can terrorize around the house. That's when a guardian angel has to jump into action. The Red Ryder's box under the Christmas tree is too big to make disappear. The tube of copper BB's that is just small enough to get lost in all the wrapping paper, that colored paper with Currier & Ives scenes or Santa and his Reindeers. An angel surely could get a small tube of BB's mixed into that mess. Especially with mom scooping up all the shredded paper and bows, sighing over each pile she tosses into the garbage bag. Mom's into her third spiced rum eggnog. She'll never feel that extra little bit of weight from the BB's. Her mind is on the roast in the oven and how ungrateful a lot her family is. No one even took notice of how expertly wrapped the presents were. That the ribbons were hand curled by running them over a scissor's blade to make them curl up just so. Each bow was selected to match perfectly with the paper. Seams on the wrapping paper so expertly aligned it would bring a tear to a Drill Sergeant's eye.

Guardian angels really need to be able to think fast on their feet and use whatever is around them. There is no on the job training. It's baptism by fire. You have to hit the ground running. Keep your wits about you. Anticipate and react. This isn't an episode of *I Dream of Jeannie* where crossing your arms and nodding your head makes things happen. Angels don't have Elizabeth Montgomery's *Bewitched* talents. No nose twitch and the salt shaker across the room obediently starts to sprinkle its content.

They do have the ability to conjure up things for themselves; they just can't use them to help those they're guarding. This job takes guile. It's accomplished by an idea placed in someone's head. The heebie jeebies, the willies - these are some of the tools of the trade. Phobias: phobias of snakes, spiders, darkness and heights are all in a guardian angel's bag of tricks. The ace in the hole of all tricks is using your pet.

If you have ever sat on your couch and stared at your dog and thought, "He knows everything I'm saying," you win a prize, because you're absolutely correct. Your pet knows all your secrets. The things you mutter under your breath. They read your body language, your scent. You give off a different scent when you are going to take Fido to the park instead of playing hoops with your buddies. You can lie to others, you can even lie to yourself, but you can't lie to your pet. It's one of the main reasons angels use our pets to help guard us.

How someone is chosen to receive the help of a guardian angel is a mystery. It is quite clear by looking around that not everyone has an angel guarding over them. Those who go throughout life without the assistance of an angel are normally labeled "accident prone" or "clumsy" many seem to find their way to their final resting place a little earlier than those who have an Angel.

Chapter 2

My guardian angel is Mora. Mora was born and bred in a small railroad town about 20 miles outside Chicago named Tinley Park. The town was actually named after the first railroad station manager, Joe Tinley. She's about 5'9", 140 lbs., looks great in jeans. She has eyes like an angel, steel blue yet warm. Her smile is a devil's smile - part smirk, part grin, like a child who has a secret.

Mora came from a working class family. Money was tight and times were tough. The country was just getting back on its feet after WWII. Her father, who everyone called Big Mike, was considered a jack of all trades but there was never enough money to put down real roots. Her mother was only a faded picture that her father kept on the night table beside his bed. Just a lady in an oversized hat held onto her head by a scarf, and big black sunglasses. Mora never knew her mother. Only a handful of times was Mora held in her mother's arms before her untimely death. Mora's mother went to bed one night and never woke up.

The family moved several times each year so her father could be close to where the work was. Mora was 17 when fate decided to step in and deal her a life altering hand in the game of life. Her father was offered a job as a mechanic. It meant moving to the south side of town. An area of town that was a step or two lower than middle class. Not poor, yet not exactly what they were accustomed to. Mora and Big Mike, took an apartment in a three story walkup on Ryder Street. A worn down, yet clean flat, that was close to her father's job and walking distance to Mora's school. Several storefronts down from their apartment sat Gunning's Blues Hall, owned by Red and Millie.

Red had worked at Gunning's back when Lillian Gunning owned it. Lillian was a stout, tough, Irish woman who, as a child, immigrated to America during the late 1800's. Ireland hadn't fully recovered from the potato famine and times were bleak. America beckoned to her the same as it had for thousands of her countrymen. Lillian was the one who gave Red his name. His Christian name was Joseph. He was born with a full head of red hair like he was a founding member of the Ancient Order of the Hibernians. One day while bussing tables a patron called Red, "Pizza," because he had never seen a red headed Italian.

It was the first and last time anyone ever called Red, "Pizza".

Red quietly placed the tray of dirty dishes he was holding on a nearby table, walked over, grabbed the patron by the scruff of the neck, and threw him out the front door, twice. The first time the poor bastard only bounced off the door jam. Lillian figured a better nickname was needed if she was going to save her customers and the furniture. Red was just a natural choice, and not only due to the color of his hair. When Red got mad it was like a Matador waving his Muleta at a raging bull. Most odds makers would give you 8 to 5 on the bull.

Red worked for Lillian for many years and learned every trick of the trade from her. First trick, be here every day and work hard. Lilly, as Red called her, knew Red had been squirreling away money for years to buy her out. Lilly was now too old for money. She had all she needed to last her the few remaining years she had left. Lillian was going to take all she had and go back to the old country. Smell the fresh clean air of the Irish countryside. Live her final years in a whitewashed cottage with a thatched roof. Warm her old bones sitting next to a fireplace. Pictures of her life would grace the thick wooden mantle, and a photo of Red would always have its place on that mantle.

The time came to sell Red the tavern. Lilly would have just given Red the place. It was his, he earned every inch of the place. She knew he'd never just take the tavern as an inheritance. Red had too much pride. He'd never stand for a handout.

So Lillian and Red met at the lawyers, exchanged money and signed papers. Afterwards they returned to the tavern, locked the doors, poured whiskeys and toasted each other on their new ventures. Lillian stood, kissed Red, and said, "She's all yours. Do me one favor," pressing a note into his hand, "Read this tomorrow, and do exactly what it says." She gave him a wink and walked away. Red choked back a tear. He wanted to say one of the many Irish toasts he'd heard her say over the years, "wind at your back." Something about being in heaven before the devil knows you're dead, but they always seemed to lose something in the translation.

"Ciao, Bella Lillian, Grazie" was all he said.

The next day Red did as he was told. He kept the door bolted. Opened the letter from Lilly and began to read it.

"Red, you have been like a son to me for many years. You have earned every inch of the old place. Now she's yours, you owe me nothing. Make her yours - paint her, move the bar, build a stage, whatever you desire. Whatever you do, I know you'll be successful. There is one last detail I need you to do for me. Behind the cash register I've left a little something. Thank you for everything."

She signed it *Lilly*, and Red could tell she wrote it with a wavering hand and watering eyes.

Red reached behind the register and felt a leather pouch. He thought to himself, "God, now what has she gone and done?"

When the ties where undone and he peered into the pouch, his legs went weak. Lilly had left him two gifts. One was a snub nose .38. The other was $5,000 wrapped in a rubber band. There was a note with the money.

"Marry Carmela. You'll enjoy life more working with someone you love".

Red was mad and happy all at the same time. He followed Lilly's instructions and made a few changes to the old place. The first was to have a new mirror installed behind the bar. The mirror had lilies etched into the glass running up both sides. He then married the love of his life, Carmela, known as Millie by everyone. Lastly, a small stage was built. Red and Millie agreed to not rename the tavern.

Gunning's had been in the neighborhood for nearly 30 years. It just made good business sense to leave it named something everyone already knew and enjoyed. Even with the changes made to Gunning's Red could look around and still see and feel Lillian's mark on the place. He'd never dishonor her by renaming the old place.

Chapter 3

Red worked the bar serving draft beer and whiskey to tradesmen and Millie ran the kitchen. It was more like she *orchestrated* the kitchen. Though the tavern was in the shanty Irish section of town, Millie prepared and served the finest Italian food in all of the Chicago area. Everything was homemade. Sausage and peppers, gnocchi, linguini and clam sauce with olive oil, garlic and red pepper. While the rest of the neighborhood was boiling corned beef, Millie was roasting beef with Rosemary and Sage. Pork butts with slits cut into them where Millie had inserted whole garlic cloves. It would roast for hours and the garlic would infuse into the meat. The entire neighborhood would be enveloped with the aromas of Millie's kitchen. No one ever left Red and Millie's hungry.

Due to many years of Millie's culinary genius, Red developed a well earned roundness to his stomach. Married to Millie it was unavoidable. Though Red was a well fed man, his appearance was never sloppy. Six days a week he was attired in black pants belted around his stomach. He would never allow his girth to hang out of his trousers, like some in the neighborhood. White shirt and apron, always sharply pressed. A suit was the dress of the day for church on Sunday. Red ran the tavern like the Mayor ran City Hall. He knew every patron by name. He knew their anniversaries, kid's birthdays, everything about them. If there was a death in someone's family, Millie and Red were the first to send food to the house. Not just a meal, but enough food to last several days. Many a wedding reception or Christening were held in their establishment. Gunning's was the cornerstone of the neighborhood.

Red also had the skinny on the entire dark side of the neighborhood. Who was cheating on their wife. Who was a drunkard. How much someone owed to the Shylocks and where they were hiding out until they came up with, the vig, "the interest." Red had his finger on the pulse of the neighborhood because he spoke with everyone daily. The fish monger, the butcher, baker, and beer vendors. Red knew it all and he never left the bar, as all news flowed to him. On any given afternoon you'd have the neighborhood bookie at table 3 eating fried calamari with vinegar peppers. He'd always stop by the kitchen and pick up Millie's numbers for the day. Two tables over was Finnegan, the beat cop, inhaling a beef brisket on rye and a pint of stout. In the booth by the window, was Monsignor Ryan. The Monsignor favored Millie's veal dishes. Red served him his Bushmill's in a coffee mug as the good father needed to keep up appearances.

Saint or sinner, everyone paid. Red would give anyone a helping hand outside of the tavern, but within its four walls, it was cash for services rendered. He also never held a grudge. Anyone who was loud or drunk, he'd give them the bum's rush out the back door. The next day they'd be allowed back in. They were always a bit contrite the following day but Red would say, "No harm done. We ain't serving holy water in here," followed by a hefty slap on the back, signifying all was forgiven but watch your step.

As busy as it was during the day it was at night when the tavern shined. Millie and Red loved music, especially Blues and Jazz. Musicians fought with each other to play at the tavern. Red was straight with the money and Millie fed them like kings. Some nights Millie would be bone tired from her tour of duty in the kitchen and head straight home. Other nights, old friends would sit in with the band and she'd stay 'till the wee hours of the morning. She'd prop her swollen feet up on a chair, light a Chesterfield, and let the music take her. The moan of a saxophone or the clean rift from a Gibson electric guitar emanating from their old 20 watt tube amps had a sound that just relaxed her soul. Afterwards when all the patrons had left for their homes, stomachs and souls full from food and song, that's when Millie and Red were in their glory. They had their family around them. Everyone eating and sharing stories from the road. Millie would serve espresso and Italian pastries and they'd play cards until dawn. Everyone would be laughing. Calling each other "whores" or "rat bastards," depending on who was winning or losing. The laughter would increase when Red would curse in Italian whenever he'd lose a sure hand to Millie. It was intoxicating.

All the big names would stop by if time and schedules allowed. There was Muddy Waters, Johnnie Lewis, Junior Wells, and J.B. Hutto who wasn't old enough to be in a tavern let alone play at one. Red would joke, "If the cops raid us tonight I'll just tell them you're my Sicilian cousin." That always got a good chuckle out of everyone. J.B. would use a whiskey glass as a slide and entice his electric guitar to join in on the laughter. The small unisex dressing room bore the names of all who played there over the years. Due to the lack of education many received growing up as sharecroppers in the Deep South most signatures were unreadable.

On hot summer nights with her window open to find relief from the heat of the apartment the sounds of Blues and the smells of great food filled her senses. Mora would lay awake at night breathing in the wonderful smells and wonder what was making everyone laugh so hard. She didn't realize the laughter was just the product of friends and family enjoying each others' company. Mora didn't have family. Yes, she had a loving, caring father but the rest of the family, aunts and uncles and cousins, were very distant. Not just geographically but also emotionally. They never bonded as an extended family. The bonds created by breaking bread with each other and of children hearing the family stories every holiday. It's the cohesiveness of having generations of family together at a table. Mora never had any of that. The sounds from the tavern awoke a burning curiosity within her. She had to know what was going on at that tavern.

In the meantime, Mora was quickly developing into a beautiful young woman. Everyone was noticing. Her father started noticing everyone noticing. He was no fool - she'd be a full grown woman in a blink of an eye. She'd be gone in a few years to make a life of her own, but for now she was still his little girl. She couldn't be locked in her room like the princess in a tower. There's always some horny knight and his steed sneaking around. Big Mike worked long hours and without any family on this side of town he was stuck. While walking past the tavern one day, he saw Millie taking a break. She was sitting on a wood slatted folding chair enjoying a smoke in the sunshine. They exchanged pleasantries, and, while not considered a regular at the tavern, he had come to know Millie and Red. "Hey, Millie! How you doing? Enjoying this beautiful day?"

Millie barely heard him, lost in her own thoughts watching the blue smoke from her cigarette rising in the sunshine. She quickly looked up as if brought out of a trance. "Huh? Oh, hey. I didn't even see you there, Big Mike. No, no, I'm just getting out of the kitchen. I'm getting old and my feet hurt too much nowadays. I can't stand there all day like I use to."

"Aw, stop, Millie," Mike replied, "You got another hundred years in you!"

Millie laughed and said, "From your lips to God's ears!" and with a groan lifted herself on wobbly legs. "How's the family?" she asked with a quick head nod toward the direction of his house.

"Good, everyone's good, thank God. Mora's growing like a weed. Good student. I can't complain."

Millie replied, "I know I see her every now and then. Bella! You're a gonna need a big stick to keep those boys away!"

Mike's eyes rolled and he let out a long slow breath. Millie half smiled. Suddenly Mike realized the solution to his problem was standing right in front of him. Millie was the sweetest lady in the neighborhood but she was also a drill sergeant in a housecoat. "Millie?" His voice had a touch too much excitement to it. "You looking for any help in the kitchen?"

Millie looked confused. "You? You looking to work? What happened? You lose a you job?" Mike grinned. Millie had been in this country since she was three but never lost her native tongue. She and Red both spoke faster than anyone else he knew. When they were yelling at each other they sounded like dueling auctioneers to him.

"No, it's for my Mora." Then he paused for one or two breaths, embarrassed to explain he wanted another set of eyes to watch his child. Millie could feel his discomfort but knew why he was asking.

She broke the silence. "Otz, she cook?" Millie gestured with her hand holding her index finger and middle finger to her thumb and shaking her hand up and down as if she was warming dice for the next throw down a craps table. "You donkeys don't cook... boiling meat! That's not cooking!" She swiftly raised her hand as if backhanding away the thought of Irish cooking. She was breaking his balls in a fun way and he knew it. "You send her to me, I show her to cook. Ciao!" She turned to walk down the alley towards the screened backdoor of the kitchen, grease from years of cooking choking the life from the screen.

That night, Big Mike told Mora that she'd be working at the tavern every day after school. She was a month away from graduation and a straight A student. Big Mike knew school and work would be no problem for her. She was a smart, respectful kid, but Big Mike still had to add his parental advice. "Do whatever they tell you to do and don't be any trouble." As if a girl of 17 would be any trouble for Millie and Red. They've handled every personality that walked through their doors for too many years to count. Big Mike's daughter would be no trouble.

Mora's eyes opened wide with amazement. It was as if Santa really did exist! The one true present she always wanted was suddenly under her tree. She snapped back to reality, "What am I going to be doing?"

"Anything they tell you to do!" Big Mike answered back, sharply.

The next day Mora reported for work at the tavern right after school. Red was checking in a liquor order with his vendor, Geno, opening every box and double checking the inventory. "Red! Why the hell do you have to check every item twice? Don't you trust me?"

Red furrowed his brow as he looked over the top of his thick black framed glasses. "Trust you! I don't even trust me! Why do you think I check it twice?" Out of the corner of his eye he noticed a young woman in jeans and a t-shirt. Curly blonde hair that consisted of every shade of blonde there was. It fell beyond her shoulders and framed her face. "Can I help you?" Red asked while nodding his head in her direction.

"I'm here to start work," she replied sheepishly.

"Here? Doing what?" Red's voice was full of confusion.

"I don't really know. My father spoke to your wife."

Red cut her off as he yelled for Millie in a baritone voice. The strength of his yell startled Mora. Somewhere in the depths of her mind she made a mental note, "Never piss off Red."

16

Millie pushed open the door from the kitchen. "Red! Are you on fire? No? Then stop bellowing like that! Who's this beautiful woman? Is this the putana you're going to leave me for?"

Red became flustered, "I don't know who she is but she says she works here." Then he caught himself, "What putana am I leaving you for?"

Geno tapped on the stack of liquor boxes to get Red's attention. "Red, come on. I got other deliveries!" Bringing his attention back to Geno, Red signed off on the invoice. Before he could return his gaze to his wife, Millie ushered Mora back into the kitchen. When Red turned back, the kitchen door was swinging back and forth, and his wife and new employee had vanished. He shrugged his shoulders. "I just own this place. Why should I know what's going on?" he muttered to himself.

In the kitchen, Mora's senses were firing on all 8 cylinders. There was fresh vibrant green broccoli rabe bathing in a sink of ice water. A stack of wooden crates stood like a Roman sentry by the screen door. The smell of onion and garlic permeated the air all around her. Dented pots and pans where arranged on the 8 burner stove like NASCAR drivers at Talladega. However it was the omnipresent heat that grabbed her hardest. It was stifling! Beads of sweat formed on her neck under all her hair. Millie smiled and told her not to worry, "You get use to it. First things, first! Tie up your hair. We can't have a no hair in the food!" Millie exclaimed as she cut a piece of butcher's twine to use on Mora's hair. Once Mora had her mane tied back, "Buena! Now we can start." Millie led Mora to the sink filled with the Broccoli Rabe. Millie selected a stem and with a small paring knife deftly removed any of the unwanted leaves and shaved down the lower part of the stem. "See, you need to take off the tough outer skin and any brown spots. Your food needs to look as good as it taste!" Millie explained as she winked and nudged Mora's elbow with her own. "Now you do!"

Mora took the knife and began to do as she was instructed. After a few stems were completed under Millie's watchful eye she was left alone to finish the task. The heat of the kitchen was made bearable by having her hands in the ice water. Millie would pass by Mora on the way to do some other job and give her an appraising look. Millie was pleasantly surprised to see Mora finish the sink load of Broccoli Rabe and was already sweeping up any debris that was lying on the floor. "Nice, nice. Good girl! Always keep your area clean."

Mora didn't need to be told to police her area. One look around the kitchen and you knew this woman ran a tight ship. If she wasn't cooking or dealing with Red, she was cleaning. A dish towel was always tucked into the drawstring of her apron. She could pull out that rag faster than the Lone Ranger could draw his pearl handled six-shooters. Grease and grime were the Jessie James and Billy the Kid of her kitchen and they'd be run out of town by Sheriff Millie.

As Mora progressed with her kitchen skills, Millie assigned her more and more jobs. Fire roasting red and yellow peppers on the top of the gas stove, while slowly cooking trays of garlic to mash and add to Millie's other recipes. Mora would watch as Millie showed her how to butterfly a flank steak and then flatten it out with a cast iron pan to make Braciole. "Not enough Pignoli! chop your garlic finer and add more oregano," Millie would say as she would add a pinch of salt or grind some peppercorns into the mixture, "And don't go crazy with the cheese, its expensive!"

Millie was true to her word, as the summer months passed Mora became accustomed to the oppressive heat of the kitchen. The heat and work in the kitchen also created a bond between Millie and Mora, more of a mother and daughter connection than an employer and employee. There was nothing they wouldn't do for each other. Millie would watch over Mora like a mother hen while she was cooking and like a mother hawk when delivery men entered into the kitchen. At those times Millie would always find a job on the far end of the kitchen for Mora. Delivery men were shooed out of the kitchen as soon as their work was done. Always with a little piece of whatever had just come out of the oven. Mora also kept a keen eye on Millie. Jumping in to lift anything she deemed too heavy for a women of Millie's age to be lifting. "Millie let me get that!" or, "Mil, you've been on your feet all day, go have a smoke outside and relax" Mora's affection for Millie and her growing abilities in the kitchen didn't escape Red's attention either. He felt a burden lifted from his shoulders knowing Mora was keeping an ever vigil eye on his wife while he was out of the kitchen. As much as they loved the tavern and all it brought them, it was a bone tiring existence. It was becoming increasingly tiring with every year that passed.

For as much as Mora had come to love the hectic life in the kitchen, there was a new passion growing in her life, music. She was still too young to stay and hear the all night jam sessions. She would listen in as musicians would set up instruments and practice. Just the gleam off a shiny trumpet or cymbal of a drum set stirred something in her. Every musician stopped by the kitchen before thinking about the stage to pay their respects to Millie. It was always big hugs and kisses with laughter and cheer between old friends. At the back of the kitchen, there stood an old wooden table. Millie would cover the table with an assortment of bread, cheeses, olives and salami for the guys. "Sit, sit! Eat a little something. How have you been?" A little something from Millie would feed a small family.

After a while Red would burst through, "Oh, what am I running, a soup kitchen? You guys ever going to set up?" Everyone would stammer back an answer as they scurried away like children who were caught with their hand in the cookie jar.

"Red. Why you always yelling at them? They're just hungry. They need to eat." Millie would say.

"Eat! They're Gavones! They're always eating!" Red would yell just loud enough for the scurrying musician to hear. Red would give his wife a wink of his eye and raise his eyebrows in the direction of the stage. He and Millie would laugh a quiet little laugh like it was some private joke between them.

All the musicians would inquire about Mora, since they'd never seen Millie with any help in the kitchen before. Millie knew which ones were sincere and which were looking to put another notch in their bed post. The horny ones all got the same reply. "Never you mind who she is! And you look at her wrong I'll cut off that little sausage of yours!" Millie always seemed to have the largest knife in the kitchen in her hand when she said it. To the ones with honest intentions she would call Mora over and introduce her to them. She would brag and boast on how beautiful she was. "You think she just a Bella! Wait until you taste her cooking!"

The musicians' eyes would open wide and they would just stare for a moment. They weren't looking at Mora's beauty. They were trying to comprehend the words they just heard. They would then shake Mora's hand and give her a kiss on the cheek. "Well, welcome to the family little sister. If Mamma let's you cook in her kitchen you just gotta be something." Mora would blush and everyone would laugh. Soon Mora would become part of the gossip among the musicians' circuit.

Mora's time at the tavern changed her. Not only had she developed into a beautiful woman, there was more, way more. There was a certain something that makes average looking women desirable, and beautiful women seem almost unattainable. Confidence, Mora had a boat load of the stuff. She'd learn to run a kitchen that served no less than 60 to 70 meals nightly. Meals that showed she listened to everything Millie had taught her. In today's world she'd be known as, "A rising star in the culinary world." Through Red's tutelage she'd also learned to *tend* bar, not just sling drinks. She learned to tell the right joke to the right patron. She could tell a blue tale to Father McCormack that would make him blush and laugh his Irish ass off, yet she'd never utter a dirty word. She could tell the same joke to Finnegan the beat cop and make it the dirtiest he'd ever heard. "Mora I swear you got a mouth like a longshoreman" he'd say while laughing until he cried.

Through watching Red she learned how to keep her mouth shut and listen - glean information from liquor loosened lips. She also learned how to keep a secret and to get rid of people who wanted to just gossip. "If they wanted me to know their business they'd come down here and tell me themselves to cut out the middle man," was the line she borrowed from Red.

Red also taught her to drink Bourbon. "It's sippin' whiskey" he'd say, "Let the others throw back drinks, but you sip and listen." Then he'd give her the "look". The "look" was nothing more than a stone cold stare. Millie could read his face like it was a novel. The burrows in his brow, crow's feet around his eyes. It's the reason they were unstoppable at cards. Each knew what the other was holding just by glancing at their partner. Mora was also learning to read that face.

Millie introduced her to smoking. After a hectic day in the kitchen, she and Millie would step outside and sit in the shade of the alley and enjoy a smoke together. Chesterfield's were Mil's brand of choice. On special occasions, a friend who had a gig in Europe would bring back some Players Navy Cut, a true coffin nail, shorter and thicker than American smokes, and loaded with flavor. They'd breathe deep and exhale blue smoke, watching the smoke dance upwards on the thermals, like a hawk on outstretched wings.

Millie turned packing down smokes into an art form. She'd hold a pack between her thumb and middle finger, keeping her index finger on top for balance, beating the pack against her left hand until all the tobacco had been packed down. A small section of rolling paper would stick out past the packed tobacco of the cigarette. Millie could light one of her smokes with one match in a class three hurricane.

Chapter 4

Lil' Son Rollins was passing through town on his way to play a gig in Detroit, yet he had to stop by for some home cooking. In his band was a bass player named Danny. The moment Danny and Mora met, there was an instant connection. Each gave the other the once over. Everyone in the room could feel it. Millie understood that Mora was now a grown woman, yet still felt the need to protect her. When they had a private moment together Millie told Mora, "Honey, he'll be gone in the morning. It's the way they are. His life is the stage and the road." Mora wasn't sure if Millie was telling her to stop or go after him. After all, wasn't it Millie who taught her that fruit is only in season for a short while?

Danny wasn't Mora's first lover. He was the first she wanted to go crazy with. Danny had spent years on the road and had been with many women. He had a real healthy appetite for women. Mora was on fire that night; it took all he had to keep up with her. When the night was through it would take a whole troop of Boy Scouts to undo the knots in those bed sheets. Years later Lil' Son Rollins wrote a song called "Rock Me Baby". It's been covered by B.B.King, Eric Clapton and countless others. There is a line in the song that goes, "Rock me babe, Rock me all night long. Rock me like my back ain't got no bone." Danny contributed that line to the song. Mora had a big part in writing that Blues classic.

Red and Millie were getting older and the tavern was taking its toll. Mora was beginning to take on more responsibilities. She double checked all receipts from the delivery men. No one tried to cheat on the bills with Mora watching over Red's shoulder. While Millie was in the kitchen every day, it was Mora who was running the show. It seemed as if the two of them had switched roles. Millie did more of the prep work and Mora handled most of the major cooking. Still Millie kept her hand in everything. Tasting a soup and adding a pinch of salt. Keeping gravy stirred so it wouldn't burn. Little things, but it ensured it was her kitchen. "Mora don't keep the pasta in the water too long it'll get funny. "She loved Mora like she was her own daughter, but pride wouldn't allow her to just hand over the reins of her kitchen.

Red started to have Mora stay late and close up more often. This was her favorite part of the job. It was at night that the tavern came alive. The way the stage light reflected in the glasses over the bar, gave a magical effect to the place. The regular patrons all bellied up to the bar. Everyone laughing and swapping stories, the sounds of conversations filled the air. The nights when bands played, Mora was giddy with excitement. She loved the feel of the air when an electric guitar would make an amp crackle or the sounds of a horn section warming up resonating through the tavern. But it was after the bar closed and she was able to hang out with the band that excited her most. Hearing all the stories of the places they had been: NY, LA, New Orleans. Those stories of New Orleans made her blood pump heavily through her veins. The stories of the music halls and the food made her head spin. It sounded like someone took Gunning's and created a city out of it. It held the number one spot in her mind of places she hoped to see someday.

It wasn't the stories themselves but the way they were told. Willie Mae Thornton, later known as Big Mamma Thornton, would tell stories about roadhouses in East Texas, Buddy Guy would jump with a, "That's right!" or an, "Aye, yeah." He would punctuate her stories as he would her songs, with just enough of a cord at the right time to balance and blend the whole thing together. "Oh baby someday you's just got to get down to Austin. The music and the Barbeque, Lord have mercy. The whole town is filled with that sweet smoke. The meat just fall off the bone they cook it so slow and sweet" Buddy would bend a cord and Willie Mae would say "O, you so nasty".

Mora would sit and listen to them all night if she could. One of her favorites was Sonny Boy Williamson, one of the best harmonica players she ever heard. One could hardly understand what he was saying but his tempo and rough laugh would keep all who were listening riveted. Sadly, there were always other gigs hundreds of miles away so their time together was always too short.

Mora was amazed by her new friends. They were treated like second class citizens in their own country. These were the founding fathers of America's own music and they couldn't eat in most diners down South. Most were uneducated by no fault of their own. What little recording they did they never received their just rewards for. In Europe they were like royalty, in their own country they had to sleep on the bus. Through all they had to deal with they were always laughing and joking and praising the Lord or thanking Jesus.

When the night was over, the glasses all washed, stacked and stowed, the patrons sent to their homes to sleep away the night's affects, Mora would light a cigar, pour herself a tall Bourbon, and cash out the register. Peeking into the kitchen, like a parent checking on a child's slumber. Making sure all the gas stoves were off, freezer door shut tight, everyone tucked in for the night. Her body would start to wind down. The ringing of the music in her body would start to subside. In the dark with only the glow of the streetlamps filtering in through the smoke hazed windows. This was the only time she felt insecure and alone while at the tavern. It was no longer a living, breathing thing, it was just a building. Soulless timbers nailed together to provide protection from the elements. She would then stash the night's receipts in the strong box under the bar, lock the front door behind her, and finally head home.

Millie had introduced her to smoking cigarettes; her love of cigars was nurtured by many of the Cubans playing in the bands.

Each would leave her with a few each time they passed through Gunning's. She couldn't run out for a fast smoke with Millie and have a cigar. They took too long to burn and a good cigar should never be rushed, as she was told. At night when she was cashing out the register, that was the time for a cigar. She would light one with a wooden match, roll it between her fingertips and enjoy the rich deep flavors. Cigars became a private treat that would be savored in the afterhours at Gunning's.

During the little time she was away from Gunning's, she would indulge herself in her favorite past time. She would borrow a friend's motorcycle and go riding. Since Gunning's was the center of the universe for the neighborhood, an array of motorbikes were at her disposal. Half her customers rode or worked on motorcycles. Her favorite was Connor's - a beautiful 1947 Indian Chief with red on black paint job. This was no petite little rice burner that you see on today's highways. No sir. This was a 675 pound, 1212 cc V Twin with a left hand tank shifter and left side foot clutch. Chromed spring fork suspension up front and a War Mascot Light mounted on the front fender. It was an all American made road machine.

Mora was a sight to behold roaring around the streets of Tinley. A red and white handkerchief, tied around her head. Leather jacket and goggles were all the protection she required while straddling the tank of the beast with skirted fender. The sun on her face, and that unmistakable engine vibration rising up through the leather seat was heaven for her. Mix in the staccato of the pipes and a 100 mph top end and it was simply intoxicating. Mora was one of the very few women who could pull it off. Working in the kitchen gave her the physical strength to handle the big Indian. Her connection from working the bar got her out of more than one or two tickets.

At one point Monsignor Ryan was asked to speak to her about her recklessness. "Mora, my dear, you're an unholy banshee on that machine. It's no wonder you haven't broken your bloody neck," his Irish brogue still thick even after many years in America.

Mora just lifted her head to the heavens and let loose with a wild laugh. "So, I'm the Omen of Death, am I, Father?"

"No, no, of course not child, it's just that you scare the bejesus out of my parishioners."

"Now look, Father, I'm just having a little fun on my Sunday," she suddenly paused, "Hey wait a minute! Shouldn't those sweet parishioners of yours be in church when I'm out riding?" Mora didn't mean to be short with the Monsignor but lately she was growing anxious, restless. Part of it was the stories that the different band members would tell her. Traveling, seeing new places, meeting new people, experiencing life. She would often wonder if she'd ever have the chance to taste life as they did.

She would never share those thoughts with Millie, afraid to hurt the one who had shown her nothing but love and respect. Never would she hurt her family. Millie knew what it was like to be a young woman, starting out fresh in life. She knew someday Mora would leave them, just had a premonition. Mora did decide that when Millie and Red retired or sold the place that was when she'd strike out for a life of adventure. Maybe buy Connor's bike and see the world.

Monsignor Ryan answered back "And it wouldn't hurt you to attend a Sunday Mass or come to confession, young lady".

Mora smiled and kissed the Monsignor on the cheek. "No need Father. We're both in the confession business, you do it behind closed doors and I do it from behind a bar. But we both know everyone's sins." She then gave him a devilish wink of her eye. Before the Monsignor could say a word, Mora had kick started the big Indian and revved the engine. Monsignor Ryan's calls of blasphemy were drowned out by the roar of the motorcycle's engine. He made a mental note to say an extra prayer for her this coming Sunday.

Chapter 5

The tavern was a neighborhood joint. Mostly everyone knew each other. However since the end of the war the neighborhood was seeing more transients. Enlisted men, who for whatever reason, decided to see America before heading back to the lives they knew before. All were changed men. They would not return home the boys their parents remembered. They all had seen the horrors of war. Frank Burrows was among the ranks of those men.

Frank grew up in Midland, Ohio. He had been in some sort of trouble since the day he could walk. The type of guy who, when he walked by, women would shift their purses to the other side of their bodies. He had a nervous way of constantly looking around. It gave him the appearance of a sparrow on a telephone wire, always on the lookout for danger. The war was a stroke of fortune for Frank. With the threat of jail time hanging over his head for his last offense, the Army looked like a way out of his troubles. He headed for Columbus and enlisted.

Being a thief had its benefits in war. He quickly became the company scrounger. Whenever the company commander needed supplies, Frank got the call. Food, movies, medicine, smokes - Frank always came through. Frank would leave the camp under darkness and head for the next unit, steal them blind, and head back to his encampment. He'd rummage through the pockets of the dead for ammo and smokes. He'd steal from the villagers and farmers of the area who had nothing. As the war dragged on, his stealing compulsion gave way to other demons. Throughout Italy there had been attacks on women. More than money was taken from these women. None of them had ever seen their attacker. He'd come out of the shadows with a knife. How to use a knife was one thing Frank paid very close attention to in basic training.

Even though Frank supplied the men in his company with food, cigarettes and ammo, he was still the scourge of the company. It took enemy fire to make most men stay in a foxhole with him. Whenever he'd hang around the other men someone would eventually say, "Frank, do us all a favor, and step on a landmine." They'd tell new recruits to sleep with their mouths shut tight as Frank would steal their gold fillings.

It wouldn't be a landmine or his indiscretions that would get Frank sent home. That act of kindness to the American troops was provided by a Mauser 7.62 cartridge fired by a German soldier outside of Naples. Frank was hit in his left thigh, shattering his femur. Upon leaving the army, Frank was awarded the Purple Heart, a noticeable limp in his gait, and a lifelong addiction to painkillers. Morphine relieved the aching in his leg and his appetite for it grew. Frank's army career ended just two weeks before VE Day.

He was no longer under the care of the doctors and nurses at the Thomas M. England Army Hospital. He was out on his own, just him, his addiction, and his new 4-inch folding knife. The medics had taken his prized knuckle knife while he was being evacuated from Italy. He quickly took to becoming the scrounger again. He started small; stealing cigarrettes and other pocket-sized items. It grew as most addictions do. Soon he was breaking into pharmacies at night for any pain medications he could grab. Once those cravings were satisfied, other old cravings started to enter his mind.

Frank was no longer the thief he was before the war. He was a highly trained combat veteran. No longer the smash and grab thief of his old Midland days. He was smarter and more cautious. He needed to be unseen. His leg had mended but the days of running from a crime scene were long over. He'd now have to put his military training to use again. Use the cover of night, get in quick and quiet, no noise, and no witness.

Criminals seem to wear out their welcome in towns faster than the average population. Frank would arrive in a new town, mostly by train or hitchhiking. People were apt to pick up a young veteran aged man in those times. Everyone wanted to do their part. Paper and rubber drives, blackout curtains on windows, and victory gardens. The chance to give a ride to a injured serviceman was just too alluring. He'd spend a few weeks bumming around, committing crimes, and then he'd be off to a new town, hundreds of miles away. Dropped off on the side of the road and given a big old thanks for his service. After he was out of the car, the driver would exhale a sigh of relief. Happy to be a good American, but relieved to be out of Frank's company. Frank just made people feel awkward. His answers were always, "Yes," and "No." You'd never have a real conversation with him. He was always too worried about giving away too many clues about himself. He also had a bad habit of rubbing his leg. Part of it was his war wound and part was his addiction. Frank just had a gift for making people uncomfortable around him.

As the steel wheels of the 11:15 out of Chicago came to a grinding halt the dark green locomotive exhaled a cloud of steam. The conductor sang out the station name, "Tinley Park!" He continued on with his song, the same song he'd sung year after year. Every train station had a different cadance to it. Tinley Park's was heavy on the "Tin" with a quick finish on the "ley" followed by a hard fast "Park". The rest of the conductor's well rehearsed song of stations was lost to Frank's ears due to the churning of the steam engine and the screech of steel wheels trying to grab traction against the metal rails.

With his slightly noticable limp, Frank made his way from the platform to the street level, drew a cigarette from his half empty pack, and looked around. With no destination in mind the points of a compass have no meaning to a wanderer. Striking a match, drawing heavily on his cigarrette, then exhaling the blue grey smoke, Frank turned left and walked up the street. Ever

31

vigilant for an opportunity, Frank's mind and eyes would begin working like he once again was on a military mission.

His mind was racing, gas station on the next corner. What's the lighting like?   How late do they close?   How many attendants?   What's the best way in and out?   A few blocks up on the right was a sign that eased his mind. A large white sign with a red Rx. A pharmacy, salvation! He would take extra care to case out this score. It would have to wait, as an impending rainstorm was approaching and the first order of business was shelter.   Hotel, boarding house, anything would do as long as it was dry.

He stepped into the gas station and inquired about housing from an attendant wearing a starched white uniform.   While he was inside the station he bought a pack of Lucky's and cased the place.   Turning to look out the large plate glass window, he thought, "What would be the best position to attack?" His mind constantly working all the angles.

Lost in thought he almost missed the recommendation from the fresh faced attendant. "O'Neal's Boarding House, three blocks down on the right. They don't serve food but Gunning's is just down from there. Best place in town to eat, even got music on some nights."

Although Frank could have stolen the pack of smokes from the chatter box kid, he didn't want to be remembered. A pack of smokes need not ruin a bigger score later on. He tossed a few coins on the glass counter and headed out the door towards O'Neal's. Stealing a quick glance back inside the gas station, the ever helpful kid in the white unifrom was pointing in the direction of O'Neal's and shaking his head, assuring Frank he was going in the right direction. Frank smirked and waved a thank you to the kid. Thinking, "OK kid, I made it through Italy, I'm sure I can find this place on my own."

Upon reaching O'Neal's, Frank exaggerated his limp to guarantee a room on the first floor. Not that he couldn't make the stairs but he'd be less likely to be seen entering and exiting the building from the first floor. Frank settled into his room. Four nondescript walls with a shared bathroom for guests down the hall. When Frank sat down on the bed the springs sank low and the bed moaned like Frank's weight was killing it. He wondered if O'Neal's had ever been a whorehouse at one time. Regular patron sleeping here couldn't possibly have worn out a bed this bad.

The rule was no smoking in the rooms so Frank stepped out on the porch and sat in one of the wooden rockers. A pail of sand was in the corner of the porch for the disposal of butts. Frank would never use it. Since basic training he had the habit of GI'ing his butts. Once smoked he would crumble the butt between his fingers until it disintegrated, leaving no trace for the enemy to find.

While out on the porch an aroma of garlic made Frank's senses perk up. "That kid mentioned someplace to eat around here." He inquired about it at the front desk and was given directions to Gunning's. First he'd clean up a bit. Get the road and rails off him. Next was a stop at the pharmacy. He wanted to take a close look at its setup. He had painkillers for a day or two, but never liked his supplies to run that low.

Once out on the street the aroma from Millie's kitchen was stronger than Frank's need to see the pharmacy. He followed the directions he received for Gunning's. Once inside the doors Frank was transported back to his days in Italy. The good days. Eating food provided by simple farmers. Peasant food, prepared fresh and skillfully. No heavy sauces or over spicing. The freshness of the food spoke for itself. He sat at a table toward the back. Ordered a cold draft and reviewed the menu. The entire menu was desirable but on a slate by the bar were the specials. Lamb shanks with garlic potatoes caught his eye like a neon sign on the Vegas Strip.

When his meal arrived at the table he was overwhelmed by the size of the portions and the aroma. Lamb cooked until just falling off the bone, sitting high on a mound of fluffy mashed potatoes infused with garlic cloves. The garlic was cooked to the point of becoming another consistency. It became a gooey, almost candy like substance. Topping it all was a simple but delicious gravy of stewed tomatoes and onions with a hint of basil and roasted peppers.

Frank wanted to devour it, it had been a year or so since he'd tasted food like this. He fought the feeling to fill his mouth quickly. This was food to savour. Every bite brought out the skills of the cook. Eyes closed. Chewing slowly to release all the flavors. Frank exhaled, opened his eyes to gaze upon Mora standing in front of him.

"Everything OK, Mister?" topping off his draft, "Need anything just give me the high sign". Mora smiled as she spoke to him.

Frank could only nod, his mouth working on a piece of lamb, not wanting to swallow too fast and rob himself of the enjoyment of it all. While his mouth was busy on the lamb, his eyes were busy on Mora. He was transfixed on her. His eyes darting from his plate to her figure, no matter where in the room she was. Then looking to see if anyone was looking at him. It gave him the appearance of a mouse, eating a scrap of food, ever vigilant of the cat. Red took notice of Frank. Not really concerned, everyone liked to watch Mora. Yet there was something.

Frank followed his meal with American coffee as expresso was too heavy for him. He broke character by complimenting

Mora and Red on the meal. Paid his tab and walked outside for a smoke. His hunger now satisfied it was time for his next task at hand. A walk to the pharmacy. Inside it was the same as every small pharmacy he'd ever been in. Soda fountain against a long wall. Against the back wall stood a high counter manned by a balding man in a starched white coat. A few aisles of sundries, some birthday and get well cards on a wire rack. Frank looked the place over as he pretended to read a few of the cards. He asked the pharmacist if he had a restroom he could use. The pharmacist cocked his head to his left and answered, "Round back here." Frank followed the man's direction and stepped slowly up behind the counter. He noticed the pharmacist looking at his limp. Their eyes made contact and Frank knew immediately the man wanted to ask if it was war related.

"A present I got while in Naples. One minute I'm standing there and the next..." An uncomfortable silence fell upon them both. One was embarrassed for wanting to ask, the other for answering. Frank just turned and headed for the restroom. He'd experienced this feeling many times since leaving the VA hospital. It's just better to keep moving, the silence never breaks.

The bathroom was paneled with chest high white wainscotting. Above it a Robin's egg blue paint job. Frank looked for what he was really here for. The window - he needed to see the window - the height of it, the size of the opening. Frosted glass in an old metal frame. Years of paint welded the frame to the sill. In a flash the 4-inch folding knife was out and releasing the window from it's encasement of paint. Once his knife was back in its pocket the only thing left to do was unlock the window. His work done, he ran water in the sink and wet his hands. He walked past the pharmacist and mumbled a thank you. The air was still thick with the silence of their previous encounter. A head nod was all Frank received from the man behind the high counter.

Back at O'Neal's Boarding House the rocker on the front porch helped ease the dull numbing pain in Frank's leg. The steady back and forth motion put him in a mild trancelike state. A Lucky burning between his fingers adding yet another layer of jaundiced yellow to his stained fingers. The meal he'd eaten at Gunning's filled his stomach – it's flavor still residing on his tastebuds. The thought of it brought him back to his days in Italy. Deep within the dark area of his mind another old familiar feeling started to ease into his conciousness. His hand fondling the knife in his pocket. Index finger and thumb tracing its outline. The familiar weight of it on his thigh.

The women of Italy started to reemerge in his mind. Their hair, their scent, the terror in their eyes. A feeling of warmth grew over him, the cigarette burning into the gap between his fingers helped heighten the feeling. His other fingers tracing the outline of his blade even faster now. Then a thought of Mora was spliced into his private mental movie. It was as if the director decided the old starlets were yesterday's news, "We need a fresh new face - maybe a blonde." Frank was the director and casting agent. The new starlet search was over, Mora won the contract and she never even knew she was in the running.

Startled by footsteps Frank was brought out of his trance. A fellow boarding houseguest asked if he might borrow a cigarette. "I'm out and don't feel like venturing out in this weather."

Frank still not quite fully back yet slowly turned to look out off the porch to see a light misty rain. Shaking his head to release the cobwebs he replied, "Sure," as he jostled his pack of smokes up and down to release a coffin nail. "Use the pail," tilting his head towards the corner of the porch.

"Oh, right, will do," said the guest as he looked over to the silver galvenized pail. Frank wondered if the grubber of cigarettes had noticed him carressing his knife through his pants.

The rain had placed a hold on his plans for the pharmacy for tonight. It would have been a perfect setup if not for his leg. Couldn't take the chance of slipping on the wet pavement. Tomorrow night, under the cover of night would do. "Good night," Frank said to his porch guest, "Need another?" as Frank handed him the two remaining cigarettes from his pack.

"Thank you!" surprised by this gift of generosity. He didn't know why but just didn't think this fellow was capable of being nice. It was something else that stuck with Frank from his time at war. A guy needs smokes you give him what you can. An unwritten code. Just hand over what you can, they'd do the same for you.

The next day was a carbon copy of the day before. Frank cursed his bad luck. This weather was murder on his leg. Felt to him like the marrow was being pulled out of his femur. He found himself constantly rubbing his leg. The weather also increased his pill consumption.

Another recon job on the pharmacy was in order and besides it beat hanging at O'Neal's. He hobbled the block or two until he was on the corner across from the pharmacy. The collar of his trench coat pulled up, brim of his hat pulled low provided protection from the weather and prying eyes. Waiting for a cab to pass he started to cross the wet street, eyes checking every angle. No need to check the inside of the pharmacy again. Time to head down the alley and give it an eyeball. Check for the nosey neighbors. Do they keep curtains drawn? Can I be seen from the street? Frank's mind worked all the angles.

As he ambled down the alley he noticed that with each step he took the incline was steeper. He lowered his gaze and realized that the alley was on a down hill slope. His mind started to go into overdrive. His body temperature started to rise despite the misty rain. He quickened his pace disregarding the ache in his leg. He positioned himself below the window he'd freed from years of paint the day before. It was several feet higher than he expected. The gift he received in Naples prevented any chance of jumping to grab the sill. Frank's eyes surveyed the alley for a pallet or anything else to give him some height. There were only galvanized garbage cans so dented from years of abuse they would never hold his weight.

As he walked back to O'Neal's a rage built in him. How the hell didn't he notice the alley sloped? He had peeked down the alley the night before. Actually taken a step or two into its shadow for privacy. He was looking up at the window for security bars. If he had only taken a few more steps he would have felt the slope of the darkened driveway under his feet.

"Maybe I can boost a ladder somewhere," he thought. "No, I can't carry a ladder around town!" his mind whirling. Firing up another cigarette, inhaling deep, exhaling hard. Dammit! The ache in his leg grew. "Alright, calm down, slow your breathing, think," he told himself. "First, what you need to do is get dry, then food and a drink." Mora flashed into his mind. Next stop Gunning's.

As he walked through the front door shaking off the chill, he took notice of the wide planked floor. Wondering why he hadn't noticed that detail yesterday. He dismissed the thought and headed to the bar.

Red had his back to him, taking stock of the bar. When Red heard the barstool pull out, he turned and recognized Frank from the day before. "Aye, back again, huh? What it'll be?"

Being recognized startled Frank for a moment. He answered, "Something to warm me up, brandy."

"Good choice. You staying for the show? It'll be a good time. Pinetop Perkins and Honeyboy are playing tonight."

Frank's eyes were blank as his mind was trying to comprehend what Red just said. He thought, "Damn, this guy talks fast!" then replied, "Uh, not staying, but I'll stop back later." He finished his brandy in three fast sips, shuddered and placed the snifter back on the bartop.

While exhaling a slow brandy warmed breathe he told Red, "That's better." Red gave him a head nod and a smile. Frank inquired about the Lamb shanks and complimented Red on his food.

"Sorry we're all out. But everything is good"

"What do you recommend?"

Red chuckled and patted his girth, "Everything, but go with the veal and eggplant."

"Done."

Red headed toward the kitchen to place the order. He noticed Frank's reflection in the mirror behind the bar. He was leaning over to sneak a peak into the kitchen. Red didn't know what to make of it, but it didn't sit right with him. Not enough to throw him out, but enough to keep a eye on him.

Frank was culinarily surprized by his meal. He was expecting cubes of veal and eggplant in a light sauce. Instead he received a flattened piece of veal encased by thin slices of eggplant, all of it lightly fried, served over rice and topped off with a balsamic sauce. He ordered a glass of red wine and devoured the meal. While finishing his second glass of wine and digesting his meal he scanned the room for a glimpse of Mora. His blood pressure jumped at the sight of her. She was working a table of six in the back of the room. All of his senses satisfied, he paid for his meal and left for O'Neal's.

The phone behind the bar rang. Red's big paw was on it by the second ring. "Gunning's," he barked into the receiver.

Through the static on the line he heard, "Red?"

"Speaking, who I got here?"

"Red, it's me, Pinetop."

"Hey!" Red's voice rose, "What, are you calling in your food order early?"

"No, no man, we're stuck in Chicago, the bus is broken, we ain't going to be able to make it tonight."

"What's wrong with it? Can't you fix it? Millie's making something special for you."

"Hell, man. I'm a musician, not a mechanic! I don't know nothing about no engines and stuff. What's Millie making?"

"You won't know until you get here."

"Man, Red, that's just wrong! Sorry to let you down, but this don't look good for tonight. We'll try to be there for tomorrow night. I'll call you. Tell Millie to keep everything warm for us. Later man."

Red replaced the receiver on the phone and gave a slight Italian curse, "Fanabala!" Then turned towards the kitchen, "Millie!" he yelled as he burst through the kitchen door. Startling both Millie and Mora.

The women looked at each other, complaining simultaneously, "I hate it when he does that!" Millie turned back to Red, "Red what's a matter?"

"The guys' bus is broke down in Chicago. They can't make it tonight!"

"Is everyone alright? They coming tomorrow?"

"They'll try."

She shrugged her shoulders reassuringly, "So we'll see everyone tomorrow. Why you gotta scream?" she chastised him.

Mora spoke up, "So, you guys go home early tonight. I'll close up and you'll be fresh for tomorrow night."

Millie clasped Mora's face with both hands, leaned over and kissed both her cheeks, "Grazie." She and Red worked for another hour or so and left for the night. As always Red told Mora to call the house if she needed anything. She never called. Red had taught her how to handle everything.

Frank arrived at his room, took the last of his pills, peeled off his wet clothes, and dried off. He changed into something dry and laid down on the wornout bed. His mind started to wander, staring at the wallpaper, trying to figure out what flower was recreated on the print. Soon he was rubbing his leg again. He needed a score fast. What did that bartender say? There was a show tonight at Gunning's? That register should be loaded later tonight. A plan emerged in his mind, Mora and money all at one place, his hand instinctively touched his knife.

Around 11:00 p.m. Mora looked down the bar. Only a few regulars nursing their beers remained. She'd give them another hour before sending them on their way. They'd complain like small children wanting to stay up past their bedtime. "Ah come on Mora, just one more round. It's early still."

She knew how to play the game, " OK, boys. The last round of the evening is on the house." Making sure to inflect her tone on the word last. The boys bellied up to the bar as they only heard, "On the house."

Frank walked down Ryder Street expecting to hear music. "Band must be on a break," he thought. As he entered through Gunning's large red front door he was surprised to see only a handful of patrons. Mora read the puzzled look on his face and explained what happened to the band. Frank silently cursed his luck. "What's with this town? I can't catch a break." First the pharamacy, now this, "Well, at least blondie is working, that's something." Frank pulled off his trench coat and pulled up a bar stool several seats down from the regulars and ordered a draft. His mind calculating all of his options. Leaving town empty handed was not one of them. He wondered about just coming back another night but hated the idea of sticking around a town with such bad luck. He was brought back from his thoughts by movement behind the bar.

Mora was pressed up against the back bar reaching for a bottle on the top shelf. On tip toes she was stretched out to her full extent. Back arched, her shirt leaving the confinement of the waistband of her jeans. From Frank's angle he could see her flat stomach, the gap between her pants and that stomach. His depraved mind had always been a smoldering ember. To see Mora stretched out was like having someone breathe a warm breath on that smoldering ember. It started to glow and then the flame began to grow, hot. It would be tonight. Tonight for sure he told himself.

Frank got up from the barstool and headed to the Men's room. As he passed the door for the kitchen, he peered in. It was empty. Finally an opportunity. He quietly snuck into the kitchen and made his way to the back door. With the practiced hands of a thief he unlocked the door without a sound. As he was heading back out to the bar he inventoried the kitchen, needing to know his surroundings for later when it was dark. Another quick look out from the kitchen door to see that the coast was clear and slip back into the bar. He stood between the stools of the bar, gulped what was left in his glass, and threw down enough money to cover his tab. He put on his jacket as he headed toward the door.

Once outside he displayed the common thief maneuver, looking both ways. Not the way a mother teaches a child to cross the street. This was a sinister action meant to see who was looking at him. Checking the windows across the way to see if any busybody was checking out the street. He lit a cigarette and headed toward the alley, softly touching the knife in his pocket. He'd wait in the shadows until he could hear the rest of the patrons leaving the bar for the night. He wouldn't need to strain his ears, the last to leave are normally the loudest.

The moment he was waiting for finally arrived. One slightly drunken patron even stopped to relieve himself in the alley. Frank was well concealed in the shadows and the fellow went on his way without ever noticing Frank. Once he assured himself the place was empty, he placed his hand on the handle of the backdoor, exhaled and pulled on the door. Mora was at the front door locking up and didn't hear the small creak from the rear door.

Frank hid in the shadow of the walk-in fridge. He wanted to hear movement to determine Mora's location and activity. He heard her as she locked the front door and headed back toward the kitchen area. The kitchen door opened slightly, a shaft of light sliced into the darkness of the kitchen. Mora glanced toward the stoves to make sure all the jets were off and walked back behind the bar. Frank closed his eyes and exhaled a slow, controlled, deep breath. His knife was in his hand and he was opening the blade.

Exposing only his right eye to the pane of glass of the kitchen door, he saw Mora had her back to him. She was looking down at the bar, counting the night's bounty from the register. Pressing his weight to the door to open it just enough to slide his body through the opening, he eased up to the blind spot just behind Mora.

Mora had stopped counting, and lit one of the small cigars she favored after the bar was closed. She reached for a bottle of Kentucky's finest and poured herself 3 fingers worth. She was trying to calm herself. She hated being in the bar after everyone was gone. It was too still and had the feeling of a funeral parlor.

Frank was slowly creeping out of the shadows, staying low, blade out front. As Mora lifted her glass to take a long sip, she caught a reflection in the glassware above the bar.

Mora spun her head and caught sight of Frank coming at her. Frank's bad leg gave way on the wet floor behind the bar. Mora took a step backwards while grabbing the bottle of Bourbon off the bar. Getting his legs back under himself Frank pushed forward. Mora stopped backstepping and turned into the aggressor. Bourbon left the bottle in an arch as she swung at his head.

Unprepared for an aggressive woman, Frank was stunned as the bottle broke against his cheek. Mora didn't hesitate, cursing like a drunken sailor, she charged in on her assailant. Frank's military training instintively took over and he blocked her advance while bringing his blade up. Mora stopped in her tracks as her left side felt as if lava was pouring from her body. She looked down to see the silver blade sticking out of her ribs.

A rage engulfed her. Her eyes steeled, jaw clenched tight. The jagged neck of the shattered bourbon bottle still clenched in her fist slashed across Frank's throat. Crimson blood splattered against the mirror behind the bar turning the etched lillies red. Clasping his throat, Frank turned to flee. Blood pumping through his fingers with every beat of his heart. A feeling of nausea overwhelmed him. He barreled through the kitchen doors only to run straight into Red's path.

When Red and Millie had arrived home from the bar earlier that evening, Millie asked Red what was wrong. "I don't know, something just isn't right," he had replied.

"Why, you feel sick? Something you ate?"

"No, no. There was a guy at the bar tonight. Something wasn't right with that guy. He made my skin crawl!" He tried to relax. Sat and talked with Millie over espresso, but he just couldn't sit still. Years of working behind the bar, meeting all sorts of people, gave him certain insight.

Millie tried calling the tavern but the phone just kept ringing. Now her nerves were on edge, "Red, I don't like this. Go down there and check on Mora." Red was out the door before she finished the sentence.

The shortest route to the bar was through the alley and in through the kitchen's back door. Red found the door unlocked.

As he entered the back door he heard the sound of breaking glass. He reached into his pocket for the last gift Lillian had left him. Red was a bull of a man, large strong hands from years of hard work. The snubnose .38 felt small, in all the years since Lillian left it to him he only handled it to clean it.

The kitchen door burst open. There stood Frank Burrows silhouetted by the light from the bar. Red could see Mora behind him with a bottle raised high to throw at Frank's head. As if in slow motion Mora's body began to sink. Legs buckling from blood loss. The bottle slipped from her grasp, crashing to the floor. Mora threw her hand out to catch her balance, knocking bottles from the first shelf onto the floor. The sight made Red blind with anger. Two shots rang out, deafening in the small tiled kitchen. Momentarily blinded by the flash of the shots, Red never heard Frank hitting the floor. He ran past his dead body and caught Mora in his arms. He lifted her body, not wanting his *daughter* to fall into all the broken glass from the fight.

Placing her gently on top of the bar, he comforted her, telling her she'd be alright and not to move. He fired three more shots into the floor in hopes of waking the neighborhood. It had the desired effect. When the police and all the neighborhood arrived they found Red pressing mounds of bar rags on Mora's wound to help stem the bleeding. Later the police and doctors would tell him his actions saved Mora's young life.

Chapter 6

While Mora recuperated in the hospital, her and Red's actions became the talk of the neighborhood. The police investigated but never filed charges against Red for the shooting of Frank Burrows. He and Mora became heroes in everyone's mind. Red apologized to Mora's father, Big Mike, everytime he saw him. "Red, it's not your fault. You and Millie saved me by giving her this job. I asked you to take her. You were my salvation" Red didn't care. He covered all her hospital bills, and gave her father Mora's pay every week even though the bar was closed for renovations.

They could never clean the blood from the etchings of the lillies on the mirror. It made Red's blood boil. Two generations of women that he loved had been marred by that piece of crap, he thought. Finally in digust he threw a tumbler glass through the mirror. The next day he had a glazier at the bar measuring the opening for a new one. "Lillies up both sides, for Christ sake's, you been in here a million times, you know what they looked like." He bellowed to the workman.

"It would have been easier if you hadn't broken the other one, Red," he jokingly said. Red shot him a look from over the top of his glasses and the glazier sheepishly returned to his work.

Red gave Millie strict orders not to enter the tavern until all signs of the fight were erased. Millie was never the type of woman to take orders, but could clearly see how distraught Red was. "Ok, ok, Red. But how soon? It's my home, too!"

In a calm reassuring voice he replied, "I know, soon, very soon."

The time came to reopen the tavern. A new mirror, with etched lillies running up both sides, presided behind the bar. A fresh coat of paint for the walls and even the bar itself had been sanded down and refinished. Millie was back in the kitchen, tired but happy to be back doing what she loved. Her heart was at ease because today was not just the reopening of the tavern but Mora was coming home! Her father said that if she was strong enough he'd bring her by, "...for a short stay."

The nurses were happy to be rid of her. Not only was Mora an unruly patient, she had the strangest visitors. All these old black men coming in to see this little white girl. Word of Mora surviving the attempted murder quickly spread through the entertainment community. As it spread the tale of her deeds grew. By the time Big Mamma Thorton heard the news, Mora had been shot twice and stabbed once. She cried out when she found Mora would be alright. "Lord knows that child got's to have some sister in her to fight a man like's that, ain't nobody ever gonna give her no's troubles no more!" then she chuckled a bit, "I can just see her, too. All that blonde hair and those crazy eyes, swinging a bottle, oh Lord blessed that child." Songs from many a stage went out to Mora.

The tavern was alive again. Everyone who came through the door yelled their greetings to Red and Millie. The smells from Millie's kitchen put everyone in a celebratory mood. Sounds of laughter, silverware against plates, glasses being raised, and toast to Mora filled the air. Finally, an old sedan pulled up in front of the bar. Out stepped a frail figure with wavy blonde hair from the passenger door. Her father running around the front of the car to lend a helping hand. "I got it dad, I'm ok," her voice strained from the exertion. Her father didn't even listen. He just grabbed her elbow to help steady her. She smiled at him and patted the top of his hand.

One of the priests sitting with Monsignor Ryan spotted Mora coming out of the car. He clinked his glass several times with a fork to get everyone's attention and announced she was coming up the front steps. Everyone in the place wanted to rush the front door to greet her, but were respectful enough to give Red and Millie that honor. Mora never made it through the front door. Millie was out on the porch and had her in a bearhug, both women crying so hard they couldn't understand what each other was saying, but they knew. Red was next, with the killing of Mora's attacker their bond was now stronger than ever. He had killed to protect her.

Once inside Mora owned the room. Everyone wanted her attention and she shared it with everyone. They all wanted to hear about the fight, insisting on blow by blow details. Millie was worried that it was all too much for her. "She shouldn't have to relive it," she warned Red.

He nodded in Mora's direction, "Look at her, she's a tough kid."

Millie disagreed and grasped Mora by the elbow and directed her to sit at the corner table. "You look pale, eat something." Millie prepared a bowl of pasta with meatballs and sausage. After several weeks surviving on hospital food, Mora inhaled all that Millie served her. Millie's cooking was the best medicine Mora could ever have. After an hour or so Big Mike told everyone it was time to take Mora home. There was no argument from Mora, she realized just how weak she was.

After another week or so of Millie's food Mora started to feel like herself again. Her strength was returning. It had been almost seven weeks since the stabbing and Mora was ready to get back to work. Sitting around the house was boring and gave her too much time to think about things. Her near death experience had given her a new taste for living. She realized

49

now that she wanted to live harder and faster than before. Her plan was to work at Gunning's for another year or two. She would save every penny she made and then hit the road for adventure.

Mora came back to work under the watchful eye of Millie. There would be no heavy lifting. A stool from the bar was brought in so she would not have to stand all day. Millie saw how well that worked out and had another stool for herself brought in the next day. Steadily Mora's strength returned, soon she had no ill effects from the fight. The tavern was also doing better than ever. There were more customers. People wanted to see the two heroes, have a drink served by the killer of Frank Burrows. Mora's stockpile of money was growing steadily with the influx of new customers. Her dreams of adventure seemed more of a reality everyday.

It was now early fall and Mora was fully recoverd in both mind and body. She had been a little restless lately. She needed to get out and get a little crazy, blow off some steam. Red had received a phone call from J.T. Brown. J.T. had known Red and Millie for years. They loved the way he played his tenor sax. He was going to share a stage with John and Gracie Brim at a little hole in the wall in Chicago. "Sorry it's been so long, but the road, you know, man."

"Just good to hear from you." Red reassured him.

"Hear you had some trouble a little while ago," J.T. coaxed.

Red interrupted him, "Yeah, but it's all good now."

"Wanna come out to our show tonight?"

"Love to, but with everything that happened, I close the tavern nowadays."

"Yeah I understand Red. How's Millie and Mora doing?"

"Fine, fine, everybody's good. Hey, you know what? Mora's been climbing the walls lately. She needs a night out. Can you leave a ticket at the door for her?"

"For Mora, no problem. Two tickets up front will be waiting for her. But it'll cost ya. A little something from Millie's oven if you know what I mean." He finished with a throaty laugh.

"Thanks, I'll make a plate for you myself!"

"Don't forget the bread!"

Red laughed and hung up the phone. He burst through the kitchen doors startling the two women standing by the butcher block table. "Mora, I need you to make a delivery for me."

"Sure, Red. Where to?"

"Chicago."

"Chicago?" both women answered in unison.

"Yeah, you bring the dinner and you get to see a show," Red explained who was playing and where. He gave her directions and told her to go home and get ready. "Don't forget to come back and get the food!"

On the way out the door she spotted Connor. She bounced over to him and asked if he wanted to go to the show. Connor explained that he had to work the next day and couldn't do a show in Chicago. He saw the disappointment on her face, reached into his pocket and tossed the keys to his Indian on the bar. "But my bike can go!"

She kissed him hard and scooped up the keys. "I'm going to have to do something nice for you!"

A sinister look came over his face as he replied, "Yes, you do and I have a good idea what it should be!"

She blushed and ran out the door. Connor's eyes never left her until she was out of sight.

All cleaned up, a care package of food in the saddle bags and the bike gassed up. She was out on the road for the first time since the attack. Mora hated that all time seemed to be identified as before or after the night of her stabbing. She decided that since she was taking the Indian that she would get to the show after the first set. Let the band warm up, feel the mood of the room, then come alive. Even thought Fall was fighting Summer to take over the season the temperature outside was still well over 80 and the humidity just sat on her skin. Better to let it cool down for the ride.

She had looked over Red's directions and they were right on the money. A good direct route, mostly highways and well lit. Mora decided that she would rather take a longer route. One that would take her through as many of the city parks and by as much water as possible. Nothing like feeling the air coming off the cool lakes at night, the smell of the clean air in the parks was invigorating. It was much more romantic than Red's sterile directions. The moonlight peeked through the canopy, its beams dancing on the street before her. Her face was glowing, like a child with a new toy. She rolled back the throttle and the big Indian's engine responded. The red bandana that she wore over her hair was ripped away. She laughed and shook her head letting the wind do what it wanted to her hair.

As she came over a small rise she saw another reason why she took this route. A hard left turn that was slightly banked.

She'd taken this turn several times before but that was always during the daytime. It was pure adreneline, get the bike up to its top end in the straight away. Hug the centerline. Slide one butt cheek off the seat to pull the bike down on its left side. Tilt her left shoulder towards the ground and let centrifical force take her around the turn.

The bike was running hot, chrome exhaust pipes barking out their presence. When she got to the apex of the turn those same pipes sent a startled doe and her fawns scurrying back into the woods that ran along the right side of the road. Without warning the warrior headlight blinded another small fawn that had strayed too far from its mother. Mora saw the fawn's frozen eyes shining back at her. She attempted to swerve but was too far into the turn. The moment she broke form, the bike's back wheel broke loose.

She didn't dare let go of the handlebars to grab the shifter. The small fawn was hit by the full force of the big Indian. Mora was thrown from the bike. The first part of her body to hit the pavement was her right arm, which snapped into mutiple pieces on impact. Her body started to roll uncontrollably. Her left ankle was the next to break. It was all happening so fast that pain had yet to take over. She felt the cool grass under her body as she slid off the hard, hot pavement. The night's humidity had settled on the grass allowing her body to slide even faster. She slid down the slight embankment towards the lake. Her left foot caught a root which spun her around, into a head first slide towards the water. She felt a popping in her neck when her head grazed a rock. She landed a few feet from shore with a splash that sent slumbering geese clambering to the other side of the lake.

She was in four feet of water, cold and clear. Once the water settled down from her entry it reflected the night's stars like a mirror. Mora tried to move her twisted body, it failed her.

The popping she felt in her neck was a snapped vertebrae, paralyzing her. Her mind screamed in terror for her arms and legs to move.

Slowly the water seeped into her clothing. The fabric drank it in like a thirsty child at a picnic. With each sip its weight increased. She was up to her neck in water. She couldn't tell if she was on her knees or not. There was no feeling below her neck, no movement. She released a scream that could wake the dead, but it fell on deaf ears. She hadn't seen another person the entire time she was in this part of the park. The scream expelled air from her lungs making her lose buoyancy. Another scream would not be tried again. As the small air pockets in her clothing exhaled their last breathes she sank further into the water. Her chin was now wet, it was the first time she could feel the wetness on her skin. She would have been thrashing in terror if only she could move. She slipped below the surface of the water gasping for her final breathe, eyes opened wide. Her last vision was of a beautiful indigo colored, star filled sky illuminated by a crescent moon.

It was several days before her body was discovered. A fisherman walking the lake noticed a reflection from the motorcycle's chrome. Everyone had been worried, she was a wild one for sure, but not irresponsible. She never would have taken Connor's ride for days without telling him. Her recuperation in the hospital was the only time she had ever missed work. Millie's nerves were shot. Lighting one cigarette from the butt of her last one. Red was quiet, his mind was everywhere. Couldn't contact J.T. Brown, his was a one night show and Red didn't know where his next gig was. He called every contact he had. The last person to see her was the attendant at the gas station, when she filled up. Hard to forget a beautiful girl on such a large bike.

Millie collasped when Mora's father told her the news. Red felt cheated. He'd saved her once, he wasn't given a chance to do it again. Due to her time under the water it would be a closed casket. Monsignor Ryan held the services. There wasn't a dry eye in the house. The entire neighborhood was in shock. Their new found hero was gone. Red and Millie tried to go on but every sight in the tavern reminded them of Mora. Soon after, Gunning's was sold. The cornerstone of the neighborhood was under new management. Millie and Red retired. They decided to move back to Naples making one side journey on their way to Italy. Red had learned of Lillian's death years earlier and now with some free time on his hands decided to do the honorable thing and visit her grave. Red laid lillies on a grave marked by a lone Celtic Cross. A biting wind rose off Lake Innisfree as Red told Lilly the story of Mora. Millie's hand rubbed his back in a sign of support.

Chapter 7

So there you have my guardian angel, no strong chinned Arc Angel. No Disneyesque pixie, hell I didn't even get the Cary Grant/Topper version of guardian angel. No, no, no. I get a Whiskey drinking, cigar smoking, card playing, pool shooting, bar fighting, take no crap, Blues aficionado, who feels just at home in a kitchen or straddling an Indian motorcycle. It's as they say, "A match made in Heaven."

Chapter 8

Mora stood lost and confused unsure of where she was. Still shaken from the terror of slowly sinking beneath the surface of the lake, with glazed eyes, she took in her surroundings. A line of other souls stood waiting to hear their names called. Suddenly a feeling came over her. Back in the neighborhood of Tinley Park it's know as, "Getting your Irish up."

"Horseshit!" she cursed, "I don't belong here. It's not my fault. Who's running this show? How long have I been here? Monsignor Ryan was right. I should have gone to church more," she thought.

She wandered around and saw nothing but other souls as lost and frightened as she. Her nose picked up an old scent and she followed it like a ravenous dog. She thought her mind was playing tricks on her but she swore she could smell chicken cutlet parmesan on garlic bread. She paused, "Millie! That aroma, it's Millie." Her pace quickened to the point of running. Ahead she heard yelling and spied a woman in a black dress, black shoes, and black handbag that was draped across the inside of her elbow. Her hair was black as coal with a few strands of grey washing through.

This woman in black wasn't yelling, she was just loud and talking at warp speed. The poor angel who was taking the brunt of her wrath was trying to get a word in edgewise, to no avail. "But, but, but," was all he could say before she would hammer him again. Finally he yelled, "Madeline, stop! I can't help you child."

"Child!" Now she was yelling and Mora could definitely tell the difference immediately.

"After what you just put me through, you call me a child?" A smile of recognition started to grow on Mora's face, this Madeline smelled like Millie and yelled like Red. Mora felt a kinship to this woman immediately.

Madeline caught a glimpse of Mora in the corner of her eye. She snapped around to face Mora. "What are you doing here?" An accent so New York it might as well have been dressed in Yankee Pinstripes. Madeline's face twisted, left eye squinted, right eyebrow arched. "Why are sneaking up behind me with that stupid grin for?" The angel who was being berated used this opportunity to exit the area quickly and quietly.

Mora was stunned for a brief moment. Stung by Madeline's sharp tongue. She quickly shook it off, years of working for Red had callused her. "What did you call my grin?"

Madeline fired right back. "Stupid, I called it stupid. You're standing there behind me with this dumb look on your face, Twizzle. What do want me to call it? And why are you standing behind me anyway?"

Mora was getting ready to fire off a retort but realized Madeline was right. She was standing right behind her and a little too close at that. Stammering a little she apologized, "Sorry. You sounded like someone I know, uh knew." Now she was getting perplexed. The aroma of chicken cutlet hit her nose again. She sniffed the air around Madeline. "Why do I keep smelling chicken cutlets and garlic bread?" she asked.

Madeline chuckle, "This Twizzle was alright," she thought to herself, "All set to jump down my throat but chicken cutlets distracted her." She slid her handbag down from her elbow to her hand. Released the latch and handed Mora half a cutlet sandwich wrapped in paper towel. Mora hadn't felt hungry and said so. Madeline answered, "Why, you gotta be hungry to eat?"

Mora nodded her head in agreement and took the sandwich. Madeline reached in her bag and took the other half of sandwich, shrugged her shoulders, and stated, "It's impolite for me to let you eat alone."

"Why were you yelling at that angel?" Mora asked.

Madeline's bottom lip crushed up against her top one. She looked all around, slapped her leg, and muttered through a mouthful of cutlet. Sonofabitch! It was as if a camper stoked the coal of last night's fire, letting air breathe life back into it. The rage built back in Madeline. Swallowing hard to release her mouth for other duties. "Where the hell did that Twizzle go now?" she cursed, as she wiped the side of her mouth with the napkin in which her sandwich had been wrapped.

Mora's eyes opened wide, "Do you think you should be talking like that up here?"

Once again Madeline stopped and gave Mora a quizzical look. "Up here? Ah, where do you think you are, up here?"

Sheepishly she replied, "Heaven?"

"Heaven! This ain't Heaven! It's Limbo." Madeline shook her head and muttered, "Twizzle," under her breathe, "These rat bastards," now yelling for everyone to hear, "Are too stupid for heaven!"

"Limbo?"

"Yeah, Limbo. You know how everyone liked to say that Florida was God's waiting room?' Well, welcome to sunny Florida. Don't forget to apply your coco butter!"

Mora shot Madeline a look that said, "Thanks wiseass." Then became sad over the thought that she never got to see Florida. She'd heard about Miami, Tampa, and the Keys from musicians. It was on her to do list, along with New Orleans, New York, and countless other places. Limbo was not on her list.

She shook away the thought and returned to questioning Madeline. "So why you're so mad at that angel?"

Madeline's eyes became wide, her nostrils flared, and took a calming breathe. "I'm not mad at him, I'm mad at everyone. They made me a guardian angel. Told me it was my duty to watch over him and keep him safe. I'd walk the earth as long as he lived." Opening her ever present black handbag she produced a photo and a Hershey Bar. "Chocolate?" she asked Mora, flashing the candy in her direction.

"I'm good, thank you," waving her hand like she was signaling a Blackjack dealer, "No more cards."

Madeline snapped off a piece for herself, tossed the rest back in her bag, then handed the photo to Mora. "That's my Vinny on his sixth birthday." Mora looked at the picture, then at Madeline several times. Her brain couldn't comprehend what she was seeing. The boy in the picture looked to be about eighty. He had childlike features but the body of an old man.

"It's called Progeria. Something goes wrong in the body and they age rapidly. Vinny died of old friggin age just six months after that photo was taken." Her voice cracking as she choked back tears, unsuccessfully. "No graduations, no first dates," her eyes welling up with tears of anger. "Nothing but hospitals and arthritis and pain." Her hyper New York accent picking up speed and raising an octive higher with each phrase. "They gave me a child to love and watch over, and then gave him a disease I couldn't..." The tears choked off the last of her sentence. "That's why I'm back in Limbo. They are too scared to let me into..." she pointed above her, "There." Mora and Madeline sat and cried together until there where no more tears left.

They would meet daily and talk. Madeline realized that she and Mora had a much deeper connection. She couldn't find the right words or time to explain it to Mora, but it could wait. Time is the one thing they have in abundance in Limbo. Mora told the tale of her life and death. Madeline didn't say it but was impressed that Mora fought Frank Burrows. There were other things Madeline didn't tell Mora. One was that she already knew Mora's story. Another was that Mora would be deathly afraid of any body of water for eternity. It wasn't a problem in Limbo, but if she returned to Earth it could be an issue. Madeline's fear was of Subway platforms. She had met her death at the hands of a platform pusher.

Madeline had ridden subways all her natural life. She was a New Yorker through and through. Able to tell you which lines to take to get anywhere in the City. Tokens were at the ready in a small stylish black alligator change purse, which resided in her black handbag. Safety was always a concern on the platforms and on the trains themselves. Madeline was smart, eyes ever alert for someone who didn't look right. Handbag strap wrapped around her arm and held tight fisted. She knew that if trouble came her way she was armed; house keys held between her fingers like brass knuckles.

What she never expected was the well dressed, clean shaven man who stood close enough to smell his expensive cologne, would have a demented side to him. As the No. 6 Train was entering the station, his hands found the small of her back. The noise and vibration from the train disguised his movement. With a forceful shove, Madeline was on the tracks just feet from the oncoming No. 6. The next morning curious straphangers could still see remnants of her belongings scattered down the tracks. A pack of gum, tokens, and hairbrush all littered the tracks of the No. 6 station. Every year on the anniversary of her death, her sister Joanna would arrive at the station, and place a wreath of flowers by the track and say a silent prayer. That night, a transit employee would toss the arrangement into a metal garbage can.

Mora and Madeline had a close connection, closer than Mora could ever imagine. More importantly for Madeline, she had another foodie around her. Someone who worked in a kitchen. Someone with Sunday gravy in her veins. Madeline called out to Mora. "Hey, Twizzle!"

Before she could finish her sentence, Mora cut her off. Her face was emotionless and her voice had a rough edge to it, "All right, what's with the Twizzle? I'm not sure if I should hug you or slug you, so what's a Twizzle?"

Madeline paused in deep reflection before answering. Twizzle had been a word, more of a term that she'd been using most of her life. It isn't an easy question to answer. Funk and Wagnall have no entry for it in their dictionary.

Madeline explained that in her earthly days she was from Harlem. 117th Street between 1st and Pleasant Avenue. 117th is how it's written but in her neighborhood it sounded like "Ahun seventeen." A crowded neighborhood with more characters than your local library. Virtually everyone had a nickname or an alias. A Catholic area where Mount Carmel Church was at its cornerstone. The social club around the corner was another well established force in the community.

The mothers on her block all wore housedresses, shopped daily for their groceries, and knew everything that was going on in the neighborhood by stopping and talking to the neighbors and shop owners. Some sat on the stoop, others perched in their windows. They were the original neighborhood watch, nothing got past their ever watchful eyes. It was a rough neighborhhod, where people used hard language. Madeline's parents would beat them senseless if they heard their daughters using such language. So Madeline, and her crew of friends, instead of catching a beating for using curse words, developed their own curses.

They were mostly Italian with street slang, Spanish and Black thrown in. Sometimes a word would be mispronounced by someone, each of the girls played with a variation of the word until they made it their own.

Cocknocker was one. It was used for a male who was a pain in the ass.

Zorkala, that one was the neighborhood whore.

Capichooch, is a person with a big head. Either they physically had a large head or sometimes it meant that someone was full of themselves.

Gomada, it meant best female friend.

Twizzle started out as a female who was a pain in the ass. It grew to mean other things mostly because it's a fun sounding word. If you were jealous of another girl for any reason she became a Twizzle. If good fortune was bestowed on someone she became a lucky Twizzle. It also became a reference to a part of the female anatomy. "Go play with your Twizzle," was a common phrase, another was, "Her Twizzle must be lined with silk." It wasn't just used for people they disliked. Friends also became Twizzles in the blink of an eye. Stutter a word or misspeak, and you were a "Dumb Twizzle."

Mora said "I still don't know whether to hug you or slug you?"

Madeline smiled "I know, ain't it a great word?"

Chapter 9

Mora's mind kept wandering back to something Madeline said about Vinny. "I would walk the earth for as long as he lived." She questioned Madeline constantly about it. Finally one day Madeline confronted her about it. "You're thinking about becoming a guardian, aren't you, you Twizzle?"

"Thinking about it," Mora answered vaguely.

"You know, it's no vacation. It's 24/7, no rest. Now don't get me wrong, you're alright in my book but you're a little rough around the edges."

Mora's cheeks flushed as if she'd been slapped, "What?"

"Don't get upset now, Twizzle, but let's think about it. You're a drinker and a smoker, those damn smelly little cigars, not even cigarettes. And who knows what else, hanging out with all those bands. You live a bit dangerously. Motorcycles," she dragged out the word motorcycle for effect, "You know guarding a child is like," she paused to get the correct phrasing in her mind, "Like making a good Risotto. You constantly have to be ready to stir, add a bit more stock at just the right time, and never take your eye off it."

Mora cut in, "Yeah, I know how to make great Risotto, don't forget the butter at the end for a nice sheen," she tried to bite her tongue but her Irish was up now and she was going to say her piece. "Oh and maybe since we're going to talk about kids like they're food; mine will be more of a nice stew. And for your information, a motorcycle isn't dangerous! It's those freakin deer that are a menace!"

Madeline's eyes narrowed, she didn't like being spoken back to, yet was intrigued to hear a good stew recipe. "You know you sound crazy," she said in Italian, "Botz!"

"Maybe I'll just add the right ingredients at the right time, turn the heat down low, put a lid on it..."shooting a look at Madeline while she said the last part. "Step outside for a smoke and drink, and just stir the pot every now and then so shit doesn't stick. How's that work for ya?"

Madeline was hurt and all this talk of food was getting her hungry. "Fine. You're so smart. Go guard one. You'll see." She then turned and walked away.

Mora planned out her becoming a guardian angel. Mora had always felt cheated out of her life. She yearned to still live it to her fullest and becoming a guardian angel was a means to an end in her mind. If she worked it right she still might see all those wonderful places all the band members had told her about. "I'll have to put in my time in the beginning, but after the kid gets a little older, I should have lots of free time," she thought to herself. "The kid's going to have parents. I don't need to be a fulltime babysitter. This just might be a sweet gig."

A day or so later, Madeline and Mora met. Time had cooled everyone's temper and both agreed that there wasn't just one way to guard a child. Madeline introduce her to the right people and got the wheels turning for Mora to return to Earth in the role of guardian angel. A date, time, and place was given to her. June 16, 1959, St. Lawrence Hospital, Bronxville, New York, at 11:33 p.m.

The day she was to leave for her trip back to Earth she met up with Madeline. "This is the most important thing you'll ever do so don't screw it up, Twizzle" she smirked as she said it and both women chuckled. It was a nervous laugh.

Then Madeline held Mora's face and told her not to be scared, "You'll do great." Mora thought about Millie. Millie had held her face the same way. She was brought back into the moment by Madeline's voice, "Don't worry. I'll check in on you from time to time."

Mora asked quizzically, "You can do that?"

Madeline's face lit up with an impish grin. "You'd be amazed at what I can do," then she lifted her arm and pointed to her black handbag, "You hungry?"

Chapter 10

In a sterile, white tiled room a woman with her feet in cold stainless steel stirrups moaned. She had been in labor for several hours and was exhausted. It was 11:31 p.m. and Doris, the tall, mocha skinned nurse dressed in starched whites checked her clipboard and then her Timex. She turned to the woman in labor, "Now honey, you needs to shake that money maker and get that child here. I got a date tonight and can't be late."

The woman in stirrups found that hysterical and started to laugh which in turn loosened up everything. Next thing I know I'm riding down the slip and slide of life arriving at 11:33 p.m. Doris got to her date on time, I was swaddled and placed in loving arms, and Mora was outside having a smoke looking up at the stars. Mora made a mental decision to stick with her plan on guarding me. I'd be a stew, not a risotto. A large part of her plan was just pure luck since she had no influence on it. I wound up in a loving, caring family. In Mora's wonderful stew Artie and Eileen were the meat and potatoes.

Today's guardian angels have it so much harder. Crack heads having babies. Girls not even old enough to drive having babies. Babies born to women in prison. Man talk about having the deck stacked against you. It's a wonder anyone takes the job anymore.

My mother was the original Martha Stewart. Halloween costumes were handmade and many won some prize at school functions. Birthday cakes were made from scratch and expertly decorated. You name the committee and she was on it; Holy Name, Altar Rosary, Boy Scouts, Girl Scouts, Bingo!

My dad was just the same. He worked all day as a conductor on the railroad, Hudson Line out of Grand Central. At night he'd do auto body work. Weekends he'd take my brother and me fishing. I have him to thank for that lifelong addiction. Anywhere he could find an empty spot of soil; a tomato plant would find a home. His garden consisted of sixty five tomato plants and hundreds of lettuce plants. The man's part rabbit! He fussed over those plants like those crazy mothers who put their five year old daughters in beauty pageants.

So while many of Mora's contemporaries were staying up late at night keeping an eye on the kids, Mora could relax as Artie and Eileen were on duty. Mora found watching a baby a bit boring, "All they do is eat, crap, and sleep!" she thought. In just a little time her attitude changed. A crawling and then walking baby is a walking, crawling nightmare if you're in Mora's profession. Three quick steps, a wiggle, a wobble, and they're falling, banging their heads against coffee tables or walking into doors. They're just an accident waiting to happen. Mora couldn't wait for my parents to finally put me in a crib for a nap. It was the only time she could relax and have a smoke, or maybe pour herself a few fingers of Bourbon.

This is when Madeline would usually show up. Mora's favorite place to hang was the roof over our front porch. It was on the sunny side of the house and she could watch the neighbors as they went by. She could hear music coming from nearly every home on the block. Mostly it was Soul and R&B. On Sunday it was all Gospel. It was also right outside my room where she could keep an eye on me.

"Twizzle, what are you doing?" Madeline would squeal. It always had the desired effect on Mora, that being to startle the hell out of her.

"Mad," Mora started calling Madeline *Mad* when she became Earthbound again. Mad was never sure if she was shortening her name or being called crazy. Madeline considered it just another reason to call her a Twizzle. It also made Madeline squint her left eye, like she was trying to see through the name. It brought joy to Mora's heart to be able to drive her friend a little crazy. "What's wrong with you? I almost spilled my drink!" she muttered, holding a small cigar with a long ash dangling from the side of her mouth.

"Me! You are supposed to be watching the baby, not out on a roof sunning your Twizzle, with a drink in your hand."

Mora just nodded her head in my direction, "He's finally sleeping." At that, Madeline's eyes went wide.

"Oh, let me see the baby!" her voice so excited it sounded like fingernails on a chalk board. "Look at those fat little legs I just want to chew them up!"

"What are you? A cannibal?" Mora would crack. After giving me a good looking over and a lesson in baby talk, Madeline turn her attention back to Mora.

"So tell me, How you doing?"

"Good. It's an easy gig. The parents are on top of everything, there's a grandmother on the bottom floor. She steps in whenever they need a helping hand. Then there's the dog. Scruffy looking mutt follows the kid everywhere. The kid pulls his hair all day long and he just stands there and licks the kid's face."

"You know the *kid* has got a name. It's Shamus in case you haven't heard." Madeline paused, "Look, I know it can be boring but it will get better. You do realize that it is for his entire life. You do get to have some influence in it you know. Nothing too direct but something subtle done now can have long lasting effects. So you'd better start enjoying him. They are a gift you know."

Mora changed after that talk. She liked music; she wanted me to like music. Music was always playing outside. She placed an idea in my grandmother's head that I wasn't getting enough fresh air. My grandmother told my mother to have a window open while I slept, "It's good for the baby." I was listening to Marvin Gaye by the end of the week. Later in life it became apparent I had no musical abilities. I could listen all day long, but would never play any instrument.

Motorcycles were still a deep passion of hers. It always seemed that every time a motorcycle pulled up next to our car the rider revved his engine. This drove my father nuts and he'd call them every name he could think of. Still it got motorcycles in my brain. I'd look for them everywhere we drove. When guys on bikes would come roaring up past us on the highway I'd always wave. Most of the time I'd get a wave or a thumbs up from them. These guys were cool; leather jackets, bandanas, chrome pipes, some girl holding on tight to them, what's not to like?

Mora was starting to feel a bit smug about her abilities. She had overlooked one small detail. Artie and Eileen were beach people. Nothing short of a monsoon would keep them off the beach.

A day at the beach as any parent can tell you, "Is no day at the beach." I was the third child, and only three years separated me from my older brother, Sean. Susan has three years seniority on Sean. The wood paneled Country Squire station wagon would be packed with everything to keep three kids occupied at the beach for a full day.

Mora watched the choreographed loading of the car with great interest. Being a mid-western girl she had never had any firsthand knowledge of oceans and beaches. Lake Michigan, which was her home town lake, is one sizeable piece of water, literally a great lake. However, it pales in comparison to the Atlantic Ocean. She was starting to get a queasy stomach as she began to inventory the items in the car. Tomorrow would be her first day by water since her death.

She sat outside my window all night. The gutters on that old porch must have looked like an ashtray by daylight. "Shamus baby, you need to learn straight off that water is not to be trusted. You want to climb mountains or jump out of planes, baby, I'm right there with you. But water…" she nervously exhaled the smoke from her cigar, her body shivered but not from the night air, "Just not water," she pleaded.

The next morning the old Country Squire station wagon headed to Jones Beach.

Located in Wantagh Long Island, Jones Beach stretches for six and a half miles along the coast. Mora rode on the top of the car. She never lost the love of having the wind blow through her hair. A mile or so before you reach the beach as you cruise down the Meadowbrook State Parkway; you start to catch the scent of the ocean, clean, fresh, brine. The Atlantic, that day, was slightly kicked up by an offshore storm. Three to four foot waves crashed against the sand, depositing shells, seaweed, and white foam.

Mora was as white as the foam. Never had she felt a power like this, she was petrified. The water that took her life was still and calm. The only ripples on the water were from her sliding into it. It was still able to pull the life out of her. The Atlantic, whether she's tranquil or raging, is raw power at its finest. Waves were crashing, blustery wind blowing in off the water, sand and salt peppering her skin, Mora sat on the blanket exhausted. How could she ever fight an ocean? "It goes on forever, engulfs you even when you're not in the water," she worried.

Then, the horror of all horrors, my father held me in his arms and took me to the water's edge. Holding me tightly he let the waves splash against my legs, lifting me when every one of the big waves came rolling in. I giggled the way happy babies do, squealing with sheer delight. I was officially christened, a beach loving, ocean swimming, body surfing, surf fishing, beach rat. It was probably one of Mora's saddest days. Her wails of pain were drowned out by ocean, wind, and the call of hundreds of black faced gulls. Every weekend during the summer months we were on the beach.

Each Friday night the packing of the car became a bigger chore. My father yelling, "Where the hell are the kids sand pails?"

Mom yelling back, "Did you check the garage?"

This would go on for hours. Everything seemed out of place and eventually all the kids would get yelled at for moving all the beach gear. It was Mora just being a Twizzle.

Mora didn't move them. She didn't have to. Sean, since the day he was born, had been building things. When he was building something it wouldn't matter if you owned a Ming vase. If it fit as part of his master plan he was going to use it. Give that kid an erector set or Lincoln logs and stand back. Two things are going to take place. Something extraordinary will be built and, more than likely, Sean is going to the emergency room. Sean always seemed to be able to get his fingers in the way of some moving part and off we'd go to the hospital. My brother's hospital records resemble the yellow pages of a small town.

Mora used Sean quite a bit in her master plan to keep my family away from the beach. Most accidents would happen on a Friday night, right in the middle of packing the car. Her plan only slowed us down never stopped us. One parent would take Sean to the hospital while the other would get everything ready and waiting by the front door.

The one nasty trick Mora did use successfully was planting the idea in my mother's head that a person needs to wait half an hour after eating before going back into the water. "You'll cramp up and drown. Now sit on the blanket and just wait." I would go play in the water for awhile, come out of the water starving, eat something and become a prisoner of the beach blanket for thirty minutes. Mora worked it where I seemed to spend half my beach time out of the water. What a Twizzle!

Mora's plan to not stand over me but instead have the right people come into my life was working out quite well. I had a good family surrounding me. Now she needed to add some outside influences. It was time to build her stew. The first ingredient would be mushrooms. She chose my friend David. David was chosen because, like mushrooms, David absorbs all that goes on around him the way mushrooms soak up any broth in which they are placed. She decided to start the first day of kindergarten. There, I met my lifelong friend, David Thomas, aka Uncle Big Head, or Uncle Stupid Head.

David can make something funny out of anything, and usually has the entire crowd around him in tears with laughter. Since David and I were the tallest in the class the anal retentive nuns who always liked everything in size order, had the two goofballs sitting next to each other. It worked well for me; I received an education and watched a comedy act every day.

Dave's entire family is funny. We were sitting on the couch in his mother's house one afternoon. *"His Girl Friday,"* was on. It's a classic film with Cary Grant and Rosalind Russell. There is a scene where several reporters are on different telephones, they are going at it in rapid fire reporter talk. David starts reciting lines from it like he was an understudy for the show. His sister, Donna, walks in and picks up the dialogue like it was written for her. Then his brother, Greg, walks and joins in, mimicking what's happening word for word. The tones, pitch and pauses were dead on. Now more actors join in on the set and David's family are taking on more characters and not missing a beat. I'm sitting there; my head's bouncing from the TV to each of them, like I was at some mad tennis match.

Many are the times I heard him describe someone as a "Booger eating idiot," or a "Jackenhimer." There was a Korean kid down the block whose name sounded, David would say, "Like you threw metal off a building, ting, tong, ping." His humor wasn't cruel even if you're the butt of one of his jokes. When he hears or sees something that is low down or foul he'll claim "Now that's roach hockey, and there ain't nothing lower than roach hockey."

Mora loved Dave from day one. He was made first, longest, and best friend for life. Years later he would marry Joan. Joan fit in with his crazy family perfectly. It was like watching the girls on my block jumping Double Dutch. One would be rocking back and forth getting the rhythm and timing perfect and effortlessly glide into the swinging ropes keeping cadence with the others. Braided hair tipped with colored beads, all bouncing and clacking together in perfect unison.

Big Head and I were the test pilots for many of my brother's inventions. Sean would roam around the Bronx with a 9/16th and a ½" wrench in his pockets. He'd come peddling up the driveway with parts he "*found*" from "*abandoned*" bicycles. Sean would then build these crazy contraptions. Sawing the forks off of one bike and adding them onto the forks of another bike to extend them out. He had probably three fork lengths on one bike. He used a steering wheel instead of handle bars and oversized sprockets and chains. Yes sir, it was a real piece of mechanical genius. Big Head and I were all set to be test pilots. The next street over from my house was Kingsbridge Road. It was as steep as Mount Everest to two twelve year olds. A couple of peddles of the oversized sprockets and a speed of Mach one was achieved. All systems were a go, careening down Kingsbridge Road at warp speed.

NASA we have a problem! The mad genius forgot to put brakes on his little invention. Big Head and I burned through the soles of our Chuck Taylor's in no time flat. We probably slowed ourselves down to a ¼ mach. It was time to take evasive actions. Find the largest piece of granite there is and crash head on. No one said test pilots were smart. That was the day Big Head and I became blood brothers.

Mora who was well acquainted with bad crashes figured any crash you can walk away from is a good crash. We carried home the remnants of my brother's invention and deposited them in the driveway. Standing there in torn bloodied clothes and ripped skin, my mom spraying us with Bactine, whose active ingredient, by the way, is kerosene. Big Head didn't come over for a few weeks after that. We still carry scars on our bodies from that day.

Madeline would stop by to check things out.

"Twizzle! How are you?"

"Hey Mad. I'm good, actually I'm great. We're moving!" she said with noticeable joy in her voice. No more oceans. It's to the hills of Brewster for this family!" she cheered as she danced a little Irish jig.

"Careful what you wish for." Madeline semi sang her warning.

Mora eyed Madeline, thinking of a response, when the smell of éclairs stopped her dead in her tracks. "Éclairs?"

"Oh yeah, you gotta try these!" as she quickly pulled a white box fastened by red and white twine.

In a critical voice Madeline said, "I see Shamus has got quite a few new scars on him. Is everything alright?"

Mora became defensive, "He's a boy and they're supposed to have scars. It builds character for later on in life." Mora then took a bite of her pastry, "Umm, these are good," Mora muttered while tilting her head back trying to not lose any of the cream from her éclair.

Madeline nodded her response incapable of talking while eating an éclair. After swallowing, Madeline changed the subject. "So, tell me about this Brewster."

"Love to but I've never been there. Artie and Eileen like it well enough. Clean fresh air, plenty of room to play, good schools, and all around safe place to raise kids."

"What the hell do you mean 'you've never been there?'" Madeline's eyes grew wide as her voice hardened.

"Simmer down, Mad. They never took Shamus with them so I had to stay here and keep an eye on him. He's always into something. You know he was drinking a beer and had his first cigarette the other day."

Madeline just gave Mora a blank stare and said, "Well the apple doesn't fall far from the tree now does it?"

"Oh come on Madeline, he's not a baby. He's going to try things. He's 14."

Madeline took another bite from her éclair to prevent her from lashing out at Mora, but a muddled "Twizzle" was barely audible as Madeline shook her head.

This tweaked Mora and she let Madeline know, "Oh and you have tons of experience guarding 14 year old boys, don't you?"

This stung Madeline and Mora was sorry she said it the moment the words left her mouth. "Madeline, I'm sorry. I overreacted. Shamus is mine and I don't like hearing from anyone that anything is wrong with him or how I guard him."

Madeline was hurt but also proud. "Well, I'm just happy to see you've taken an interest in Shamus. There was a time in the beginning I wasn't so sure you deserved to be a guardian." Trying to change subjects Madeline asked, "So, why Brewster?"

"Artie's a conductor, as you know, so he needs to live by a train line. The house has a big yard from what I hear, so he'll lose his mind planting vegetables. It's also surrounded by woods. Now that Shamus is getting older and the woods are right in their backyard, Artie will have an easier time teaching him to hunt. You know Artie's a deer hunter!" her voice crackled with excitement. "He's taken Shamus once or twice for rabbits and birds. He took to it like a duck to water." Madeline could hear and feel the hesitation when Mora said the word water.

"Still haven't got past the water and deer thing have you?"

"Leave it alone and don't interrupt. My Shamus will be a deer hunter. I guarantee it."

"Well it's nice to see you're not fixating on this Mora," Madeline said while rolling her eyes. They parted company after Madeline was secure in Mora's guardianship of me.

Chapter 11

I wasn't the only thing growing and changing in the world. The Blues were being replaced by the very thing they inspired, Rock 'n' Roll. Mora would hear songs on the radio and smile in amazement. A kid named Elvis had a song a while back called, "You Ain't Nothin' but a Hound Dog." Everyone was calling him the *King of Rock 'n' Roll* and acting like *Hound Dog* was his very own song. "I like his version of it but Big Mamma Thornton was singing that song when I was alive," she thought. Later on she said the same thing about a song called "Ball and Chain" sung by a girl with crazy hair and bad skin from Texas called Janis Joplin. Then all these English groups started coming to America. Mora was always shocked to hear British singers do interviews. They would sing in perfect American English but talk with Cockney or London accents.

She'd hear the Stones and think of Muddy Waters. George Thorogood sprang from Johnny Lee Hooker. It was Eric Clapton that brought back the most memories for her. Sometimes you can feel Blues Boys influence on him, other times it's Bo Diddley or Buddy Guy. Many years later she would be floored by another kid out of Texas. "That Stevie Ray Vaughn, now that's the real deal right there. That boy could actually make a dead girl like me feel my blood pumping. He even dresses like a black man!"

Rock 'n' Roll was on the move and so was my family. Looking like the Clampett's in reverse we loaded the U-haul and headed up 684 North to Brewster. The Brewster of my times was a railroad town. It used to be a mining town way back when and still had some vegetable and horse farms. It was surrounded by lakes and reservoirs. Those lakes and reservoirs kept me busy in my early teens.

Brewster is nestled in the hills about an hour North of Manhattan. It has the most picturesque setting of any town. When you crest the last hill on 684 and look down on the area, it's breathtaking. My family moved there in autumn and the trees were ablaze with color. The lakes and reservoirs would mirror the trees and sky. It's the place where Currier and Ives envisioned vacationing.

As we crested that last hill, Mora cocked her head like a Labrador Retriever that just spotted a squirrel. A sound resonated off those yellow, orange, and red festooned hills. It was the "Sound of Music."

No, not Julie Andrews prancing around the hillsides of some Nazi invaded country. This was Rock 'n' Roll. Brewster had one other very outstanding characteristic about it. The town boasted no less than seventeen bars in a two mile stretch of Route 6. They fell into two categories: Little hole in the wall Saloons and Taverns or Rock 'n' Roll bars. Most were dark, smoke filled, watering holes frequented by locals. The only time they were ever truly busy was when it was deer season. There were close to 50 different bars in a 100 mile radius that had bands playing nightly. It wasn't until later in life that I found out that not everyone grew up with the ability to see live bands any night of the week. A large part of Mora's plan just fell into her lap the day my parents bought the house in Brewster. She would be able to hear bands playing almost every night of the week if she wanted to. I would also be able to hunt deer in my backyard.

The hole in the wall bars would be filled with accountants and civil servants from New York trying to escape from their wives. All wearing red and black flannel shirts, sporting three day beards to try to act like they were Paul Bunyan. Getting into the great outdoors was a big deal for these great hunters. They'd dress in layers of wool underwear and Woolrich pants and jackets. Heavy wool socks slipped inside hunting boots that never saw the outdoors unless there was a snowstorm that hit the city. Gun belts with enough rounds to hold off the German army were worn around their waist. They'd wake up at 4:00 a.m. and head to the nearest diner, order sausage and eggs with coffee. All inhaled without the mandatory lecture on the dangers of cholesterol from their wives. Once at the parking area designated by the Department of Conservation these new aged Davey Crockett's headed into the woods for a good 100 yard march, all tiptoeing as if Elmer Fudd gave them stalking lessons. Their elusive prey was searched for behind every rock and bush. Each would find that magical spot where the sun would poke through the canopy, sit with their red plaid covered bodies against a tree, and fall fast asleep. It's truly a miracle that whitetails aren't on the endangered species list.

One of the oddest watering holes was Jerry's. Jerry's had the distinction of being situated at the highest elevation of all watering holes in Putnam County. A fact that Jerry informed everyone and anyone who ever walked into the place. Not that many people actually went into Jerry's or even knew the place was open for business. The rumor was that it originally was a chicken coop. I cannot disprove this rumor and can easily understand why it started. The place was maybe 8 feet across by 20 feet long. Anyone over 6'5" rubbed their head against the ceiling. That fact could easily be the reason I never once saw any players from the NBA hanging out in Jerry's. The place had been painted bright pink sometime in the late 40's. The sides of that building were never tickled by a paint brush ever again. When I first saw Jerry's, it was an extremely muted pink. The pink of chewing gum that came with baseball cards. The muted pink color made the building look as if was a nursing home for retired Flamingos. Older birds, that could no longer deal with the humidity of Florida.

The parking lot was festooned with an array of rusted vehicles that would never again see asphalt. They started new lives as condos for field mice and raccoons. Once inside it was like walking into a madman's funhouse. As you opened the front door a string which was fastened to the door stretched. This in turn would send a toy monkey on a skateboard sliding down the string. As the monkey slid, its little monkey hands would bang a pair of cymbals. This wasn't a cute little monkey; fact was it was an ugly little sucker that would scare the hell out anyone not expecting it.

When I first met Jerry he reminded me of some old vaudeville comedian who missed the bus for the next show in the Borscht Belt of the Catskills. He'd never play the grand ballroom at Grossinger's or open up for Shecky Greene at the Nevelee. He had missed the bus for the Catskills and just put down roots in the pink chicken coop. I learned Jerry's real story later on. He was a trained Opera singer, certainly had the pipes for it. Somehow life decided that his stage should be in a pink chicken coop and not the Metropolitan Opera House.

He was still doing his act though, three shows a day whether there was anyone to hear it or not. Ask for a book of matches and that's exactly what you got. Jerry had hollowed out the pages of some thick volume book and filled it with books of matches. He'd hand you the whole book. Drinks were served in glasses that in a previous life served as vessels for jelly. It was one of those places that always had Christmas lights up behind the bar.

The juke box was filled with Sinatra and Dean Martin and Opera classics. It was his place and he was going to play what he liked. Jerry would sing along and serenade any woman in the place. If you were smart enough to look past all the gags in the place he'd give you a real education on Opera. He'd lean against the bar and sing along with Marilyn Horne or Maria Callas. At times I thought his voice would shake the old place apart. Jerry would also do play by play on the Operas. He'd give you the real inside scoop on what they were singing about. The, who loves who, who's no good, that one's a real Putz, he'd say with a bit of a Yiddish accent. When you understand the story and then throw in those powerful voices, Opera's got something to it.

After Madeline's first episode with the monkey and his cymbals she always was busy when Mora said we were headed to Jerry's.

Chapter 12

Mora watched over me for a day or so making sure I wasn't killed in an avalanche of moving boxes. "Madeline would never let me live it down," she thought, then becoming reflective, "Is live it down the right phrase for someone in my situation?" Shaking the thought from her head she investigated the rest of neighborhood. Nothing about the neighborhood gave her any real concern. She started a mental pro's and con list. The reservoir down the road was marked with a big check mark in the Con column. There is a really cool hairpin turn the old Indian would have loved about halfway up the main road. She placed a mark in the Pro column! A few more items found their way onto both sides of the list but all in all a safe neighborhood.

As night fell and the entire family found sleep hard to resist after a day of painting and unpacking, Mora walked barefoot in the cool, dew laden grass in the backyard. The cool grass growing carefree never suspecting large portions would fall under the blade of Artie's spade. 100 feet by 40 feet would be turned over for a vegetable garden. Every kid growing up wanted to be a cowboy or Indian from the movies. Artie wanted to be the sod buster.

There was a rock the size of a Volkswagen about midway down the backyard. It was fast becoming Mora's favorite spot to have a whiskey and a cigar. Far enough away from the chaos of the house but close enough to keep an eye on me. Each night at dusk she'd sit there and watch deer come out of the woods to graze on Artie's grass. Mora would watch them closely. She'd take a sip of whiskey, point her cigar in their direction, and say, "Enjoy it, you Twizzles, I got a plan for you!" When I'd fall asleep she'd whisper tales of hunting and camping. Great adventures in the outdoors I'd grow up to enjoy. She'd smile a vengeful smirk and her eyes would grow wide thinking about what was in store for those damn deer.

Our house was situated on top of a hill and if conditions were just right Mora could hear music playing. Waiting until everyone was asleep she'd leave to go exploring, convincing herself that this was part of her guardian duties. "How could I possibly let Shamus wander about, without doing a little scouting first? The boy might get into some kind of trouble," she would tell herself. She would follow the music across the hilltop and around the lakes.

At one point she was torn on which way to go. The smell of burgers and the sound of laughter emanated from the South. Music, hard and loud, was coming from the North. She turned her head from North to South several times as if she had center court seats at Wimbledon. "What would Madeline do?" she wondered, then decided to go South, following the aroma of burgers.

She found herself standing in front of an old building, sided in wide, rough hewn planking. A sign whose lettering was losing the battle against weather and time read "The Old Homestead". "This place has got some history I bet," she thought as she wandered in. Inside there were twenty or so patrons bellied up to the bar. The air was thick with the blue haze from cowboy killers burning away in the ashtrays. Everyone either watching sports on an old television mounted high to the ceiling by the men's room or listening to the bartender telling some story.

The man behind the bar was a legend in these parts. His name was Norm. The sign above the building may have read "The Old Homestead" but everyone called it "Norm's." Norm lost his sight years ago. I'm not positive how. It became one of those urban legends. Didn't really matter, it happened so long ago that virtually everyone knew him as the blind Norm. Norm's voice was booming. Norm had a voice that sounded like he gargled with rocks. He could easily be heard above any crowd.

Mora being the type of woman who loves characters, immediately took a liking to him.

Anyone who ever had Norm pour them a cocktail had one of his thick fingers in their drink. He would keep one finger in the glass so he knew when to stop pouring. People who were new to the place didn't always realize he was blind. He knew the bar like the back of his hand. He could tell where you were standing and he would come right to where you were. Norm would take your order, turn around to where he kept the liquor bottles, and start pouring the drink order. Turn back around and place them right in front of you. It was all very fluid. The trouble normally started when a new customer wasn't paying attention and just held out his money. Norm wouldn't know where to grab for the money and tell the guy with his booming voice, "You want to help me out here a little, Bud?" The customer would then realize what he did and get all embarrassed.

Sometimes, new customers would try and get away from paying full price for drinks. They were normally stupid young kids. They'd order twenty dollars worth of drinks and hand him a five. Norm would take the bill; look the kid square in the face, and say, "I'm blind, not stupid, asshole! Now pay for the drinks or I'll toss you out of here!" What they never knew was that Norm was so beloved in Brewster that there was always a regular sitting in one of the corners keeping a watchful eye out. Whenever they saw someone trying to pull a fast one, instead of getting involved, they would just tap on their glass or the bar, to signal Norm that he was being ripped off. It was a wonderful system and helped Norm's legend grow. Mora would shake her head and chuckle whenever she watched it unfold. Thoughts of Red would soon follow and make her a bit melancholy.

Norm's was quickly added to her list of places I should frequent. Not only did she enjoy the people but other requirements were also met. First, Norm's served up one of the best burgers you ever sank your teeth into. No little frozen patty. This was fresh ground beef, about an inch thick, on a Kaiser roll. Large order of steak fries, lettuce and tomato. Second was the "Mystery," Norm's version of a Bloody Mary. It had the right consistency, full of flavor, with just a bit of a bite to it, and a stalk of celery. The celery wasn't a garnish. It was a tool. You used it to keep the Tabasco, black pepper and other bits of flavor from settling on the bottom. Mora's first thought was that, "Madeline would love these!" It fast became Brewster's cure for a hangover, which was only fair since it was the cause of many of those hangovers. Whenever I traveled to see folks who lived in Brewster at one time or another, they'd always ask me to bring them a bottle or two of the "Mystery" mix.

Norm's became one of Mora's main stomping grounds. On any night something was bound to happen with the cast of characters who hung out there. One night, one of the regulars, a big fellow named Jimmy, was getting very drunk. He was sitting on a barstool next to the men's room. Jimmy took a bowl of peanuts with him into the bathroom. A minute or two later, he emerged, stripped naked, with the floor mat wrapped around his shoulders. The bowl from the peanuts was being worn as a crown. Jimmy then burst through the bathroom door singing. "If I were the King of the Jungle," Like Dorothy and Toto had just blown in from Kansas. The whole place gave him a standing ovation.

Norm turned to another regular named Wolf and ordered him to drive Jimmy home. "Wolf, give Jimmy a ride home. He can't drive in that condition."

Wolf replied, "Why not, he's driven naked before!"

Norm hesitated at Wolf's reply, shouting, "Naked! Oh Christ, get him the hell out of here!" Mora clapped with gusto and whistled at Jimmy like she was hailing a cab. It was the Gong Show and American Idol all mixed together with a few shots of Tequila thrown in for good measure.

Chapter 13

Mora had a very difficult balancing act for the next few years. Since she wanted music and travel she needed to instill a freewheeling side to me yet keep me out of trouble and harm's way. She had it easy so far with a loving, caring family to look after me. The little boy she whispered to at night heard everything she said and was starting to awaken as a wild eyed teen. Now my family is not one of those families that poses together in photos all wearing the same sweatshirt, with the family name on it. Christmas is our time of the year for us all to get together. We are all individuals, each has their own calling. Sean's thing is cars. Antique, hot rod or rusted out pieces of crap he just lives for them. To me a car is just something to get me from point A to point B. So I'm never hanging with him going to a car show. Somehow smoky bars with Rock 'n' Roll and pool tables just seemed to call me. It's almost as if someone was guiding me.

These were the start of my high school years. It was also time for Mora to add another ingredient into that stew of friends. The next ingredient came in the form of a guy named Mike Tompkins. Mike is the peas and carrots of Mora's stew. Tons of color had just been added to her stew. Mike and I became thick as thieves from the word go. Mike was a wild man. Mora had her reasons for choosing Mike but also made her work harder at her job than ever before.

I met Mike in Spanish 101 taught by Mr. Acrish. It was first period of the first day of high school. I knew nobody, Mike knew everyone, or they knew of him. He was no bully, never once acted tough, and he didn't have to. Mike was not the type of guy who was going to take any crap from anyone. By third period we were having a beer together behind the school.

From the very first time we hung out together, Mora needed to be on her "A" game.

I had walked over to his house. His dad, Bill, was on the front porch having a cup of coffee and a smoke while reading the day's newspaper. He asked where I lived.

When Bill asked you something it was as if a Drill Sergeant asked you a question. It was direct and there was no avoiding the question. Mike's dad was from the *Greatest Generation* and he was one of their best. He lied about his age to join in the service of his country. He toured Italy at sixteen, carrying a carbine the whole way. 50 years later he lay in a hospital bed suffering from clogged arteries. In the bed next to him lay an elderly Italian gent who was ready to meet his maker. The guy was talking a mile a minute in Italian. The nurses all looked at each other not understanding any of the gibberish he was speaking.

Now I grew up with Italians my entire life but knew nothing of what this old guy was saying. Bill, as white bread as you could be, turns and starts speaking fluent Italian like he stepped off the boat yesterday with an eggplant under one arm and a salami under the other. He explains to the nurses what the old guy was saying and the rest of us sat there in awe.

Folks, when John Wayne looked in his dictionary for the meaning of the word tough, he saw Bill's photo. Sergeant York would have had him on speed dial in today's world.

When I answered him, Bill looked over the top of his paper and said in a dead, flat tone, "That's close to eight miles from here. You walked?" I nodded affirmatively.

Mike told me years later that his father always wondered which one of us was the bad influence. Bill said, "Mike's in the woods across the street," and pointed the way with a half burned Chesterfield.

Once inside the woods I could hear a ruckus about fifty yards farther in. I walked towards the sound. "Shamus, stand back you're in my way!" I looked around but saw no one through the foliage. I took several steps away from where I had been standing when Mike came out of the canopy. He must have been watching "Robin Hood" on T.V. the night before. He was climbing up trees then reaching or jumping onto smaller trees making them bend over and return him to Earth. "Give it a try, it's a pisser!" he called. I tried it on one of the lower trees.

"Don't be a pussy, climb a tall tree and try it." Mike challenged.

This is when one of Mora's phobias, planted in my brain years ago, kicked in. As a toddler we lived on the second story of my grandmother's house. The stairs leading to our apartment were quite steep. I was always trying to climb up the banister or slide down it. My mother caught me at one of my attempts. She banished me to my room screaming that I could have, "Broken my neck!"

If David Letterman ever did a Top Ten list of phrases that would make Mora's skin feel like a thousand spiders were crawling on her, "You'll break your neck!" would be in the number one spot.

She jumped into action immediately. As I slept, she would whisper in my ears about falling from some high place. She'd shape dreams so I developed acrophobia, a fear of heights. These days I no longer have a fear of heights. I have a deeply rooted, healthy respect of heights. Due to Mora's meddling, Ringling Brothers may have lost out on one of their greatest high wire acts. We'll never know for certain.

Mike is up in the tree tops acting like some crazy spider monkey. I'd hear him leap onto some poor unsuspecting Oak, his weight doubling over the poor sapling until his feet touched the ground. He'd then release the small tree and it would catapult itself into an upright position again. This routine was completed several more times all the while he berated me to try it again. Each time he'd climb a few feet higher.

I was standing in the shadow of a large Hickory when I heard a different noise; sort of a combination POP and SNAP followed by the sound of a body crashing through the canopy at a high rate of speed, then finally, the sound of a body slamming into the ground. The air in Mike's lungs fled his body with the same zeal school children use for the final bell before summer recess. Mike grunted he was, "Ok," and, "To just leave him lying on the floor of the woods until the fall leaves covered his corpse." Mora was feeling quite proud of herself, but knew she had her work cut out for her.

Mike's older brother, Billy, was our chauffeur until we all acquired our own drivers' license. He'd drive the family pickup, a late 60's model Ford 150. Cruising down Route 684 doing 80 mph and we'd climb out of the cab and into the bed of the truck just for the fun of it. Sitting in the bed of the truck brought back fond old memories for Mora. Wind in her hair and the sun on her face always brought out her smile although the vehicular gymnastics raised her blood pressure to unhealthy levels.

On scorching summer days, everyone in Brewster headed to water. Some had pools and others would join beach clubs situated on one of the many lakes in the area. We used the Dean's Corner's bridge and the reservoir in Carmel, our neighboring town. The bridge crossed the coldest water. It was located a few hundred yards away from the dam's output. The drop from the bridge was 50 feet and you hit the frigid waters below. None of Mora's bag of tricks could keep me from leaping.

This, of course, answers a parent's age old question, "Well, if all your friends jumped off a bridge, would you?" The answer is yes. Especially when there are teenage girls in cutoffs and wet t-shirts involved.

The cliffs in Carmel were another great spot. Everyone would pile out of their cars and run through the woods towards the cliff's edge. We would all leap off the cliff in unison. Skinny bodies garbed in Chuck Taylor sneakers and cutoff denim shorts. There would be the occasional arrest by the police for trespass and illegal swimming but these were very infrequent. An overweight cop wearing a gun belt, flashlight, handcuffs, and all the rest of their paraphernalia, had as much chance of catching a scared kid running through the woods as the Washington Generals have at beating the Harlem Globetrotters.

Mora was fast learning her abilities paled in comparison to the teenaged free spirit. My parents were having the same dilemma. The best she could do was slow us down. She came up with a brilliant idea. "I'll scare the crap out of them," she thought. She set about spreading rumors about very large trout being caught at the base of the cliffs. It worked.

One day we all did our usual routine, running like madmen, hurling ourselves off the edge of the cliff face. I don't know who was more scared. It was either the long haired kids in midair or the old black guy in the rowboat. Everyone twisting and turning their bodies to avoid putting a body sized hole in the old guy's boat. He probably still wakes up with night sweats. All these crazy white kids looking like the Japanese raid on Pearl Harbor and him sitting on the Arizona. After that we always looked before we leaped.

"Are you insane? You could have killed someone!" Madeline screamed.

Mora just flicked the ash from her cigar. "Wondering when you'd get here," her voice had a nonchalant tone to it. "Now before you get all crazy about how I handled this. Let me give you a few details. Shamus and his friends, and all their friends are mental cases. They are always jumping off of or out of something. A few beers and smoking I can understand. Driving fast I get. This..." she launched her cigar butt off the edge of the cliff, then she resumed, "This Flying Wallendas, Johnny Weissmuller, me Tarzan, let's do something stupid thing had to stop! I'm powerless to stop it. Best I can do is slow them down a bit."

"Well you are partially to blame, you know. You're the one who thought it was cute when he used to jump off of all the furniture as a child. A few more nightmares would have done him a world of good." Madeline's voice had a very maternal sound to it.

"I'm not guarding some little pussy here. He's fine. Just a little spirited. All I have to do is guide him through these teenage years and I got it licked." Her voice now had a defensive tone to it.

"Don't think I don't know about those adventure tales you've been telling him at bedtime. I know what that's all about! You can't use Shamus to get revenge on those deer. It's not right to use him this way. It will backfire on you. There are certain paths the living are suppose to follow. We aren't allowed to interfere," Madeline warned.

"Who's interfering? His father hunts, and his brother hunts, so of course he'd be a hunter. If he's going to be a hunter anyway..." Mora just let the rest of her sentence linger in the air.

Madeline just shot her a look that said stop talking. "Can I give you a little advice? I know he's doing fine," Madeline rolled her eyes, "Smoking, drinking, crazy stunts. He's perfect." Before Mora could interrupt her she continued on in a slightly louder voice, "But isn't he about the same age you were when you got your first job?" Madeline's face was a blank canvas. A professional card shark wouldn't have been able to read her expression.

Mora's face was the exact other side of the coin. Her eyes were wide with excitement. "That's a great idea! Get him a job, less time with his maniac friends." Her skin was turning red from embarrassment for not thinking of it on her own.

The crew of cliff jumpers had returned from our climb up the cliff face. Everyone breathing heavy and dripping wet. Without a word we all just charged and leapt off for another free flight. Madeline turned to Mora, "You must be so proud," then held up her black bag and asked, "Fried chicken?"

Chapter 14

Mora was sitting on the big rock in the backyard, sipping a whiskey, and watching smoke trails from her cigar spiral up until an unseen current would erase them from sight. With no ambient lights to wash out the stars, she was able to see all the stars in the heavens. It relaxed her and let her mind wander.

She wondered if she was interfering with my life as Madeline mentioned? Mora was brought back from her thoughts by a very faint sound of music. There would be no Norm's tonight. Tonight we find that music! Just over the first hill and down to the far side of the reservoir sat the Fore "N" Aft. The walls were vibrating and people were standing in line to get into the place. Mora noticed a few familiar faces from Norm's waiting in line. The guys were taking passes out of their wallets and women were digging through their purses for them.

Mora was curious about them and saw a pass slip from some fellow's hand. It was a 4 inch by 3 inch piece of card stock that was folded down the middle. Upon inspection she realized it was not only a pass for entry into the club but also contained information on drink specials. The inside contained a calendar showing when which bands were playing. "Live music five nights a week, free beer until 9:30? This I got to see!"

She stuck her head inside and found close to 150 people milling around the bar and the stage area. The first person she noticed was the manager, Chris. He was checking ID's and collecting the dollar or two they were charging for admission. He was stamping people's hands, so they could leave and reenter without paying again. Chris was also the lead bouncer for the place. He had a very unique way of stopping fights. He would lean on people and place them into submission. Being a man who tips the scale well above 300 pounds it was a very effective strategy.

Once inside she was a bit puzzled by the décor. It resembled the bowels of an old wooden ship. There were whaling harpoons, crabbing nets, lobster pots attached to the walls, even an old rowboat hung above the bar. She thought, "We're up in the hills so why the whaling theme?" Shrugging her shoulders she moved on. A large three station bar occupied the middle of the main floor. Another single station bar known as the Coppertop was up by the dance floor and stage area. This area should have been called Tinnitus. Seating was found all around the perimeter and a game room was anchored in the back with a Pac Man, and a couple pinball machines. A foosball game sat in one corner.

Outside there were two main parking lots. There was one on street level and another down behind the building. The one out back is what brought in, I believe, all the revenue for the bar. On the two days a week the bar was closed the owner must have rented out the lower parking lot to NASA so they could test their lunar rover. I'm fairly certain the owners also received kickbacks from every muffler shop in town. It's easy to imagine the manager of Midas Muffler driving by to thank them, "That parking lot put my daughters through college!" In reality it was a very smart business idea to keep the parking lot in such bad shape. They never had to worry about people speeding, doing donuts, or any other muscle car activities. You crept slowly out of that parking lot trying to save your muffler and the fillings in your teeth.

As Mora headed up to the stage area she was struck by the power of the band. The bands that played at Gunning's were little 3 or 4 piece bands. The largest guy normally played the bass. Another would be on electric guitar and a small drum set would be behind the other two.

The band on stage at the moment was more country than a rock band. They were loud for what Mora was used to. She knew nothing of roadies, sound engineers or pyrotechnics. She was in for a rude awakening hanging out at the Aft. Country wasn't really her style so she headed for home. She eyeballed the pass once more. Slapped it against her left hand and stashed it in the rear pocket of her jeans. All the little pieces of her plan were coming together.

I was still too young to work in a bar. Madeline was right though, a job would keep me out of trouble. Within a week I was stocking shelves and retrieving shopping carts at the local grocery store. I was hired with another kid named Brian Finch. Brian was a devious bastard and had a wonderful plan. The time clock was by the restrooms. He figured that since no one had known him or knew what he looked liked, would come in acting like a customer trying to use the restroom. He'd quickly punch in and then leave the store, later on he'd return to the store punch back out. The only time he was really there was to pickup his pay check. It wasn't a bad plan for about two weeks. Never saw the kid again, but you got to love his spirit.

A new manager was hired to run our store. Rocco Nicko was his name. I liked Rocky right away. He called everyone, "Hump". "Hey hump!" he'd yell and ten different people would turn around. Some people were good humps, some were dry humps and some bad humps but everyone was a hump. Rocco had the greatest hump expression for those times when everything is going wrong. "Well hump me running." Whenever he said it the vein on the side of his bald head would pop out. It made it appear as if his head would explode. Tommy Rodik, a coworker of mine, would almost wet himself whenever Rocky would say it. He couldn't even explain why it was so funny to him. He would start laughing uncontrollably when trying to explain it. Tommy would walk around imitating Rocky "Well hump me running!" Then just start laughing like it was a private joke known only to him. Rocky had this enormous laugh. It wasn't just loud; it grabbed you and pulled you into itself. Whenever Rocky told a story, anyone within earshot was pulled in. He would start low and slow like he was telling you a secret, yet just loud enough to catch the attention of anyone close by. By the end of the story there would be a crowd around him, his voice was booming, and he had everyone laughing until they cried. With his next breath his face was dead serious and he was yelling, "What the hell is everyone standing around for? I'm not paying you to stand around with your dicks in your hands. Get to work you lazy humps!"

Rocky told everyone that if he ever caught you stealing he'd pull your heart out of your chest and eat it. I'm fairly sure he meant it. The very first time he said it to me I looked him square in the eye and said, "Rock, don't worry, you'll never catch me stealing." Rocky stopped, staring at me long and hard trying to understand what I had just said. He could have taken it one of two ways. Either I was never going to steal anything or he was never going to catch me. Now Rocky had these piercing blue eyes. They would bore a hole straight through you. Time felt like it stood still as he stared me down trying to see if I'd flinch. Rocky blinked and then he called me a "hump" and walked away. Rocky never caught me. No one ever did.

It became a game taking things from Rocky. You never took too much. There is a certain amount of loss from breakage in a grocery store as long as you stayed below those levels no one suspected anything. All the other stock clerks were doing the same thing. We finally had to keep our own inventory so things didn't get out of hand.

Soon it became an Olympic sport amongst us. In one summer you had to have taken one of every item, from every isle. At the end of the summer it was a tie between me and a coworker, Johnny. There was no awards ceremony, no flags were unfurled or anthems played. Only two reformed nitwits toasting each other in the parking lot. After that neither of us took another thing from the store. Johnny would laugh and say, "We stole Tampons, what the hell is wrong with us?"

Madeline had just finished a high and mighty speech to Mora regarding her duties. "Protecting Shamus does not included covering him in illegal activities," her voice thick with morality.

Mora interrupted her, "I didn't help or hinder."

"You had no hand in any of this?"

Mora shook her head from side to side, crossed her heart and gave Madeline the Boy Scout salute while saying, "Scouts' honor, I watched but didn't interfere."

"Shamus and these other knuckleheads did all this without any outside help?" Madeline questioned again.

"I know," she paused for a moment, "Good thing they don't work for Fort Knox. The country would be broke."

Actually there was just one more item taken but it wasn't really my fault. I was standing on the loading platform with one of the butchers, a little Irish guy named Patty. Patty was having a smoke and knocking back a shot from a flask. "Keeps me warm," he said as he raised the flask in a mock toast to my health. "Those cutting rooms are awful cold and this rain doesn't help my bones at all."

I couldn't argue, it had been raining for the last day or two and everything was drenched. There were torrents of water gushing out of leaf choked gutters. As we were standing there a delivery of meat arrived. There were stacks of boxes filled with hunks of grade "A" meat all vacuum packed in plastic bags. Patty turns to me and says, "I'd love to have me a box of them," nodding his red head towards the boxes.

"No problem" I said to him.

"What are you, daft? You could never get them out of here." Shuddering in his white blood smeared butcher coat, while adjusting its blood stained collar.

"If I get them out of here, you do all the butchering," I replied confident as a poker player holding a Royal Flush.

"Deal, but how could you do it?" Patty was now enthralled.

"Ok, first, give me a cigarette. Next you sign the invoice." I put my hand up to cut off his complaint, while inhaling a long drag off the butt. "Just sign it and watch."

I snatched the paper work from him after he had scrawled his chicken scratch of a signature on the dotted line. I walked over to the end of the loading dock and fired the butt of my cigarette through the cascading water. I then held the paper work he just signed into the waterfall. At the time our country had not signed any treaty against water boarding meat invoices, so I hadn't broken any international laws. Turning back to Patty I said, "You just signed it and I bet you couldn't tell what it says now."

An evil grin sprouted on his pointy little Gaelic face, "But how in blazes are you going to get it out of here?" curiosity now creeping into his voice.

"Shut it, you carnivorous little leprechaun!" I silenced him.

As the meat delivery truck was leaving, the milk truck was pulling up. Timmy was the driver on our route. He was a gambler and liked any kind of action. It didn't matter to Timmy. Dice, cards, football, or horses - if it could be bet on Tim wanted a piece of the action. Rocky and Timmy were always betting each other on something. Whenever they were together, their conversations were about how some ball player screwed the pooch last night and cost them a bundle. I once saw them throw 50 bucks apiece down on which fly would fly away first. Rocky won.

Timmy climbed up on the loading dock greeting everyone. "Nice freaking weather; if you're a duck's ass!" he said. "What's happening boys?" Timmy could tell action was in the air, his eyes looked everywhere. He looked straight at Patty, "What sort of revolution does the I.R.A. have planned for today?"

"Need a case of steaks, Tim?" I gave him a wink of the eye.

"Where am I dropping them off to?" were his only words.

You got to love a guy who catches on fast. I tossed him the key to my house and gave him directions. "Leave a gallon of milk in the fridge when you leave"

"Regular or chocolate?" he laughed.

"Both." I replied.

Later that night I entered my house with Patty in tow, to find large puddles of blood surrounding cases of meat stacked on the kitchen floor. There were two gallons of milk in the fridge, one was chocolate. The six pack of beer I had planned on downing that night was missing from the fridge. There is just no honor amongst thieves. It was my Coup de Gras and I toasted it with a glass of ice cold chocolate milk while Patty cut steaks.

I worked the day crew for awhile when Mora decided I needed to get ready for working at the Aft. Somehow she influenced Rocky to switch me to the night crew. It wasn't really hard for her. Rocky was already thinking about shifting me to the night shift anyway. He had no proof I was involved in any nefarious activities but his gut told him his bottom line would do better if I was under lock and key inside the store with the night crew. It also gave Mora time to head to the Aft or Norm's knowing I was safely locked away for the night.

The hours were midnight to eight in the morning Monday through Friday. I worked with a good bunch of guys. All family men trying to do the best they could in life. Every night around 2:30 a.m. we'd stop for lunch. Conversations were always about sports or whatever trouble their kids had gotten into that day. Sitting on milk crates in a warehouse eating cold deli sandwiches gets old real fast.

I spoke with Rocky about a plan I had. I'd go in to work a few minutes early and buy a steak, potatoes, and charcoal. At around 1:00 a.m., I'd have Kenny, the crew chief, unlock the front door. I'd toss some charcoal into a shopping carriage that I'd push into the middle of the empty parking lot and wait for the coals to get nice and hot. A little while later I'd go out and place potatoes I had wrapped in foil into the child seat of the carriage. Once I thought they were close to done, back out I'd go, and throw the steak on. The crew thought I was insane. After a meal of steak and potatoes I wasn't so crazy. It quickly became a nightly event and the mood of the crew improved tremendously.

What started out as a culinary stunt by me grew and grew. By the time I had left the night crew we were eating great dinners every night under the stars. A side benefit sprouted from our little alfresco dinners. The first night I started cooking, the state police pulled in to see what I was doing. The State Trooper barracks was only a half mile North on Route 22. They would pass our store all the time. The trooper drove in the parking lot to see some tall skinny kid wearing a black leather jacket barbecuing out of a shopping cart. I wonder what the code was when he called that one into headquarters.

They rolled up on me real slow, blinding me with their million candle watt spotlight. The driver's window lowered and a clean cut officer asked me what I was doing. Knowing I was doing absolutely nothing illegal I flipped the steak making the fire jump and hiss. "Why I'm cooking a steak, officer." Apparently it was not the answer he was looking for.

The officer slapped the gear shifter into park and stepped out of the car. "You can't do that out here."

"Why?" a lilt of innocence in my voice.

It's a good thing Troopers didn't carry a taser at the time. From the look on this guy's face I would have been lit up like the Rockefeller Center Christmas tree.

Quickly losing my wiseass tone I explained that I worked here and was making dinner for the crew. I then offered him and his partner dinner. They declined, but joined us on other nights.

Once they had a K9 with them. One of the guys, Malcolm, would freak. He was a pothead and thought every police dog was used for sniffing drugs. The dog was a white German shepherd named Caine. The joke was lost on the kid. The night crew became friendly with the Troopers and offered the officers a few of the broken bags of dog chow.

It was a good deal for everyone. We had our own security force, the K9 unit got free food, and no one from the night crew ever received a ticket for any traffic infraction. Mora and Madeline watched the entire scene unravel from the small hill at the far end of the parking lot. Mora was proud of how I brought the night crew together and how I handled the police. Madeline was proud to see I let the steak rest before cutting it.

Chapter 15

Working the night crew I never had the opportunity to piss away my pay as fast as my buddies. It was becoming time for some new wheels and our Saudi friends had us in a choke hold over oil. Mora had the solution, two wheels and chrome. Her appetite for bikes and my salary however were on different sides of the scale. The big Indians she loved were few and far between unless you knew the right people and had buckets of money. A Honda 550 was more in line with my pay scale. She'd try to compromise and, *"Harley, Harley, Harley,"* became her new mantra. Something about those big bikes just gave her goose bumps. I wanted something that would sip a gallon of gas and be able to go horizontal in a hairpin turn. I won, it was only fair. I was the one working at night while she was hanging at Norm's or the Aft.

It was my first motorcycle. I had no license and a permit on which the ink hadn't yet dried. The rules on the permit stated that you need to have a licensed rider within a hundred yards. It's hard to comply when you have a whiskey drinking angel whispering in your ear for a ride. The first hour was spent getting the feel for the bike. Yes, I said the bike, I never named it.

Wannabe, weekend riders on well waxed Harleys and wearing matching leathers name their bikes. "I'm taking Spike out for a run this weekend," like they're talking about taking a Cocker Spaniel out for a walk.

No, mine was just a machine to get me from place to place. It was as reliable as a postman; I rode it all four seasons. Let me tell you why you never see a motorcycle in a Currier and Ives scene. Because it's freezing! There drawbacks to having a wild woman as a guardian angel.

I spent that first hour riding up and down the street getting accustomed to it. Gearing was one down, four up. The first few times the handle bars tried with all their might to take out my front teeth. By the second hour I was screaming through the gears. Mora was getting a bit bored sitting on the back watching the same house go by for several hours and wanted a change of scenery. The next time down the street I made a left at the stop sign. I headed down the hill, cruising along without a care in the world. Mora had sunshine on her face and wind in her hair. What could possibly go wrong?

It's funny how the sound of a siren is muffled under a full face motorcycle helmet. You don't actually know the police are behind you until you notice the red lights in your mirrors. This was a county sheriff. I had minor influence with the state troopers but sheriffs were a whole different deal. It just so happened that I was pulled over next to a wide open field. For a fleeting moment I considered going cross country on the sheriff. Then the vision of Steve McQueen trying to escape the Nazis in "The Great Escape" entered my mind. It hadn't really worked out all that well for McQueen so I dropped the thought. I pulled off my helmet ready to throw myself on the mercy of the officer when a hundred or so bikers came roaring down the road. Some old guy pulled over and took my back. "Yeah, officer he's with us, my fault entirely. I should have kept up with him, just slipped my mind. I'll keep him in the middle of the pack from now on."

I took my permit and my lecture from the sheriff and went riding with those guys for the rest of the day. The old guy with the white handlebar mustache turned to me after the sheriff left and said, "We've all been there; saw it on your face as we pulled up. Now get smart and get your license." The money I would have spent on fines went towards hot dogs and beers at a little place by the Kensico Dam. I don't know how Mora did it, but she always found new friends and great places to eat. Mora soon realized that the Big Indian she favored would be hard to beat when cracking the throttle going down the highway. The little Honda, however, would kick it's ass off the starting line in a race. The horsepower to weight ratio was in the Honda's favor. Since it had a smaller wheel base it would beat the Indian in the turns every time too. Mora was fast becoming a fan of the smaller bike. I always seemed to find an excuse to go for a ride. It wasn't long before I knew every back road in the county.

Chapter 16

Mora was in an exceptionally good mood. That summer I turned eighteen which meant I could now accompany her to see bands at all her favorite bars. Hunting season was in full swing and her quest to seek revenge on the deer population could resume.

Early in the day I harvested an 8 point buck. After field dressing and hanging it for skinning, a shower, shave and short nap were in order. I awoke around six and got ready for some Saturday night fun. Working the night shift gives one a definite advantage when it comes to staying out all night long. It did however cause some strain in my home life. I was an official night owl and my parents weren't. They couldn't understand the reason for staying out until "All hours of the morning" I couldn't see living any other way so it wasn't long before I was living on my own.

Since my stomach was growling a Norm's burger was in order. Norm's would also have a good compliment of local hunters; a little bragging was in order. I parked the Honda and entered through the side door. I walked to the bar to place my burger order and grab a cold frosty one. Norm was in his customary position behind the bar but looked out of sorts. Roundman, another of Norm's regular bartenders, stepped up and told me that Norm had been drinking with a few of the boys since he got here. There were the customary jokes about him being blind drunk, by I didn't join in. Roundman looked past me and called over Fergy, "Ferg, do everyone a favor and give Norm a ride home, would you?"

Ferg obliged and started walking Norm out the side door. Norm had taken his normal position, holding onto whoever was guiding him by their left elbow. He turned them into his personal Seeing Eye dog. Fergy apparently never received his diploma from Guiding Eyes Dog School.

The door they where exiting through was only half open. Norm was walked straight into the door and gashed his forehead. "You're doing a fine job there Ferguson!" Norm growled. The entire bar busted out in laughter.

Later, Ferg returned from driving Norm home. He said that Norm was telling him when and where to turn. "I told him I knew exactly where he lived" Fergy said.

Norm's reply was, "Well, you did so well getting me to the car, I ain't taking any chances!" We all toasted Norm.

With a burger in my belly and the tales of the hunt told to those who would listen, I drained the last of my draft. It was time to point my bike North and head for the *Fore "N" Aft*. It was barely a mile and a half from Norm's so I made it in no time at all. I parked next to the front door with all the other bikes. It's always a good rule to park with all the other bikes, safety in numbers. The building was already vibrating from the band onstage. I walked in and said hi to big Chris working the front door. Chris tossed me a blue shirt with the Aft's insignia on it. I gave him a confused look. He explained that all his bartenders were sick and needed someone to work the bar.

I knew how to order a drink but didn't have a clue on how to make one, which I promptly explained to Chris. He raised his eyebrows, gave me a dead stare and asked me, "I'm sorry, were we bought out by the Ritz without my knowledge? We serve shots and beers, a couple of juice drinks. If anyone asked for a Martini tell them they're in the wrong bar. Sean's working the front bar if you have any questions ask him." Sean worked the whole night dancing behind the bar, kissing every woman he could, cracking open beers and jokes. I was a beer soaked mess.

Madeline looked at Mora and asked "Are you sure he's cut out for this job?"

Defensively she answered, "It's his first night! Give him a break. No one says it's a lifelong career, just a little job for awhile. Besides I get to see bands and keep an eye on Shamus all at the same time."

Mora was right. I took working behind a bar like a duck takes to water. My parking lot cookouts and stocking shelves were soon a thing of the past. It was the bartender's life for me. As I progressed making cocktails and working the crowds, Chris assigned me to work the nights with better bands.

Twisted Sister would play Wednesday night, Sapphire on Thursday, and the Good Rats on Friday. These would be high volume nights. These were the heavy hitters. Well established bands with good front men backed by great musicians. Twisted Sister went on to do a video on MTV and their song; "We Ain't Gonna Take It" did well on the radio. We saw them when they dressed like psychotic women freshly released from the asylum. Dee Snyder was their front man. He'd get the crowd pumped and ready to party fast. It didn't hurt that beers were free until 9:30 p.m.

The Good Rats are still the world's most famous unknown band led by Peppi Marchello. Peppi has this great raspy voice that was just made to sing Rock 'n' Roll. While glamour bands were becoming popular, with their makeup and crazy costumes, Peppi would wear what looked like your everyday generic high school gym shorts and a sweat shirt. A baseball bat was ever present, on which he played air guitar or would use it to beat the hell out of a galvanized garbage can. The can was full of rubber rats that Peppi would eventually toss out to the crowd. The rubber rats were another great marketing plan. Some people collect baseball cards, others collect coins or stamps, there are some who would collect those rats.

The Good Rats weren't just some gimmick band. They went on to play with bands such as the Grateful Dead, Springsteen, Billy Joel, Styx, and countless others. They paid their dues and played all the major venues in all the major cities but never received FM radio airplay. I truly believe that DJ's were petrified of having a madman like Peppi on their shows for interviews.

Out of all the bands and musicians that Mora was able to see with me working the Aft, her favorite was a band called Sapphire. Sapphire had one of the best equipped bands I ever saw. I'd be setting up my bar as they would be setting up the stage. Now I can't play an instrument and couldn't carry a tune in a bucket, much to Mora's dismay. She tried to influence me to play an instrument but she had to settle for a tin eared outdoorsman. However, from seeing enough bands over the years, I can tell quality equipment.

If a budding garage band found a genie in a bottle, I know one wish would be to have Sapphire's equipment. Every major manufacturer of great instruments were represented on stage. Les Paul, Rickenbacker, Hammond, Fender Telecaster, and Ludwig double bass drums were all represented. Their sound was pumped out by stacks of Marshall amps and Cerwin Vega cabs. One Marshall 1 x 18 cab was covered in red Tolex. The band referred to it as the "The Coke Machine." Over the years more and more subwoofers and tweeters were added. They even had a dry ice fog machine they called Seymour, as in *see more* fog. No one ever said that a rock band couldn't be corny.

Her two favorite musicians were in Sapphire, Jimi Heslin and Jimmy Edelmann. Heslin's hair and beard were thick and jet black, he always wore dark sunglasses. The sunglasses were part of the allure for Mora. They reminded her of the old blues musicians that played at Gunning's. All you ever really saw of Heslin was a small bit of forehead, nose, cheeks and lips.

Jimi played a Gibson Les Paul. They just always had a fat sound to them. Mora could never decide which she liked better, his Cherry Sunburst or the Goldtops model. Whichever model it was, Jimi could play it for all it was worth. Jimi must have been born with a guitar in his hands. His left hand slides up and down the neck of his Les Paul in an effortless motion. Fingers pressing strings to frets so fast it makes his hand look like a spider trying to run across a hot griddle.

Edelmann was the drummer. I had one of my most memorable nights behind a bar because of Edelmann. Heslin comes up to me and explains that Jimmy is going to come out from behind the drum set and play a drum solo using every fixture in the bar. The solo would end up behind the bar where Jimmy had stashed a set of rum soaked drumsticks. He would then proceed to play all the bottles behind the bar with flaming drumsticks. I had two small roles in this drum solo. One was to have a lighter ready to set Jimmy's drumsticks ablaze. The second, and far more important item, was to pour a pitcher of water over Jimmy's head so his hair wouldn't catch on fire.

Being an employee who knows how to follow orders, I immediately set to accomplishing my task. I had lighters strategically placed behind the bar ready to "Flick my Bic." A thought came into my mind that maybe it would be a good idea to use two pitchers of water. Jimmy had quite a bit of hair and two pitchers are better than one. I got the water ready and placed it in the ice bins under the bar so they'd be out of the way while I was tending bar. Herein lies the catalyst for a great night behind the bar.

Heslin informed me about the drum solo around 4:00 p.m. He never mentioned it would happen in the third set, sometime around 2:00 a.m. The water had been sitting on ice for hours. Edelmann stepped out from behind his drum set and proceeded to wail away on everything that would make a sound. He got a beat going and everyone had their eyes and ears glued on him. Jimmy is now behind the bar playing his way towards me. He picks up the rum soaked sticks with one hand while tapping out a beat on a bell hanging behind the bar with his other hand. Jimmy points the sticks at me and tells me to light them up and then pour the water on his head.

I touch flame to sticks and instantaneously, rum drunk, blue and yellow flames are dancing the El Fuego up the drumsticks. I then grab the pitchers of water and douse Jimmy's head with them. Edelmann stops tapping out his beat on a bell hanging behind the bar. His body is convulsing from the frigid water I just doused him with. Jimmy stabs the flaming drumsticks into the ice bins and they extinguish with a hiss. His eyes are bugged out and his teeth are chattering. I'm half deaf from the amps but start to make out that he's cursing me and apparently multiple generations of my family.

He starts to defrost and gets this wild look in his eyes. He picks up the soda gun from behind the bar and starts spraying me with Coke. I started to feel like one of those clowns at the fair and decided that before my balloon burst and he wins a prize I should defend myself. I grab the closest soda gun and fire back with ginger ale. Our soda fight brought cheers from everyone on the other side of the bar. That is until we decide that he and I were thoroughly soaked with syrupy soda and everyone else should enjoy the fun. We turned and fired on the crowd.

Oh the inhumanity! Jimmy and I looked like those white cops you saw from the early sixties demonstrations. Fire hoses in hand, blasting the crowds of protestors marching on Selma or Washington. Heslin and the rest of the band came back out on stage to see what was happening, a look of terror and amusement on their faces. They could be amused, they were the only ones not covered in soda. When the band wasn't playing you could hear people trudging through a quagmire of soda. Chuck Taylor sneakers or biker boots, Lil Abner's, or 3 inch pumps, no shoe escaped our little Le Brea tar pit of soda.

Mora sat perched on Heslin's "Coke Machine" stack quite satisfied with her preemptive strike, waiting on Madeline. Madeline made her way through the crowd in her black sequined cocktail dress and small black clutch. "Tad overdressed aren't we?" Mora quipped.

"Actually one of us is well dressed and one is wearing worn out jeans and a ripped Aft t-shirt," Madeline retorted, "Oh, and isn't that sentimental? 'We rocked your mother' is on the back of your shirt. What mother wouldn't love to see their child in that?"

"These jeans aren't worn out, but worn well, and if you really want to talk about being a mother..."

Madeline cut her off before Mora could finish her thought. "Let's not be crude, Twizzle. I'm here to compliment you. That was fast thinking. The thought that banging on alcohol with flaming sticks might cause a fire never occurred to these geniuses?" Madeline turned towards the stage and looked at Heslin, shaking her head from side to side. A look of disgust overtook her face, "Rock Stars," her voice dripped with sarcasm.

"Hey, it's only Rock 'n' Roll, no one got hurt. I was on it," are the words that Mora spoke but her heart was pounding over the fact that Madeline noticed what she had done. For as independent as Mora was Madeline's approval meant everything to her.

Every night at the Aft was an adventure. Big Chris was my tour guide for the ride. Mora just has this love for folks who are characters, be it a Scallywag or Saint. Chris was a man of size both physically and mentally. One night he's standing by the front door. He's burning through Parliament cigarettes and Jack Daniels. In his big mitt of a left hand he's holding the NY Times crossword puzzle. Now he's keeping an eye on the 300 or so patrons, stamping hands, making change, checking Id's. On top of those duties he also is aware of which stations need ice and fresh glassware.

Chris is the one who taught me the lesson on how to spot a fake ID. First off you don't really pay that much attention to the ID. If the kid who hands you the ID doesn't look right at you, something's wrong. You look at the ID and then him and do it again. Then quickly ask them what their Zodiac sign is. If they hesitate or stutter, just hand back the fake ID and send them on their way. Now the band is playing some cover version of the "Doors" at decibels that could peel paint from the walls. All the while Chris is handling everything while doing the crossword puzzle, in pen and not missing a single word.

He would mess with you while doing the puzzle. Some pretty girl would be waiting in line to get in the bar. Chris would time it so she was just walking in the door and ask "What's a 4 letter word for a cheap woman, begins with an S?"

I'd pause and think, then reply "Slut?"

Now the girl is losing her mind yelling "What did you call me?"

Chris' face would just light up with an evil ass grin. Then hand the girl a free drink pass and turn to me "Shamus, we don't speak to our customers that way."

Chris would break balls but he was truly concerned for everyone at the Aft. One night we were running short on change and Chris asked me to go to Norm's and get change. I showed up to work on my Honda so Chris told me to use his car. Heslin was standing nearby and looked over the top of his ever present black sunglasses. He leans over to me and says "Wow, I've known Chris over 10 years and I've never seen him loan his car to anyone."

Chris tosses me his keys and starts giving me instructions about his car. I felt like a teenager whose dad was letting him drive the family car for the first time. Once inside Chris' car I realized this guy is a car fanatic. It was an older model Plymouth but it was immaculate inside. I head to Norm's, get change and asked for a bottle of Mystery mix to bring back for Chris. All business done, I hop back in his car and proceed back to the Aft. I'm headed North on Route 6 when this Southbound car moves into my lane and sideswipes Chris' car. The entire drivers side is creased and crumbled. The bottle of Mystery mix hit the dashboard and exploded. Chris' immaculate car was now wrecked on the outside and it looked like I butchered a pig on his front seat. The cops show up, some I know from the old A&P barbecue days and some from working the Aft. The kid who hit me was the younger brother of one of the other bouncers. One Sherriff asked, "Is that Chris' car?"

"Yeah" I replied. He just rolled his eyes and whistled. The paperwork was handled and since the car was still drivable I headed back to the Aft.

Chris was working the front door but hadn't seen me pull into the parking lot. I've been gone for close to an hour and a half for a ride that should have taken 10 minutes. I'm covered in Mystery mix so I looked as if I had been stabbed. I walk thru the front door, Chris was pissed I was gone so long but once he saw my condition he became very concerned. "What happened?" he questioned. I just walked past him depositing the sack of change in his open hands. I hopped up on the bar and swung my feet over the top of the bar. Snatched a bottle of Jack Daniels and hopped back across the bar. I leaned over and grabbed two tumbler glasses off the bar. "We gotta talk" I said and nodded my head towards the exit. Once outside I sat on the hood of Chris' car and poured three fingers worth in both glasses. I extended one glass to Chris. He took it and said "I'm not going to like what you're about to say am I" and swallowed the three fingers of JD.

"Nope" I replied and did the same. "Now, none of this was my fault, I wouldn't even smoke in your car." All this time we are facing the passenger side of the car. It was untouched in the accident. When the word "car" left my lips a light bulb went off in Chris' brain. He took a step back and looked up and down the passenger side. He then sauntered around to the driver's side. He just stared at the car and then at me. I was bracing for him to explode. Instead he just reached across the roof of the car with his empty tumbler and jiggled it until I filled it to the appropriate height. The appropriate height, of course, was being to the brim. Misery loves company so I did the same. "Do I need to get you to a hospital?"

"Nah, I'm fine."

"Fine? You look like you've been on the losing side of a knife fight."

I realized he was looking at the Mystery mix I was covered in. "Oh that. Well, you see, while I was at Norm's, I picked you up a bottle of Mystery mix."

"That was nice of you. Before or after you trashed my car?" Chris said sarcastically.

"Before," I paused to collect my thoughts and continued, "Long story short, the inside of your car looks worse than the outside." Chris tried to open the driver's door. "Oh yeah, that don't work anymore. You have to slide in from the passenger's side. Be careful there's glass everywhere." Chris lit a Parliament cigarette then stretched his hand out to jiggle his glass again. "Top it off, Chris?" I asked sheepishly. He nodded in the affirmative. He sauntered back over to the passenger's side, opened the door and peered inside.

He just shut the door and asked again, "You're ok? you sure?" When I nodded yes he just shrugged his shoulders and said, "Well, it's only a car, I'll look for a new one tomorrow." Then he threw his arm around my neck and we went back inside and put a hurting on rest of the bottle. He never held it against me that I was driving when his pride and joy was wrecked.

He did however have me work security the night Joe Savage played. Joe was this crazy looking bald guy. His schtick was that he dressed up as different characters. One was sort of half caveman, half Indian. Other nights he'd be dressed in a loud looking Zoot suit. He sang songs named *"Free Booze"* and *"Makin' Love on a Buffalo Rug"*. He'd come out with a Boa Constrictor wrapped around him. Another part of his act was to fire up a chainsaw. The night I worked security he carved his name into the wall by the stage with his chainsaw. I was stationed by the fire exit about 10 feet away while he's practicing calligraphy on the wall. By the time he was done I was covered in wood chips and deaf in my right ear. His wife Nikki would do a Janis Joplin tribute that was terrific. She had this Scotch and soda sounding voice, real smoky and sexy. After one long night behind the bar I was laying on the bowling table. Nikki comes out of the main office and grabs my feet and shoves me down the table headfirst. My eyes where shut so I never saw her coming. The next thing I know bowling pins are above my head and she's telling me to "Get back up here I need to pick up the 7-10 split!"

Together they were a great act to watch. One night while playing a club in Massachusetts, Joe's pet Boa got loose and somehow wound up in the air ducts. You just got to love live Rock 'n' Roll. Years later I read that once again his snake got loose, with tragic results. The snake killed his young daughter.

The Aft is where I met Linda Blair from the Exorcist, which later got me on Late Night with David Letterman. I was dating Camille, whom I would later marry. She called me and said that she received 4 tickets to the Letterman show from a co-worker. She was taking a girlfriend from work and asked if I knew anyone else who wanted to go. I told her I'd check and call her back shortly. I hung up and Fergy walks into Norm's. I give him the lowdown and 10 minutes later we're on a train to New York. The entire trip down he's asking me if I know where Rockefeller Center is because he would never be able to find it. "I get lost in a round room," is his expression. I assured him I would be able to find *30 Rock*.

We met Camille and her girlfriend, Linda and proceeded to get in line for the show. Some intern came out and announced, "Tonight we're doing a bit called Brush with Greatness. If you have ever met anyone famous and would like to tell your story to David on air, raise your hand." Ferg and I both raised our hands. We tell them our stories and because we are both from the same town we get picked. The four of us get ushered into a nice air conditioned studio, sign release forms, and join the actors' union. All is great in the world until we both catch a case of stage fright. Like two athletes before a big game we went into the men's room and psyched ourselves up. When Letterman came out we did our bits. I explained that I met Linda Blair while she was hustling people on the pinball machine and Fergy told his story of meeting Dr. Joyce Brothers at some local hotel. The staff on the Lettermen show had special effects for our bits. I had snow falling on me as I read that Linda Blair had taken me home and scraped off my chest hairs with a broken bottle. Ferg had a stagehand sitting behind him who tossed a skeleton's arm over Ferg's shoulder. Lights flashed and thunder sounded which helped hide the fact that his cheek was twitching because of nerves. Luckily they did a close up of my face or everyone would have seen me rubbing my arm like a junkie in need of a fix.

Mora was more interested in the goings on behind the scenes. Television was just that box in the living room of our house. The studio she was on now intrigued her. Paul Schaffer and the band were warming up. Light and sound people were making whatever adjustments were needed. She remembered back to when the bands played at Gunning's. They were small bands but everything had to be set up just so. This was the same thing, just on a much larger scale. Mora was taking it all in like a child watching the Macy's parade. After the taping of the show we hit the town for a nice dinner and then headed back to Brewster on the 10:05 p.m. from Grand Central.

Grand Central had recently gone through a revival. All it's marble was removed, numbered, polished and replaced in its exact location. The old girl was once again a gleaming palace. Mora grew up in a railroad town but had never experienced anything like Grand Central. She gazed upon the constellations which adorned the ceilings, from the upper balconies the thousands of commuters looked like ants rushing off to work or back home. She wanted to share her experience with Madeline but decided against it remembering her fear of trains.

Chapter 17

By the time we had arrived back in Brewster, the Letterman show had already aired. We enjoyed our 15 minutes of fame. The local paper even did a phone interview with me. Fame is fleeting and within a few days we were old news and resumed our normal lives. I went back to working behind the bar but with a slight celebrity status. When the bands would take a break the crowd would head to the bar. It was Gonzo bartending at its finest. It worked out real simple. Four bartenders versus hundreds of thirsty patrons all juiced up on reefer and Rock 'n' Roll. Toss in the fact that everyone is deaf from the wall of speakers and screaming at you because they can't even hear themselves. You read lips more than you actually hear what anyone wanted. You quickly learned to pop the tops off of Budweiser, Molson, and Heineken bottles in one fluid motion. Alabama Slammers were the popular shot of the day. Made right, it tasted like fruit punch. 7 liquors, some ice and Sloe Gin for coloring was all that was in it. After a little practice you could hold 7 bottles at once and pour a shaker full in seconds. It made for a good show and tips flowed.

The trouble with Slammer's is they sneak up on you. One night this sweet looking little blonde comes in with a gaggle of her girlfriends. They order up a round of beers and then want to do some shots. They ask for a recommendation. I just started making a jigger of Slammers and say, "Here try these." They're all happy and giggling tossing back a jigger or three of the devil's fruit punch when I warn them to be careful. "They're not called Slammers for nothing!" Then I see that look all bartenders have seen. The person you're serving is this fun, happy go lucky person one minute then the next their eyes sort of look right through you. There are several different scenarios for what can happen next. They either start babbling in some non-human tongue or start stripping off clothes. For some reason this is normally an after effect of Tequila. Crying and telling you their entire life's story is another option. In the case of Blondie it was the worst scenario. She turned into one of the puddle people. It's as if the bones in her body turned into a liquid. One moment she is standing in front of my station and the next she's on the floor. I jumped over the bar to pick her up and soon realized that it was impossible to do it alone. Every time I started to lift her she just poured through my arms. Her girlfriends tried to help but they dropped her several times. Finally our top bouncer, Pete, who everyone called Bam Bam, lifted her by her belt and carried her to her friend's car. Bam Bam was a huge guy. In college he was an All State Heavy Weight Wrestler. Pete was ridiculously strong, but a mellow and friendly type of guy. He'd walk in and pat you on the shoulder while saying hi and knock you off your feet. He quickly was named after Barney Rubble's kid.

After everyone was served and the bands would take the stage again, I'd head outside for a smoke and to give my ears a break. My body still feeling the reverberations of the music, it's like being on an offshore boat for hours and then taking the first steps on dry land. Your brain convinces your body that it's still on a rocking boat.

I'd routinely stop by the top of the steps that lead down to the back parking lot, lean against the railing and watch the haze of Columbia's cash crop rise above the cars. Fergy would usually be there giving you play by play on what was happening in the cars that were rocking up and down while parked. He'd take on the persona of Howard Cosell, broadcasting an Ali fight.

"Those two are really trading some good licks in there. A quick right and her bra is off. Now wait, she's really going on the offensive. His back is up against the driver's window. His shirt is in tatters. They're both starting to look like a pair of greased snakes in there," actually holding an imaginary microphone to his mouth while doing play by play. Fergy would finish when the car stopped rocking. It was always fun to watch the couple emerge from the fogged windowed car, buttoning shirts and adjusting belts while scanning the parking lot for witnesses. As they reached the top of the stairs, Fergy would just look at them with disgust and say, "You animals," and then crack up laughing. The girls would quicken their pace while the guys would just kind of saunter into the bar. The saying on the back of Mora's shirt didn't mean, just with music!

Chapter 18

In this wonderful stew that Mora was creating, Fergy would be the onions. Like an onion he has many layers. Like Fergy, these layers of the onion are tightly packed and highly organized.

Ferguson should be the poster child for O.C.D. His cigarettes have to be packed a certain way. He turns them around in the pack so that the filter is facing down. When cleaning his truck he waxes the inside of the hood. His lighter sits in exactly the same spot on his truck's console, always facing with the striker facing away from him. When I questioned him about this little quirk of his, he answered, "That way, when I grab it, it's already in the proper position in my hand to use."

Over the years, Ferg and I have done a few fishing trips down to the Florida Keys in search of Tarpon. They are the flashiest of all the game fish. Powerful fish that will destroy any gear not rated for the job. A Tarpon can grow to well over 200 pounds and strip a hundred yards of line from a reel in seconds. It will take an angler half an hour to get back that same amount of line. They can easily jump ten feet out of the water and will frustrate an angler by landing on the line setting itself free. While a Tarpon is alongside the boat being revived, they thrash wildly and there is an ever present danger of a shark attack.

On one particular trip Ferg was in rare O.C.D. form. Watching him pack for a trip would keep a psychologist employed for years. Every item checked and rechecked again and again. Socks folded never balled. Laces for sneakers positioned inside the sneaker never just hanging outside. The mandatory ounces of reefer and rolling papers stashed inside a zipper compartment in his luggage. Yes I said reefer. Sometime in his life I firmly believe Ferg received a blood transfusion from

Bob Marley. A couple of joints per day are just about right to keep his "levels" balanced.

At this time Ferg was living on Florida's West Coast. I flew down to meet him and we would drive the 300 miles to the Keys. Fergy's anally clean truck was our usual ride. We would meet Captain Paul of Strip Strike Charters at Papa Joe's, mile marker 79.9, the following morning. Mora wasn't unfamiliar with weed. The Blues musicians would "get ready" to play by taking a quick break out on the bus or the alley out back. But she wasn't used to Ferg's quantity of use. The contact high she received however did help to calm her nerves. She had been on edge. Between the flight to Florida and the thought of us on an 18 foot skiff in the Florida Keys had her nerves raw.

Ferg was also on a mission to acquire a totem pole from an artist he'd seen on a previous trip. I was all in for giving him a hand transporting his totem pole. Mora being the Twizzle that she is figured that if I was going to make her crazy with this fishing trip the least she could do is repay the favor. The totem pole Ferg was after was close to six feet tall and had a two and a half foot circumference. It was covered in the mandatory big face as if it was the wooden cousin of the famous Easter Island totems. It might have well been since it weighed close to 400 pounds.

The artist was conveniently located just outside the entrance of the Drop Anchor, our residence for the next several days. All hotels in the Keys seem to have some type of nautical name to them. I'm willing to bet that many have rooms with names like the "Sunset Suite." The artist had a dozen or so totems of various shapes and sizes. They were neatly lined up on the side of the road. They were connected to each other by a thick cable which ran through eye bolts screwed into each pole. We pulled up and Ferg immediately needed to buy his totem pole. Mora apparently had a hold of Ferg's ear the last several miles of the trip.

We parked and got out of the truck and the artist exited his office through the driver's side door. He placed his Mountain Dew in the bed of his truck and shook Fergy's outstretched hand. After looking over several of the pieces, one with a pineapple carved into the forehead of the top face was chosen. I turned to head back to the sanctuary of the air conditioning of our truck.

"Shamus," Ferg yells out to me, as he's walking back in my direction, "He wants $500 for the big one. What do you think?"

Now being a bartender does give me certain insight to the human character. It does not however, endow me with the knowledge on the current market price of wooden totems sold street side. "Offer him $300," I said. They settled on $425.

Again I turned for the truck and its life saving air conditioning. Again Ferg calls out to me. "Hey, where you going? Give me a hand getting this into the truck."

He might as well had been speaking the language of some lost Amazonian tribe. I stared at him in sheer disbelief. "What?" I questioned.

"I bought it, this is the one!" His face beaming like he just bought a Van Gogh from some unsuspecting old woman at a yard sale.

"Why don't we just pick it up when we leave?" I replied in complete amazement.

"I don't want someone to take it," he sounded like a small child who wanted a puppy from a pet store window.

"Take it?" my voice lowering several octaves, "This friggin thing weighs a ton and it's chained to several other tons of sculptures!" my hands gesturing to all the totems like they were panelist on a talk show. "Excuse me," I yelled over to the Mountain Dew swilling artist, "Hey Picasso, ever have one of these stolen?" He just scrunched up his face and shook his head no. "See Ferg, it'll be safe!" I pleaded.

"Then why does he have them locked together?" The simplicity of his question stopped me dead. Common sense just took an upper cut to the jaw. I knew the fight was over. My corner man had thrown the towel into the ring.

Back into the air conditioning and cruising down the shelled driveway of the Drop Anchor, our Easter Island God resting peacefully in the bed of the truck. The pain in my testicles from lifting Ferg's treasure into the bed of the truck was starting to subside. "We'll check in, I'll crack a beer, and give Captain Paul a call. Everything's going to be fine," I thought.

We checked in and Ferg asked for a room in a more secluded part of the motel grounds. He wants a place where he could smoke his reefer in peace. The lady behind the counter exhaled deeply, her little protest to renting to fags.

We pulled the truck around and unload our bags. Ferg had to choose a specific bed, God bless O.C.D. life must never be boring. After our gear was stowed I grab a cold one out of the cooler and sat down. Ferg's across the room rolling up a Bob Marley special. He looks over and says, "Give me a hand bringing in the Totem before I fire this up."

"You're friggin insane!" I said as I resign myself not to fight a losing battle and ready myself to wake the sleeping God from his resting place in the back of the Ford. Somewhere in a scrapbook there is a picture of me standing next to the "Totem from Hell" in the Sunset Suite of the Drop Anchor. I wish there was some type of lens I could put on the camera to expose Mora. I'm sure she's on the other side of the Totem laughing her ass off.

With the totem secured and a cold beer in my belly a hot shower was in order. With the road and totem washed from my body, thoroughly refreshed and ready for another cold one. The fresh smell of reefer permeated the air in the room. I quickly lit a cigar for a bit of cover scent. It didn't really make a difference as we were the only ones registered in the motel. Fergy peered out the window through the slats of the blinds. He coughed from the huge toke he'd just taken and laughed. Ferg waves me over and points out the window. One of the workers at the motel was a tall, skinny Jamaican fellow. He's dressed in kitchen worker's garb. Black pants and a white chef's coat. He was also wearing a cap that covered his immense dreadlocks. That style always made the Rasta guys look like they were wearing Jiffy Pop hats.

This fellow is wandering around the courtyard trying to locate the aroma of his home country and Fergy laughed hysterically. "Check it out, I chummed in a Rasta!" It became the mantra for the trip.

Captain Paul was Mora's saving grace on this trip. Paul is a consummate professional. His boat is always in top condition and his gear is checked before and after every trip. He could be boarded at any time by the Coast Guard and they'd never find an issue. Since Florida has a zero tolerance law about Fergy's passion, Captain Paul required that Fergy leave all his "gear" on shore. Paul is no prude and with living in the Keys, the home of the *Save the Bales Foundation,* I'm sure he's seen his share of illegal activity, but this is how he makes his living and he's not endangering it for anyone. Mora began to release some of the tension in her body knowing that the Captain was in charge.

She should have remembered Madeline's mantra, "Never let your guard down."

The next morning we're up at the crack of dawn to meet the boat at Papa Joe's. Papa Joe's is a famous watering hole in Islamorada, where many of the local guides moor their boats. It's known for its outstanding sunsets and rumrunners. We greeted Paul and stowed gear. Paul had already been out netting bait that morning so it was off to the Tarpon grounds. Paul had been having most of his success fishing the incoming tides by the Seven Mile Bridge. We anchored up with our stern facing the bridge. Lines were baited and allowed to drift back to the shadow line of the bridge. Mora was comfortable with this arrangement because she was able to watch us from the bridge and not have to be on the boat. We had good success landing several Tarpon in the 60 to 80 pound range. Paul informed us that the bigger girls will start feeding on the tide switch.

True to his word as the tide started to slack Ferg hooked into a 125 pound fish. This fish went airborne several times during the fight. The captain barked orders on how to best fight the fish. "Get your rod tip down by the water and pull her sideways! If she goes left you pull right! Never let off on the pressure." Paul orchestrated the entire fight while standing on his poling platform. The fish was almost done; Paul climbed down from the poling platform and tells me that he wants to release the fish on the other side of the bridge. Lately the sharks have been feeding aggressively on the side we're on with this type of tide.

He runs down the game plan with me. "I'll handle the fish. When I tell you, release the anchor. I have a float on it and we'll comeback for it later. Then drive us over to the other side fast, so we can take photos and release this fish. Watch the currents; they shift around under the bridge." This probably would have been a good time to mention that I had never driven a boat before but Paul sounded so confident in my abilities. I've been on boats for most of my life, know terminology and all sorts of knots, but had never driven one before.

Ferg gets his fish boat side and Paul grabs the leader. Captain Paul sticks a gloved hand in the Tarpon's mouth and holds onto her bottom jaw. The fish is still a bit green and is trashing wildly. Paul has a constant eye out for sharks and sees a fin 60 yards off our port side. "Shamus, get us to the other side fast!" he yells with more than a touch of excitement in his voice. I released the anchor, fired up the engine and slapped the throttle forward, hard. A little bit too hard.

Instead of coming up on plane in a controlled fashion the bow jumps out of the water. Paul's boat rockets towards the bridge at full speed. All I can see is the bridge abutment coming right at us. I turned the wheel hard to starboard. This motion rolled Fergy, Paul, and the Tarpon into the bottom of the boat. Mora is up on the bridge screaming for me to slap the throttle back down and get control of the boat. As I look up from the Three Stooges flopping around on the bottom, I see another bridge abutment headed straight for us. I now turned the wheel hard to the port. This rolls the boat on its side as we pass the abutment. Once we clear the bridge I turn the wheel again and cut the engine. The boat comes down into its proper position in the water.

Captain Paul is white as a ghost but he held onto the Tarpon like a mother holds a baby. Ferg's "levels" are as low as they've been in years. The Tarpon orgasms a thick coat of slime all over Paul's blue N.Y. Yankees shirt. He turned to Ferg and hands him the fish. "Get your photos and let's get that fish back in the water." He then turns his attention back to me, "What the hell was that?" The veins in his neck had bulged out so hard I thought they would burst. He jumps back behind the wheel and screamed. "Man you couldn't have slid a dollar bill between us and the bridge! I've never been that scared before. Go take pictures of Ferg."

Paul's hands were shaking hard. I photographed Fergy's fish and helped release her after moving her back and forth to get water over her gills. A quick jerk of her head and a splash with her tail and the Tarpon was free to fight another day. Ferg's attention was now on me. He just looks me in the eye and shakes his head. "Man!" was all he said. I now knew how those girls felt when he used to call them animals, as they walked up the back stairs of the Aft.

Paul tried to steer the boat for Papa Joe's but his hands were covered in fish slime. I offered to drive home and they both screamed, "NO!" Everyone busted out laughing and all was forgiven. As we headed for home I reminded Paul that he forgot the anchor. No one can curse like a fishing boat Captain.

Mora leaned against the rail of the bridge, drained from what she'd just watched. With shaking hands she struck a match and lit a cigar. "Sharks, Tarpon, and speeding boats. What else could he possibly get into?"

Madeline startled Mora by answering, "Oh you never want to ask that!" Mora jumped and dropped her cigar off the bridge. Madeline told her that on a good note she found a wonderful place for conch fritters. Through many trips to the Keys Mora was able to taste the foods and flavors of the Conch Republic.

Chapter 19

From their perch atop the Seven Mile Bridge Madeline and Mora blushed as they heard Captain Paul cursing over leaving his anchor. "Nice stew you're creating there, Twizzle," Madeline prodded.

"Not bad but I'm not finished yet. I've been thinking."

Madeline interrupted her for a quick shot, "Really? You thought this out, had an actual plan?" Madeline's head nodding to Captain Paul's departing boat.

"Shut it! I just need another set of female eyes on Shamus. This stew needs some tomato paste and basil, balance it out, add another layer of flavor." She did it with Jody. Mora did it very subtly. Jody and I have known each other forever it seems. The funny part is we don't know how we met. Someone asked us how we met one time and we were both stumped. Jody is definitely Mora's kind of woman. She's comfortable in either a kitchen or the Aft. Those reasons are why Mora chose Jody. It's in the kitchen where she shines and Mora knew I could never pass up a great smelling kitchen. She's also a wiseass so there was no way our paths wouldn't cross at some point.

After returning from my vacation in the Keys it was time to look for a new lodging. The small bungalows I'd seen in the Keys intrigued me. The closest I could come to them in Brewster were the summer cottages in Putnam Lake. Jody was a "Laker", a title bestowed on anyone born and raised on the shores of Putnam Lake. I recruited her assistance in finding a home by the lake. We'd been friends for quite awhile at that point and I could always count on Jody. A few days later she told me of a house for rent. The lady who owned the house lived in New York and would only rent to married couples. We had spoken several times by phone but as luck would have it my wife worked swing shifts and the landlady kept missing her. "Great! Can't wait to meet you!" I said as I hung up the phone. She would come up the following weekend to interview us. As I hung up the phone I thought to myself, "Well now you're screwed. Even a Russian mail order bride would take at least two weeks for delivery."

I was sitting on the hood of my car trying to figure out where I was going to find a wife in a week. Jody pulls up in her jeep and asked what I'm doing. I looked up and the expression on my face scared her, "Shamus, what the hell are you up to?"

"Nothing, honey." Now I've known Jody for quite a few years and have never called her "Honey". I called her a few other things but never "Honey". After a little coaxing she agreed to be my pretend wife. The landlady and her son interviewed us for close to an hour. All the normal questions you'd expect. Where do you work, how long have you been there? Then the son asked, "How come you're not wearing wedding rings?"

It hit me like a ton of bricks that I'd forgotten that one little detail. Jody answered back without missing a beat, "I was scared to lose them with all the packing going on at our old apartment. I gave them to my mother to hold on to." Then Jody quickly changed the subject about gardening and took the landlady's arm and strolled around the house asking all sorts of questions. Mora was stunned. She knew Jody was good but even Mora was impressed with that boldfaced lie.

Two years later the landlady returned when it was time to sign a new lease. Jody was away on vacation so I had another friend, Marion, play pretend wife number 2. Jody's dark haired and Marion is blonde. They look nothing alike. I could tell the landlady's son knew something was up but he was receiving his monthly check on time and decided to keep his mouth shut.

I'd leave the Aft around 4:00 a.m. by the time we had the place cleaned up. Then a few of us would go for breakfast at the closest greasy spoon. After breakfast I'd either go fishing or play a round of 9 holes at a local golf course. Home around noon to crash and burn until 8:00 p.m. and do it all over again. We referred to it as revolving. This lifestyle was fun but didn't leave a great deal of time for house cleaning. Jody came over one day and spotted a half a glass of milk that had been on my dresser for some time. The milk was starting to sprout a green fungus. Jody was like a mad dog on a bone. She wouldn't stop ragging me about the milk. I finally told her it was a house plant and that I was going to give it to her for Christmas.

That's exactly what I did. For months I fed the fungus white bread soaked in milk. By the time Christmas arrived you couldn't see the glass anymore. It would have brought a tear to the eye of a mycologist. The cures for many diseases were in that glass. It didn't matter that I spent months cultivating this gift or that I spent hours wrapping her present. My thank you was, "Shamus, get that thing out of my house! What is wrong with you?" Her head shaking as she rubbed her forehead. Great gift, wrong woman. Marie Curie would have done back flips for a gift like that.

Jody shook her head quite a bit at me. A bunch of friends and I were headed to a Frank Zappa concert in Hartford one night. Jody came over early and walked in the front door. I was watching a football game and cooking dinner at the same time. I had a kerosene heater in the living room and placed a frying pan on top of it. My steak and potatoes were doing quite nicely sizzling away in the pan. Jody walked in and immediately started shaking her head, "What the hell are you doing?"

"Cooking dinner, want some?"

"No. Why don't you just use your stove like a normal human being?"

"Can't see the game from the kitchen." A slight tone of confusion was in my voice. It was so obvious that I had the perfect setup. Cooking in your living room, why wasn't everyone doing it? It's been 25 years since the cooking incident and she still reminds me about it.

Around this time Jody had been seeing Jimmy. Jimmy played in a band named Paralax. It was another tight band that played the Aft. It was through Jimmy's band that Mora started to understand the difference between her old Blues bands and my day's hard charging Rock 'n' Roll. Just like Mora's bands, the bands I was watching were filled with talented players and some really good voices. They did however do something that Mora's musicians never did. *PYROTECHNICS!* Nothing shouts out Rock 'n' Roll like a good explosion.

Mora had watched the roadies setting up the 1 inch pipes and couldn't imagine what they were. She found out sometime around the third set. Paralax was playing an old Little Walter tune, "*Boom Boom Out Go the Lights,*" except when they go boom, they really go boom. Mora had been standing a little too close to the stage shaking her ass and screaming like a groupie when the flash cannons went off. Apparently someone confused teaspoon and tablespoon when it came to the black powder they were using in the cannons. Madeline was deprived of her fun. For a week she kept saying to Mora, "It's only Rock 'n' Roll" but the joke was lost on Mora due to a mild case of deafness.

Chapter 20

Mora didn't need to hear any Blues today. Her mood was as blue as any music she ever heard at Gunning's. Her Shamus would be as old as she was when she died, on his next birthday. She knew how to guard someone younger than her, that just came naturally. Soon she'd have to guard someone older than herself. A thought that chilled her to her marrow crossed her mind.

Shamus, if she did her job well would be an old man one day. How long do I protect him she wondered? She saw the older folks around, frail and weak. Her life was cut short. Never knowing what it felt like to have her body betray her. Weakened muscles, arthritic joints, memory failure were never known to her. Mora's death was terrifying. The slow sinking below the surface of the lake with no control of her body was horrific. She wondered if the ones lying in some hospice bed dying of old age didn't have the same agony, only prolonged.

Her thoughts turned to Connor. The last kiss she ever tasted was his. There was a spark, both felt it. What happened to him? Was he happy? Did he have a family? Could she have had one with him? Is he lying in one of those hospital beds? Her mind erased that thought and brought back a memory of Connor astride the Indian. Muscles taut, chrome gleaming, a smile stretched across his freckled face. The memory brought a tear to her eye and a smile to her face.

I had just returned from an annual white water rafting trip. That year's destination was the New River in West Virginia. Mora was always in a foul mood around the time of these trips. The rivers my crew of buddies and I rafted were picked to have as many class 5 rapids as possible. My crew, as far as Mora's stew was concerned, were the salt, pepper, paprika and other seasoning combined. Each brought their own flavor to the stew yet they all melded together perfectly.

Guides on these trips always named each of the bigger rapids on the river. It was always something like "The Widow Maker" or "The Washing Machine." I often wondered if they changed the names weekly or seasonally.

Mora hated these rivers as much as she hated the ocean. She made peace with the cliff diving we did. It was just jumping into calm water and quickly climbing out to do it again. The rivers, however, were swollen from snow melt or from dam releases. Through the eons, torrents of water had carved deep gorges into the earth. A violent match of rock versus water, so deafening one cannot feel their own heart beating in their chest.

It was the time spent off the water she enjoyed most. Stories told by the crew over cold beers. Any screw up by anyone was fodder for stories over dinner. These were my buddies; they knew good restaurants, how to order and take care of waitresses and bartenders. One trip took us to a little town 40 miles from nowhere. This little town survived on rafters during the spring and summer. Moose and bear hunters kept it going during the Fall and Winter.

We hit the local greasy spoon the first morning. My crew is composed of all big boys with big appetites. Mora loved to watch us order and eat. No one is ordering lattes and scones. It's coffee, hot and black. Eggs and slabs of bacon served with plenty of buttered toast. It's amazing how that combination counter affects the closing of the local bars the previous night. We walk into one little place and start rearranging the tables to accommodate us. Kenny and Leroy took charge of the tables. Pierre had chairs stacked up and dragged them over to the tables. Vinny and TC confiscated condiments and silverware from the surrounding tables.

Mabel, the waitress, who looks as if she's been working in the place since the last nail was driven into the wall, is now totally thrown off her game. Her game belongs in the minors. She never got the call to play in the big leagues. Pierre stands 6'5 and weighs a hair under 280. Mabel starts with him, taking the order for breakfast. Pete, as we called him, eyeballs the table. With head nods and shoulder shrugs we relinquish the job of ordering on his capable shoulders. Pete orders 8 coffees black, 3 platters of eggs, scrambled and a slab or two of bacon. Mabel dutifully writes his order. She then adjusts her grease stained apron turns to me and asked me for my order. Mora shook her head and called her a Twizzle. The rest of us just burst out laughing.

The local sheriff happened to be sitting at the counter. He'd watched us overtake the greasy spoon like a Navy Seal team on a mission. He put his coffee on the counter and asks us all to step outside. My buddy Tom, TC as we call him, took charge. TC has done business throughout the world and is extremely fluent in cop speak.

The rest of the crew was ready to get involved but I waved them off. In these situations it's always best to have a professional do the talking. It's also a bad idea to have a crew of guys that look like a Rugby team get in the face of an armed local cop. The judge in these towns somehow is always related to the local peacekeeper. Rafting a river is a better alternative than resting your bones in a drafty jail cell.

TC walks over to the constable's cruiser. After letting him posture for a bit, the customary adjustment of the gun belt and touch of the wide brim of his hat, TC gives the appearance of listening to him like a child being read a fairytale. TC's eyes are staring straight into the officer's eyes, TC never blinks. He gives him a slight tilt of the head like it's his right ear that will take in all the cop has to say.

The officer stops to take a breath. Like a fencer with foil in hand, TC sees his opening and lunges. Now there is not a single human alive that has ever won an argument with TC. They may think they have, but in the end, TC always gets his way, and somehow makes whoever he's discussing a point with feel like they have won. Everyone comes out a winner, but TC wins just a little bit more. A hardy handshake later, TC has not only won, but has invited the officer for breakfast and drinks with us later.

Mabel stopped dead in her tracks when she walked through the saloon doors from the kitchen to see us all reseated with the officer at the head of the table. The officer is regaling us with stories of rafters he's personally saved from the river. We give him his due and applauded at the correct times. Apparently we were just a bunch of good ole boys and there must have been some sort of misunderstanding. We finished breakfast and tip Mabel with enough cash for a girl's weekend away from this one horse town. The next morning she was a ray of sunshine when she saw us walk in. The officer on the other hand was a few shades of green from a night of hanging with us good ole' boys.

Mora was actually starting to think it was time to give me a little free range. Apparently I knew how to use the people around me to their best abilities. The crew that she wasn't so sure about a few short years ago became the best people to be around. They have your back no matter what the circumstances.

Chapter 21

I was sitting in Norm's with my hands wrapped around a Norm's Burger. A buddy of mine, Billy, strolls over. He explains that this weekend he's throwing a 25th wedding anniversary party for his parents at the local Elks Lodge. Billy's parents are wonderful people. They are the type of folks that always have a pot of coffee on the stove and want you to sit and partake of some. One cup seems to turn into three and you somehow have spent several hours swapping stories about the past. It's my kind of way to kill an afternoon. Billy says he has everything covered but he needs a bartender. I say, "For your parents, no problem, and don't even think of offering me money."

Billy rumbles up a laugh and says, "I had no intention to. Hell, you owe them at least a grand in coffee money for the time you've spent around their table!" He was right. He's a cheap bastard, but he was right.

The day of the party had arrived. I showered, shaved and dressed in the customary black slacks and white shirt. I climbed aboard the Honda and headed for the Elks Lodge. I arrived an hour early to set up the bar to my liking. Ice bins loaded to the brim and bottles of everyone's favorite beers jammed into the ice. Liquor bottles lined up like soldiers awaiting inspection, labels facing out, red plastic spouts facing left. A stack of colored napkins spun with a rocks glass so they spiral on top of each other making it easier to grab each individual napkin.

The DJ soon arrived and set up his equipment. It paled in comparison to what I was accustomed to at the Aft, but it was enough to handle tonight's entertainment. The guest started to arrive and the room started to hum. Being behind the bar affords you a certain perspective on people and the world. The fact that there is a plank of wood separating you from the crowd gives you a different view on what is happening. The curtain is drawn back and you see the wizard for what he is. Neither good or bad, just different from the view on the other side of the bar.

Everyone hit the buffet line, after seeing me first. Free booze makes the bartender a very popular fellow. The DJ kicked up the music and his red and blue flashing lights washed the dance floor. Toasts were given and Stevie Wonder himself could see that Billy's parents were still in love with each other after 25 years of marriage. After the toasts were made and the cake was cut the dance floor was open again. By the end of the night sleepy children were dancing with their parents. Their heads bobbing up and down on parents shoulders as pools of spittle leaked out on mom's cocktail dress or dad's only good suit. A suit which was only released from the confines of the closet, for weddings, funerals and Easter Sunday Mass. Shirttails escaped the grip of waistbands and ties were either off or loosened their vampire grip on their victim's neck.

As the night was drawing to its conclusion, goodbyes were said to everyone countless times. The room was void enough for me to start the second half of my job, the breakdown. Every Elks Lodge or Moose Hall has some old guy that runs the place. They're a good bunch of fellows, always quick to help or show you where things belonged. After the room was swept and garbage hauled out to the dumpsters, I was ready to depart.

I unbuttoned the top collar of my shirt and was ready to jump over the bar. Billy's little sister, Liz stopped me. She asked me to pour her a JD on the rocks. She needed to unwind a bit. She was the one who organized the party and fretted over the details. She asked me to join her in one. I never drink at a private party that I'm working but this one was over. The dance floor was even broom swept. I replied, "Sure, one." Another part of bartender duties is to listen to stories on how the party was thrown together, especially if the one telling the story is a cute redhead. A bartender's duties are all encompassing.

Liz proceeded to enlighten me with all the covert activities. The late night calls to relatives. Coordinating caterers and bakers, so everything would be seamless. Arranging hotel rooms for out of town guests and taxi's to and from various locations. It was all very cloak and dagger stuff, all committed under the watchful eye of her seemingly clueless parents. Billy's parents might not have known the date or time, but they knew a party was brewing. They knew the way parents of small children know when the kids are still awake in their beds at night, when they should have been fast asleep hours before.

Somewhere in the midst of this story I relinquished my responsibilities as bartender and Liz took over. Now Liz is a small girl. If she ever stepped on the bathroom scale and it read three figures, Ralph, their dog, would have had one paw on the scale. When Liz pours three fingers of JD she uses Andre the Giant's fingers. Another curious fact about Liz is her father's nickname should be Geppetto, because his little girl has a wooden leg. I knew if she kept pouring I'd be waking up in an Elks Lodge. I told her what a wonderful job she had done, rewarded her with a quick hug and headed for the door.

Once outside I took a few breaths of fresh air to clear my head. I hopped on my bike and headed for home. A mile or two of back roads and I'd be showering in 10 minutes. As I passed the first cornfield, a doe that was grazing on the grass on the side of the road lifted her head. "No big deal," I thought to myself, "She'll run back into the corn." Mora tensed as if the devil himself blew in her ear.

The doe started running alongside me and never veered back into the field. Soon she was trapped between the Honda and the guardrail. The exhaust from my muffler was spurring her on. If I sped up, she ran faster. If I slowed down, she did as well. I was starting to become unhinged, afraid she was going to run right in front of me. Mora's mind was spinning out of control. Visions of her accident flashed through her mind. The thought of me tumbling across the blacktop caused her to panic. Visions of her Shamus being maimed or killed clouded her mind. A moment of clarity struck her. Use the kill switch on your handle bar she whispered to me. I reached up with my right thumb and hit the switch.

I don't know who invented it or what it's normally used for. I owned the Honda for years now and never used it before that day. The kill switch, when engaged, simply turns off the motor. Once the engine was off I continued to roll but now the exhaust wasn't scaring the doe and she simply let me pass on by.

I was soaked in sweat. Any effects from the JD were long gone. I pulled over and lit a cigar with trembling hands. Mora joined me. She was a physical and emotional wreck. Tears streaked down her face. She wasn't afraid of losing her opportunity to see the world. She was petrified of losing me.

Madeline watched us from across the road. A feeling of dread overwhelmed her also, but for different reasons. Mora spied her through tear filled eyes. She immediately ran to Madeline and nearly toppled her over. Mora's head was buried in Madeline's bosom, between spasms of uncontrollable sobbing she explained what happened. Madeline just stroked her hair trying to console her, "It's over baby. Shamus is alright, and you did fine."

Mora started to gain control of herself and back away from Madeline. Madeline retrieved two napkins from her bag and handed one to Mora. "Here, clean yourself up," she said as she extended one of the napkins to Mora. The other she used to clean Mora's snot from her chest.

Mora stammered, "I was so afraid. I don't know where the thought of using the kill switch came from."

Madeline used her thumb and forefinger to wipe the edges of her mouth. She took a long slow breath and released it even slower. "That was me," she said without making eye contact.

Mora raised her head, "What?, How?"

Madeline patted a boulder they were standing next to. "Sit. We have to talk." There was a long pause before Madeline continued. "It was me. I have the ability to communicate with you like you do with Shamus."

Mora looked at Madeline like a confused child watching a magic trick.

Madeline released another long breath. "I am," she paused to collect her thought, "Was, your guardian angel!"

Mora felt like she was struck by lightning.

Madeline continued, "I've been a guardian angel," then paused again to find the right words. "It seems since before the sky's been blue." Without hesitation Madeline continued her tale. "I was good at it. Good enough to cover two souls. I watched over you since," she paused again, "since your mother left you. You were growing so fast and had Millie and Red watching over you. You were in such good hands that I was also given Vinny to guard. The night you died I wasn't there to intervene because I was at Vincent's deathbed. I thought the feelings of dread I felt that night were for Vinny. I never suspected you were in trouble. I sent Red the night that man attacked you. I felt you needed me then but Vinny was taking all of my energy. The night of the crash..." Mora stopped Madeline cold with a bear hug.

Mora realized that in one night Madeline lost both of the souls she was to guard over. She wasn't mad at Madeline for not saving her. Instead her heart bled for her. Mora had come very close to losing me. How could she be angry with Madeline? Mora was still reeling from almost losing me. Madeline actually lost both souls she was guarding in one evening. It also became clear to Mora why Madeline could be such a Twizzle over how she protected me.

Madeline wriggled free of Mora's grip. Taking her face in the same way Millie used to, she kissed Mora. Madeline explained that at first she didn't realize it was Mora when they met that night in Limbo. "I neglected you for years, Vinny took every ounce of my energy. You had grown so, not just bigger, when I left to care for Vinny you were a girl. The next time I saw you." Madeline started to cry, "It was that night when you saw me screaming at that angel in Limbo"

"You weren't there, the night...the night I was attacked?" Mora asked quizzically.

"No, that was all you. I sensed something was wrong and sent Red. I knew he could handle anything. That night Vinny had a bout of pneumonia, he was in an oxygen tent for 3 days and I never left his side. It was also the night that I knew you didn't need me anymore. You fought like a caged Tiger that night and Red and Millie were there for you."

Mora's mind sizzled, "Red and Millie, how are they, where are they? My father, where is he? What about Connor?"

Madeline interrupted her, "I don't know their fates. I can only guess by the way they treated and loved you that they have their places in heaven."

Madeline told her she loved her and that she had just used up the one and only chance she'd ever have to intervene on her behalf again. She left her soon after and I resumed my journey home. Mora realized it was the first time that Madeline hadn't offered her food since she'd known her. It didn't matter after what she'd just gone through. Food was the last thing on her mind.

Chapter 22

After the incident with the deer Mora knew that she needed some extra help guarding me. The wonderful stew of friends she was surrounding me with needed a few more ingredients. I needed a woman in my life the way she needed Millie.

This stew she was creating needed garlic. Now garlic in its raw form is hard and acidic. Put it over some low heat and let it mellow and it's sweet like candy. My garlic came in the form of Raphaella Conran. I was in my 20's and Rae, as she was known, was in her 50's. I was good friends with her sons. Those boys were her reason for living. Right or wrong she had her boys' backs at every turn in life.

Rae, could be the sweetest most caring woman in the world. She could also be your worst nightmare. This woman taught me one of life's great lessons. Call a spade a spade. Everyone was welcome in her house the first time. They were treated like royalty, but if Rae thought you were a phony or a bullshit artist, you would never see the inside of her home again. There was no grey area with Rae. Either she loved you, which was one of life's great feelings, or she would have nothing to do with you. I showed up with a red head I was dating at the time. I liked her but she had to pass Rae's test. I knew three minutes in, that she would never pass muster. Rae simply gave me the look. Days later she told me to have my fun but, "Don't ever count on that one." Rae's instincts were always golden. Years later I introduced her to another woman. Her look was one of approval.

Rae's thing was Christmas Eve. She and her husband, Bill, lived in a small log home. Their home contained three bedrooms and one bath, shared by eight people. They made it work because of her strength. The Christmas Eve table was set up in the living room. The tree which was decorated under her watchful eye sat in the corner. That poor tree stood straight like an Army Private for his inspection. Every ball and piece of tinsel was hung in its proper place.

Christmas Eve night the menu would always be the Seven Fishes. It's an Old Italian tradition. You serve nothing but seafood at every course. Shrimp, Scallops, Crab cakes, Lobster, Mussels, Clams, Bacalao, which is salt dried cod. She would soak it in water for several day, changing the water several times a day to remove the salt. It is very labor intensive. When I asked her why she didn't just buy fresh Cod Fish she'd answer "I'm not making Cod I'm making Bacalao. Now stop asking stupid questions and get out of my kitchen."

A day or two before the big Christmas Eve dinner Rae was preparing Deviled Eggs. Tommy Mac and I were sitting around the table. Her sons weren't around but Mom was home and that's all you needed. She was pumping out Deviled Eggs by the dozen. Each one split perfectly down the center. She didn't use any fancy cooking channel gizmo for the job. Just a trained eye and a wooden handled knife. Mac, as everyone called Tommy, and I, were trying to keep up placing Deviled Eggs onto trays as fast as she was giving them to us. Very soon it became the classic *I Love Lucy* skit in which Lucy and Ethel are eating more chocolate off the moving belt than they are boxing in the candy factory.

Rae knows all that goes on in her kitchen. This, and the fact that she takes no nonsense from anyone, is why Mora brought her into my life. Rae figures she should have about eight dozen Deviled Eggs. She turns to see only about six dozen laid out on trays. Prisoners in penile colonies never took the beating we received with her wooden spoon. Rae went through many wooden spoons on us. You knew you were going to get the beating for dunking bread into her Sunday gravy but it was worth it. For Rae's gravy, I'd take that beating every time.

It was a perfect time for me to know Rae. I was in my late twenties and could eat like I had a Tapeworm. Her sons were all around my age and we would try to inhale all she made. The NY Giants couldn't eat all she made. Christmas Eve at Rae's house would have Mora in the best mood of the year. That small home was loaded with people. This was an open house but it was only filled with those Rae loved. Christmas lights twinkling, the smell of all the foods, and the sounds of people that love each other filled the house. This wasn't a group of folks singing Christmas carols. The conversations where about everything: sports, women and politics all at once. It was like having dinner at the N.Y. Stock Exchange. A plane could have crashed in the driveway and we would never have heard it.

Mora loved every minute of it. The food was the best that could be had. More importantly she knew she had another set of eyes on me she could trust. Rae would explode like dynamite on a short fuse when I'd tell her where I had been. "Skydiving? What the hell is wrong with you? You must have a screw loose jumping out of a plane!" Her hands would come together like she was praying for my soul with every ounce of her energy. She couldn't fool me though. She hung on every word.

I knew Rae as a woman in her fifties. Raising six, sometimes seven sons, including me, took its toll. One I know she gladly paid. There was also another Rae. It's the doe eyed, tight skinned beauty that is in the picture as you headed into the kitchen. That woman I could tell was a fireball. It always seemed that when I told her of my adventures she was always seated below that photo. I was telling my stories to both women. While the older woman was chastising me, I know the younger woman in the photo would have joined me in my adventures. I was reckless, but I know she told her girlfriends those same stories like I was one of her own and she was proud of it.

Chapter 23

You could almost hear Roger McGuinn of the Byrds singing, *"To every season turn, turn, turn,"* in the air. Life took a quick left turn for everyone in Brewster. The Fore "N" Aft closed its doors after 26 years. The saddest part of its closing was that we were never able to give the old girl a proper send off. Though, on second thought, if a true send off had occurred, I truly believe the National Guard would have been called in for crowd control.

Sex, drugs, and Rock 'n' Roll would have to leave a forwarding address. They no longer resided on Rt. 6. We all became orphaned children that fall. Artie and Eileen, along with many other parents from the surrounding area, popped the corks on many a bottle of champagne, that day. Years later, the building, after going through many owners, was burned to the ground. Eileen had a suspicious aroma of gasoline about her that night, but nothing could be proven. Every other parent in town would have supplied her with an alibi.

My years behind the bar at the Aft taught me much about life. One major lesson was that when life hands you lemons...now if you thought it was going to be make lemonade stop reading because you haven't been paying any attention to details! When life hands you lemons, grab a salt shaker and good Tequila. Find a good woman, play some Rock 'n' Roll, and enjoy the evening. Hit the local diner for a good breakfast and in the morning, find new horizons. *Lemonade?* What the hell were you folks thinking about?

As the nation's taste had earlier changed from Blues to Rock 'n' Roll, a new sound was emerging, Disco. Disco then somehow led to New Wave and Techno. The smoke filled bars that Mora and I favored, gave way to flashy glass and chrome, superficial as hell, dance palaces. Hell, even Heslin bought one. I even bartended for him for a short while. Now these meat markets did attract a crowd that didn't mind showing lots of skin and throwing money around. But the music was enough to make Mora puke. Driving bass, thumping out a singular beat. I guess it's great if you're on the dance floor. If you're behind the bar it's a bloody nightmare.

For me there were just too many people dressing as if they were auditioning for a shot in an MTV video or Miami Vice. Guys had weird hairdos. Robert Plant had great hair. The guy from Flock of Seagulls had a pissed off hairdresser on designer drugs. I was bored and it was time for a change.

Mora had been going through a time of self evaluation ever since finding out Madeline was her guardian. She had become very reflective of late. Her plans for revenge on the local deer population had succeeded, as well as her music fix, yet there was more she desired. Travel was always part of her plan; to see the places she had heard so much about from the musicians at Gunning's. Mora had done quite a bit of traveling with me but hunting camps in rural America wasn't what she was really interested in. NY, Miami and New Orleans were the cities she yearned to see.

The smoke from Mora's cigar danced along the rafters of my storage shed as Mora sat taking inventory of my gear. Fishing rods of all weights and length lay in rod holders attached to the rafters. Half a dozen tree stands were leaning against one wall. On the other wall was a small table with a fly tying vice bolted to it. Above it was a shelf loaded with spools of thread in every color of the rainbow. Clear plastic boxes stuffed with fur and feathers also resided on the shelf. The scent of eggplant parmesan cut through the musty smell of the shed broke her concentration.

Madeline had kept her distance since the evening of my near demise. Mora had missed her and her black handbag of endless treats. She found it amazing that since her own death she didn't need food to survive. However, whenever Madeline stopped by, they always ate. It was more of a social event to break bread together.

Madeline spied Mora from the shadows.

"Madeline? Come out, come out where ever you are!" Mora sang. "That eggplant smells wonderful. What are you doing in there, creeping around in the shadows?"

Mora knew Madeline was still apprehensive to approach her. Mora decided to alleviate any of Madeline's fears. "Hey, get over here. Enough all ready with all this sulking around. I told you that night, I don't blame you. I've been dead for over 25 years, its water under the bridge. Now, breakout the eggplant, I'm starving for some reason!"

Madeline sheepishly emerged from the shadows of the storage shed looking around for a place to set her bag on so she could serve the food. Mora realized that Madeline didn't realize everything she needed was around her. In a few seconds Mora had produced a folding table and chairs. Plates and utensils were pulled from a pack hanging on a nail. A knife could have come from anywhere. Knives are given to sportsmen on nearly every birthday or Christmas. We normally only use one, but friends and relatives insist on buying us one on every occasion. Madeline unpacked her bag with a devilish look in her eye. First she removed the eggplant from her bag, next was a loaf of warm crusty Italian bread. Madeline gave Mora her patented NY head nod, "We need glasses."

Mora looked up to see Madeline pulling a bottle of wine from her handbag. "Wine? Is it my birthday?"

"No, wiseass, your birthday is in November. I just wanted to have some fun with you, but if you don't want the wine, I'll put it back."

"No. No. No. Some wine would be nice."

Madeline was using the heel of the bread to wipe clean her second plate of eggplant. Mora was topping off Madeline's third glass of wine. Madeline turned her head from side to side eyeballing my gear. "What the hell is all this stuff?" Her words slurred slightly from the wine. She let her head fall back as her eyes gazed upwards to see all my fishing rods. "How many rods does one man need?"

Mora spoke up like a salesman at Cabela's Sporting Goods explaining the use of each fishing rod. "See that thin long one, that's a noodle rod. We use that for Salmon fishing in the fall."

"Why only in the fall? Don't Salmon swim in the summer?" Mora wasn't sure if Madeline was making fun or tipsy from the wine.

Mora explained the reason for fly rods in several weight classes. The reason I needed to own six tree stands. "Shamus only hunts certain properties when the wind is blowing from the right direction. So he needs several stands hung in all different locations."

"Well, aren't you just a wealth of information. I might have to change your name from Twizzle to Curt Gowdy!"

"Shut it!" Mora said as she topped off Madeline's wine.

"Good thing I'm not driving." This made both women start to giggle uncontrollably. Once she caught her breath Madeline pointed to the corner of the shed and asked the purpose of the red tank. She could tell from the way Mora tensed up that she'd hit a nerve.

Mora's voice cracked with tension, "That is proof that Shamus can be such a little shit."

Madeline broke in, "That's such a filthy word. Use Cocknocker, it sounds so much nicer."

Mora just eyeballed her and continued, "That is a memorial to my failure as a guardian angel. His entire life I have spoken, pleaded, and cajoled with him to stay away from the water. You know how it hurts me. Why can't he feel it?"

Madeline looked at the cylinder and gave Mora a look of confusion. "But what is it?"

"Scuba, it's a scuba tank! I suffered through his fishing off every pier and rock jetty he could find. How hard did I cry every time he traveled down those rivers in rubber rafts? But scuba is the last straw. Shamus is in for a big surprise if he thinks I'm letting him go beneath the surface of the water. I've watched him do it several times now and it haunts me."

Madeline interrupted, her voice steely cold, "And just what the hell are you going to do?" This stopped Mora's rant.

Madeline continued her voice hardening "Look around you. We're standing in a room full of what he does. He could hurt himself with anyone of these things. This tank is no more dangerous than your motorcycle. These hoses and gauges, are you going to cut or smash them? I don't understand why anyone likes any of this!" her arm swinging in an arch around the room, "He's always running around the woods with arrows or guns!" Madeline exhaled deeply shaking her head at the entire subject. "He could just as easily hurt himself doing any of the things you inspired him to do with your little late night chats."

Like a child that has lost an argument, Mora pouted her lips and in a sullen voice replied, "Well no."

Madeline pushed the discussion further, "Makes sense to me that, if you interfere with any of his training or dives, you could put him in harm's way. Which, by the way, you were put here to protect him from exactly that."

"But when he's underwater there's nothing I can do to help him!"

"Then you better make sure you do everything you can while he is above the surface. Make sure he checks and rechecks his stuff," Madeline urged while gesturing towards my regulator, "Put it in his mind to always have someone with him."

"They're called dive buddies. Mike is his dive partner. He's the one who enticed Shamus into this. Mike and that damn Jacques Cousteau. Still can't believe Artie and Eileen let him watch that show. I let that one slip by me. I could have stopped this way back then. I just never thought he'd do this."

"Mike? The one who thought he was Tarzan, always jumping out of the trees?" Madeline's tone had a slight hint of superiority, "The same kid you picked for Shamus' best friend? I thought he moved to Arizona?"

"Texas, and he's back," Mora corrected curtly, her stare hardening, warning Madeline she was treading on dangerous ground. "They're headed to someplace called New London next weekend on a lobster dive.

"Oh yummy, I love a good lobster roll." Madeline said with excitement, and then her tone hardened again, "I can feel you planning something, Mora. Be very careful and remember, go easy. Try a subtle approach, not your usual bull in a china shop routine." Madeline saw Mora was ready to jump down her throat and cut her off. "Need I remind you of the Putnam Lake incident?"

"What? I was subtle! I used his dog, Tanya, to prevent Shamus from walking out on the thin ice that day."

"You had her knock him to the ground and he tore the cartilage in his left knee!"

"That's on Tanya, not me; I just placed the idea in her mind that the ice was unsafe."

Madeline's NY temper was nearing boiling point. "You placed a thought in Tanya's mind, and man's best friend attacks its owner? The person who took the dog in off the streets! That must have been one hell of a thought."

"Attack him? She merely tripped him up and he banged his knee."

"He banged his knee! He has a six inch long surgical scar and a plastic kneecap," Madeline fired back.

Madeline knew the conversation was going nowhere fast and resigned from the argument and the garage, "Have a nice time in New London and save me some lobster." She drained her glass and was gone.

The following weekend Mike and I were headed up to New London, CT. Mike had learned of a location for a shore dive spot on a small island called Fisher's Island. Fisher's Island is a quaint New England fishing village. About 100 yards southeast off Fisher's is a huge rock known as Race Rock. It received its name due to the fact that it lies in the exact location that Long Island Sound meets the Atlantic Ocean. On an outgoing tide, especially during a full moon, the water races through the area between Fisher's and Race Rock. Time your dive incorrectly and you would be facing an extremely long, hard swim home from Greenland.

Fisher's Island is reached either by plane or ferry. We'd leave at 4 in the morning to be first in line for the ferry to insure a full day of diving. New London Submarine Base Station is in the same harbor as the ferry for Fisher's Island along with several fleets of fishing boats. Watching all the activity of the busy harbor helped pass the time while waiting for the ferry.

Once on Fisher's, it was a quick jaunt down to the beach. I'd exchange pleasantries with the Striper fishermen who were packing up from the previous evening. 10 foot surf rods, sand spikes, windbreakers and beach chairs were piled into their vehicles. Scuba tanks, buoyancy compensators device, which divers use to raise and lower themselves in the water column, Hawaiian slings for spearing fish and assorted bags of equipment were exiting our van. Sanderlings and Plovers worked the beach checking every piece of seaweed for whatever morsel it would yield. Schools of Peanut Bunkers would thrash at the surface trapped between ravenous Bluefish below them and Blackface Gulls and Terns hovering above them picking off any injured baitfish from the surface of the water.

Mike and I were working as feverishly as the Sanderlings around us. BCD's and regulators were attached to tanks. Pressures were checked, straps adjusted for proper fit and finally the neoprene dance would begin. In the Northeast, where the water temps are never really warm but for a few short weeks in September, divers wear 5mm neoprene wetsuits. These suits are designed to keep you warm in frigid waters, help protect against scrapes and cuts from barnacle encrusted rocks, and the stings of jellyfish. It is this same design that will suck the life out of you while standing on a sun drenched beach. You get your gear all ready, then pull on your wetsuit and hit the water as fast as you can.

Mora would walk down the beach, looking for shells, or just watch the Fiddler Crabs scurry back into their burrows, anything but watch me enter the water. The one thing she hated most fascinated me. For Mora, sinking below the surface of the water was a terrifying act. For me, it was magical. Sound changes, light changes, your breathing changes. You become aware of every breath you exhale as the bubbles from your regulator dance past your face. On land we are the dominant creature. Under the sea we are as helpless as newborns. You must learn to slow your movement down to conserve air and not spook all the sea life from sight.

Mike and I had become quite proficient at conserving air and the underwater stalking of our prey. Flounders would be speared with the Hawaiian Slings as they tried to conceal themselves in the sandy bottom. We would place red film over the lens of our flashlight so as not to spook lobster and force them further back into their lair. We would watch striper chase squid and crabs crawl along the rocks foraging. The natives taught us which techniques worked best and adapted those to fit us.

Sound travels four times farther and faster underwater. It is also extremely difficult to tell what direction sound emanates from underwater. I kept picking up on a strange sound I couldn't identify. It wasn't the usual whirl of the Johnson and Evinrude outboards used by fishing guides and lobstermen. It had a much higher pitch that felt as if it penetrated your body.

Mike must have heard it, too, because he turned to me and gestured to his ears.

We always like to exit the water with 300psi in our tanks. We checked gauges and were still above 800psi. Mike signaled to me to surface so we could take a visual of our location compared to where the van was. With BCD's filled, we bobbed along the surface discussing our exit strategy. Mike questioned me, "What the hell do you think that sound was?"

I shook my head and said that my only guess was, "Maybe a whale?"

Our bodies both felt the same penetrating sound once again. We eyeballed each other and in unison said, "What the hell is that?"

As soon as the words left our mouths the nose of a nuclear submarine from New London broke the surface of the water several hundred yards from our location. As spectacular as it was watching the submarine's breach from the water, we both felt this was not the safest place to be. It takes mighty big props to move a sub of that size and we didn't want to be within the same Zip Code as them.

We dumped the air from our BCD's and shot straight to the bottom. Mike had just taken a compass heading before the sub appearance so we headed back for the beach and the van. When we had first surfaced and saw the submarine we were only sixty yards off the beach. We made it back to the beach in a few minutes.

A New England beach is far different from a beach in the Caribbean. The soft sand of a palm lined beach is replaced by softball sized rocks. Eons of wave action have rendered these rocks smooth and slick. Rocks that have waited patiently for a dumbass diver to come strolling across them wearing wet neoprene booties. Slime covered rocks that once they feel the weight of a tired diver, balancing a weight belt and scuba tank on his back, will shift. As I felt myself falling I luckily was able to spin and let my tank take the brunt of the fall.

Mora watched me topple onto the rocks from her perch on a sand dune. She had been arranging the seashells to spell the name Connor. As she looked up to see me slam into the rocks she muttered in true Twizzle fashion, "Well maybe if you weren't out playing Sea Hunt you wouldn't have fallen on your ass."

We reached the van and dumped the tanks and weight belts on the ground. As we unzipped our wetsuits I noticed a helicopter coming in fast and low on the horizon. Mike informed me that we had company coming in from the road. I turned to see a blue and white police car bouncing over the rough beach road. "Did you park in a no parking zone?" I asked Mike.

"I don't think they send a helicopter after you for parking infringements," he replied as he nodded to the helicopter that was now kicking up what little sand there was on rock beach. I was glad I hadn't removed my wetsuit as it provided me protection from the stinging sand.

The police car arrived just about the time the rotors from the helicopters stopped turning. The cop who exited the car looked like an off duty lobster fisherman. His skin had the worn look of someone who makes their living on the water. What stepped out of the helicopter was much more impressive.

I have no knowledge of military rankings but Mike made a comment that someone important was here to see us. I asked how he knew, "I'm pretty sure he's a Warrant Officer by his markings but it's the two gorillas with the automatic weapons flanking him that tells me he's important."

We were here strictly for diving. There wasn't even a cold beer in the van, so I was fairly confident we weren't in any type of trouble. The police officer asked us for ID's and vehicle registration. The Warrant Officer ordered us not to move, in a voice that meant business. Since he's the guy with automatic weapons backing him, and arrived by way of helicopter, we gave him his due and froze in our tracks. He introduced himself as Warrant Officer Gibbens and wanted to know who we were and what we were doing here. He then pointed to the van and the gorillas went to work tearing through our gear. For some reason, those two guys reminded me of the shorthaired pointer I used to pheasant hunt with my buddy Freddy. All tensed up and ready to flush birds, straining with every fiber of their bodies just waiting for the command. I wondered if Warrant Officer Gibbens would scratch them behind the ear for doing a good job.

"Do you have any weapons?"

"Dive knives and Hawaiian Slings and my sharp wit" Mike answered.

"What are you doing on this beach?" Ignoring the last part of Mike's comment.

Mike point at all the gear and sarcastically said, "Diving." Mike never said the word, "Asshole," but it was heavily implied.

"You are in a restricted area."

On the drive up to the ferry that morning I was bored and actually looked at the U.S.C.G. navigational chart for the area. We were nowhere near to the restricted area. "Not according to the latest navigational charts," I said.

This man wasn't used to be spoken back to and his eyes looked as if they would explode out of his head. He also knew I was dead right. He immediately changed the subject. "Do you have any cameras in your possession?" the Warrant Officer barked.

"I believe I have a cheap Wal-Mart special in my dive bag," I said pointing to my red bag. One of the gorillas was on my dive bag like it was a three dollar whore and it was his first day of shore leave.

"This camera will be confiscated." His tone informing me it was a non negotiable point.

It was a Wal-Mart cheapo with no pictures on it, it was all his. The other gorilla gave him a sign that the van was all clear. Warrant Officer Gibbens seemed confident that we weren't international spies and called his gorillas into formation and they all did an about face and hightailed it to the helicopter. The rotors spun up kicking sand and scarring gulls. The Navy was gone as fast as they arrived.

Since that day I've always rooted for the Black Knights of Army in the annual Army/Navy game.

The police officer who had been leaning against his cruiser the entire time finally spoke up. "Don't sweat it boys. The Navy gets real touchy about folks being in the area when they're testing new toys."

Mike shook his head, "No problem."

I said, "Sure, you didn't lose your camera to National Security."

Mike and the cop both rolled their eyes and laughed. We sat around talking about diving and fishing and all things related to Fisher's Island. We found out that the island had an unmanned airport that over the years we would use with Mike's buddy, Jim, piloting for us. We also exchanged telephone numbers and were told to call him whenever we were going to come to the island. He'd give us the real scoop on the tides and weather. Info like that is priceless.

Mora was walking the beach when she spotted a bottle with a note in it. She popped the cork and removed the note. Only four words were written on the paper.

Real subtle,

Love Madeline

Mora stashed the paper in her pocket. Took a long hard drag on her cigar, shook her head and called Madeline a Twizzle then fired her cigar into the white foam of an incoming wave.

Chapter 24

Another part of Mora's plan was emerging. The leaves of autumn were starting to put on their best faces. Maple and Oak, Hickory and Ash were dressing up like Cinderella's step sisters getting ready for the ball. The poor Evergreens would play the part of Cinderella. Same old green dress, every year. It looks nice when accessorized with some snow around the boughs but no girl can get away with wearing the same outfit to every party. The others would dress for the fall extravaganza in beautiful red and yellows and oranges which would be highlighted by the clear blue autumn sky. They would even drop a few leaves at their feet, shoes should always match a girl's outfit.

Hunting season was upon us. Growing up, there was a gun cabinet in our home. Shotguns, .22's and my dad's scoped, levered action 30/30. All standing ready like soldiers waiting for inspection. An inspection they would have passed with flying colors. Each had just the correct amount of oil on moving parts, bores scrubbed clean, ready for the white glove inspection.

Sunday afternoon was spent watching the American Sportsman. Curt Gowdy and Phil Harris hunted deer and pheasant all over the country. They would fish the flats of the Florida Keys for Tarpon, Permit and Bonefish. It was everything Mora had told me about. It was everything I wanted to do. Yet I needed to put my own twist on it.

While all the Elmer Fudd's from NY would run around the woods with their shotguns I went armed with a bow. It was a more intimate way to hunt. You need to spend countless hours in the woods watching and learning your prey. Gear needs to be in tip top condition. Thousands of arrows fly through the air at targets throughout the off season just to keep muscles and mind in shape. Every detail is checked and double checked before a hunt begins. Camouflage clothes and scent control are a must.

Mora loved every minute of it. The more dedicated to my craft I became the more I harvested. The wrath of Mora's vengeance was being fulfilled. All women are the same, cross them and they'll never forgive or forget. Bambi and all his relatives were definitely on Mora's hit list. Never piss off a Twizzle, folks.

Another benefit resulted from hunting. Hunters all belong to one big family. Through hunting I've been all around the country. I've stayed in tents, cabins and lodges. Friends would plan vacations to Cancun or Aruba to drink frozen concoctions and brown their bodies in the equatorial sun. I planned trips to inhospitable mountains, bug infested swamps, and cornfields. The hours I've spent in airports waiting for my bow case to come around the luggage carousel should not be counted against my time on Earth. No matter where I've been, all hunters are family. I've hunted with captains of industries and poor crackers trying to feed their families. They will share anything they have to help you on your quest. Most of the time spent together is over meals, usually in a white canvas mess tent that smells of bacon grease and coffee. There is always a day or so of rain. Those days are filled with black coffee and card games, everyone sharing stories from past hunts. Knives are tested for sharpness, usually by shaving the back one's thumbnail or by taking a little hair off one's forearm. Tooling on leather sheathes are gone over like curators inspecting a long lost Dali painting. Photos of wives and children get passed around with everyone wiping the bacon grease from their fingers before handling the photos. It always reminded Mora of the days with Millie and Red and the dinners with musicians. Laughter, food and people sharing stories, it always brought a certain level of comfort to her.

Madeline never joined her when I hunted from the white canvas tents but on one particular hunt in Virginia I was hunting out of a friend's cabin, so she paid Mora a visit. She found Mora sitting behind me at a dining room table. On the table were half a dozen or so handguns and several rifles of various calibers and manufacturers. All shooting was over and each weapon had been checked and double checked to make sure they were unloaded. It was time for cocktails and cleaning. I arrived at this cabin in the woods with several guys I worked with at the time. Martin was Vice President of the company and owner of the cabin. He had invited us down to do some shooting and enjoy the property he had just purchased. Martin and I were both hunters since childhood and very comfortable in the outdoors. The other two gentlemen, Santo and a Chinese fellow named Chen Lu, had never felt anything other than concrete under their feet.

Martin's cabin sits on several hundred acres of pristine forest in Virginia. The first day we all went to do a little scouting of Martin's property. He gave us the grand tour of the property. Making sure to show me several deer stands and educated me on their history. One in particular was called Lucky's stand. It belonged to one of the original owners of the property. Many years later I would shoot the biggest deer ever taken off Martin's property from that stand: a beautiful 10 point, chocolate antlered buck. Not one animal was spotted in a 3 hour hike due to the fact that Santo and Chen Lu managed to either trip over or step on every twig and branch in the forest. After awhile we realized it was futile to attempt stalking any game with these two in tow. "Screw it let's just go do some shooting" Martin decided.

Now I've been around guns my entire life and have shot all varieties of weapons. Other than at a gun show I've never seen this much firepower at one place before. Martin had several tables full. Each time we were finished with one weapon he produced another. I knew even for Virginia this much shooting would have the neighbors calling the State Police. After we had shot for over an hour straight Martin pulls out an AK47. This gun's been tricked out. It has a switch on the side which can make it go from semi auto to full auto with a flip of the switch.

Martin hands it to me and points to this field of saplings. "Shamus, clear that damn field."

He didn't have to ask twice. I was Scarface and I introduced the saplings, "To my little friend," my compliments to Mr. Kalashnikov. You designed one hell of a killing machine. Martin received a cleared field and a winter's worth of kindling and it only took a few minutes and three clips of bullets.

So now we are all scrubbing down the firearms when we hear a knock on the door. I placed the revolver I was cleaning onto the table and smiled, betting myself that a Virginia State Trooper would be standing on the other side of the door. I should never bet against myself. In walks the poster boy for State Troopers. 6'5", a chin that looks like it's carved out of granite and shoulders that tell you this guy lives in a gym. His hand is on his gun and he informed everyone not to move.

Martin starts in with "Well, howdy. Come on in. Is there a problem officer?"

The trooper replies that he's had reports of automatic weapons being fired.

"Oh, not from us sir. Now, we were shooting hot and heavy, but no automatics," Martin lifts his glass to toast the trooper.

The trooper looks over what's on the table and asked about the AK47. I'm the closest to it so I show him that the bolt is open and hand it to him. Instead of grabbing the rifle by the stock he wraps his paw around the barrel. Big mistake, two minutes before the barrel was smoking hot. Now it's just screaming hot. Not wanting to let on that he just burnt his hand, the guy holds on and gives the rifle the once over. Declares everything to be in fine order and hands the gun back to Martin. "Y'all have a nice day now, gentlemen," and then departs. We were all polite enough not to laugh until he was a half mile down the road.

Martin says to me. "You, fucker! I'll probably get a ticket every time he sees me from now on!"

"Yeah, but you'll ask him "how's the hand" every time he hands you that ticket" I replied. Martin laughed and shook his head up and down in agreement.

Later that night we all sat around the dining room table swapping lies and playing poker. Chen Lu had never played poker before but was just itching to learn. We played close to forty hands and by the 10th hand he was getting the hang of it. He wasn't winning a dime but he was enjoying himself. Chen Lu is a very intelligent man. He has all sorts of diplomas on the wall of his office for chemistry and engineering. What he is lacking is a diploma in street smarts. The entire night he was seated in front of a 4x6 mirror and couldn't understand why he wasn't able to bluff anyone that night. Santo even beat him on one hand without ever looking at his own cards. When all was said and done we gave Chen Lu back what he lost and explained that the first rule of poker is not to sit in front of the biggest mirror you could find.

Martin's cabin always had a steady supply of characters stopping by. One of Mora's favorites was Duke. She couldn't help it she's female. All women love Duke. Duke is like white lightning. You know it's strong. You know your whole body is going to shake and your face is going to get all distorted and yet you still try it. Sunday morning you'll find him in church, the rest of the week he's out making sure he has a few sins to confess.

He's a good ole southern boy with a handshake that lets you know he's worked hard all his life. A laugh that's deep and raspy. Grew up dirt poor and had a better life than most millionaires. I doubt most lumberjacks spend as much time in the woods as Duke. Duke and I hit it off right away. He wanted to know everything about Manhattan and I just liked to listen to him talk. He has this low slow way of talking and when he gets to any one of the good parts of a story, he leans in and talks even lower like he's telling you a big secret.

Now with me being a *Yankee,* Duke thought he'd have a little fun. Martin's property has one hell of a mountain on it. Duke was trying to entice me into hiking up the mountain with him to check for deer sign. He just wanted to walk the legs off a kid from NY. Duke made one little mistake. It's a very common mistake, people hear you're from NY and they assume you're from the city. I grew up in Brewster and the hills of Virginia are no different than the hills of Brewster. I went step for step with Duke the entire day. After a few hours he realized he'd been had. Mora was giddy with excitement to tell Madeline how I out foxed Duke.

Chapter 25

Mora's mind was in overdrive. She needed a way to reel me in. Like a shot from a 12 gauge, it hit her, "He needs to fall in love. Not just a weekend plaything, a full time girlfriend."

When Madeline caught wind of Mora's plan she explained to her, "That is a boundary you can't cross," her voice was cold and hard. "You surrounded Shamus with the best people you could find. Each has had everlasting effects on him. Picking who he loves is so far beyond your abilities you will never understand it. No one can do it. Just trust that you set him on the right path."

I meet the right person, Camille. We meet in the wrong place, a disco. It was two rock 'n' rollers in the wrong place at the right time. She was everything I, and Mora, could ever want. A smart ass, fast talking, loyal, great cook, party animal, "have your back no matter what" woman. She's as good with a pool cue as she is with a spatula. A woman whose clothes and hairstyle changed so often it kept me on my toes. Mora was creating a stew. Camille would be the bread that you sop up all the stew with. Stew's nice but its better with bread.

Our first date was seventeen hours long. There are times, I truly believe, I'm still on that first date. There are also times when I believe that if I had shot her the first time she drove me crazy, I'd be out on parole by now. Camille's a Twizzle but she's my Twizzle. She's everything Mora would have chosen if she had a hand in the matter. Camille has certain traits that endeared Mora to her right from the beginning. Camille does not share my love of the water. Camille loves to travel and when Mora found that out she felt like dancing an Irish jig.

Mora was toasting her good fortune with a double JD. She was bursting with pride over the fact that Camille feared water as much as she did. Finally my time in and under the water would be over. Plus, she had nothing to do with it.

Madeline stopped Mora just as she lifted the tumbler to her lips. "Twizzle," Madeline said in a singsong voice, "You're celebrating a World Series win before the first pitch of spring training. There is much to relationships you don't understand. Who says just because Camille doesn't love the water she'd deprive Shamus of his passion of it?"

The tumbler of JD slipped from her finger and burst into shards as it struck the ground.

It was becoming very evident to Madeline that Mora needed some time away from Shamus. Mora had been becoming very possessive of Shamus lately and with a new woman in his life that was a bad combination. She had been working on a plan and now seemed as good a time as any to implement it. "Twizzle" Madeline said with authority, "We need to get you out of here for awhile. A little vacation is in order and I know just the place."

"A vacation, I can't leave Shamus."

"Mora, how long have you been with Shamus, twenty-five, thirty years? I gotta say, you are unorthodox, but your methods work. It's time for you to take some time for yourself." Before Mora could mount a protest Madeline cut her off, "Don't worry. Nothing could happen to Shamus without you knowing about it. Your bond is as tight as any I have ever seen. You'd know it if he sneezed. Besides that wonderful stew of yours needs time to simmer, and Camille is there to stir the pot when needed."

Mora reluctantly followed Madeline. Their destination was an old shack on the edge of Limbo. Limbo was the holding place for souls that were waiting to find out whether they were headed to Heaven or Hell. Needless to say there was a very fun but nervous crowd in Limbo. No holy roller personalities and no psycho killers. The two fringes usually get to their final destination immediately upon leaving life behind. No one is saving a seat in Limbo for Mother Theresa or Charlie Manson.

A sign carved from a Cypress plank announced that they were entering an establishment named, "TWIZZLE'S." Mora looked at the sign and a smile started to grow on her face. "Named it after yourself huh?"

"After us" Madeline replied tartly.

Madeline opened the door and Mora peered inside. Her eyes drank it all in. She looked back at Madeline with eyes wide. Mora was speechless. Madeline was grinning like a child who just told her friend the biggest secret in the world.

In a quiet and confused voice Mora asked, "How?" Mora's confusion arose from the fact the outside of the building was an old shack; the inside was a pristine kitchen. Many parts of it brought back memories of Millie's kitchen. Again Mora turned to look at Madeline with a look of confusion. Madeline was beaming knowing Mora couldn't wrap her brain around the whole idea.

"Twizzle, how do you think I am able to always have a little something in my bag for us? After I lost you and Vincent, I needed something in my life that I could do so I wouldn't go insane. Food has always been that one thing in my world that centered me. So I set about creating a little place for myself. After all the stories I heard you tell about Millie's kitchen I used those stories to help create this," Madeline spread her arms wide, "You like it?"

Mora stood there in stunned silence. She opened her mouth but no sound emerged. She nodded her agreement instead.

"Come, come!" Madeline squealed like a parent at Christmas wanting to show a child another present. She backed through the service door of the kitchen to enable her to keep her eyes on Mora. "Look, I figured this would be your domain."

As Mora entered the room off the kitchen, a view of a large wooden bar and 10 tables overwhelmed her.

"Check it out!" Madeline had her arms draped over a jukebox in the corner.

"What is all this?" Mora asked.

"It's ours. I created it shortly after I lost Vincent and you. Remember that chicken parmesan you smelled the first day you were here? That was maybe the second or third thing I ever made in this kitchen. I always knew you and I would run this place."

"Madeline, I don't know what to say. It's beautiful, but why does anyone need a restaurant in Limbo? Everyone's dead. They don't need food or drink. You, me, we don't need money."

"This isn't about money. I listened to all your stories about all the great times you had at Gunning's. That's exactly what these folks need. Everyone's lost and confused. Remember your first few days here? You always said that the people at Gunning's were your family. Let's do that here!"

"I can't. I have Shamus to watch over."

"That's not exactly true. You need to care for him and protect him but you don't need to watch over him. It's not good for you, Shamus or Camille. Two women living under one roof never works out well," Madeline warned.

"That's it. He no longer needs me," Mora's voice cracked with hurt.

"Now, don't be a drama queen. No one said that your duty was over. I told you from day one your service doesn't end until Shamus is no longer living."

Mora eyes filled with tears and she screamed, "No!"

Madeline realized her last statement scared the hell out of Mora. "Shamus is fine. I'm sure you'll be together for quite awhile. I have a feeling you...you, my Twizzle, have some very important work ahead of you. But Shamus isn't a child anymore. He doesn't need you hanging around him every minute of the day. There is a need for your talents here."

Mora had to agree. After countless hours afield and hundreds of dives, I have never had an injury to talk about. I've endured my share of lacerations and bruises but you don't fish barnacle encrusted jetties or hang stands 30 feet in a tree without your share of scar tissue. Scars are just payment for entry to the party. It wasn't that Mora sat around on her ass eating cookies, she has had her fair share of saves over the years.

One of Mora's best saves happened on an Elk trip in the Hells Canyon region of Idaho, a place that has never been so aptly named. My guide and I were traversing a high ridge on an ATV. We had left camp around 4:30 a.m. to be able to arrive at the high mountain meadow he had scouted the week before. Dave, my guide, and I had doubled up on his ATV because of a mechanical problem with the one I was to use. We were crossing one of many rock slides that morning when the ATV started sliding downhill sideways. Apparently the extra weight of me and my gear was too much for the ATV. *The Little Engine That Could* had never been read to this little machine.

This had been my third western trip with my guide, Dave Loos. Dave is one of those unflappable western fellows. I've seen him packing out the last of a client's Elk while a forest fire was cresting the mountain of which he was walking down. It was his third trip up the mountain and he would not allow anyone else to go with him. It wasn't for safety reasons. It was because he didn't need to be slowed down. After tossing the last of the Elk into the bed of the truck he took a sip of water and calmly stated "It's getting mighty hot up on the side of that hill, we should get out of here."

"Forest fires do tend to get a little warm, let's go," I replied.

It was a moonless night and the headlights on the ATV were useless on the 40 degree slope we were riding across. The ATV would slide sideways for a few feet until the tires would grip and shoot us forward again. We were close to halfway across the rock face when we started sliding again. Something was different though. Dave couldn't get control of the ATV. I was holding onto his shoulders and I could feel him tensing up. Then I heard him curse. Dave doesn't curse so I knew we were in trouble. I also knew it was my weight that was causing the trouble.

I caught the glint of moonlight off of a patch of grass and something told me to bail off the back of the ATV. I grabbed my backpack and rolled off the back holding my bow high. It was the right move. The ATV without my weight was able to scurry across the rocks without incident. I gingerly made my way across the rocks on foot. When I got back on the ATV, Dave was grousing about my departure. I let it slide as guide bravado. Later that day, we traversed the same rock face on the way back to camp. In the light of day we were able to see and use a game trail that was hidden from us earlier. Dave stopped a little past halfway across. He showed me the grass patch where I had exited the ATV. If I had missed the grass by only a few feet I would have slid a few hundred feet down the loose rocks. Mora had timed my exit perfectly.

"What if Shamus needs me?" Mora questioned.

"You go," Madeline replied nonchalantly.

"How?" Mora questioned again.

"You take the number six to Grand Central then the shuttle to Times Square."

Before she could finish, Mora interrupted, "Funny," her voice dripping with sarcasm.

Madeline became serious, "Twizzle, have no fears. When you're needed you'll be there in an instant."

"And I can go just to look in on him?" she asked almost afraid of the answer.

"Yes and don't be coy. It doesn't become you. We both know you want to check in on Camille too." Madeline took on the persona of a grandmother scolding a grandchild.

"I'm going to have to think about this for a bit first."

"Sure that's fine. While you're thinking let me show you around some. That is, if you can think and walk at the same time?"

"Twizzle," Mora sneered back, but she was also intrigued.

Madeline again changed persona acting like a model at a car show. Standing in front of the bar extending her arms. Using both hands to accentuate the one and only beer tap.

"One lousy tap, some bar we're running here." Mora bemoaned.

"We're not! You haven't agreed to anything yet," Madeline pointed out quite smugly. "Now grab a mug and pour me a Guinness, creamy head and all."

It had been decades since Mora had been behind a bar. Yet it all still felt natural. She hoisted a frosted mug from an ice bin beneath the bar, slapped the tap forward and with the correct tilt of the mug, poured Madeline a perfect Guinness.

"Now pour a Heineken for yourself," Madeline ordered.

Mora stopped and stared at Madeline as if she had farted in church.

"Just do it, Twizzle."

To Mora's amazement a golden liquid poured forth from the tap where just a moment before a chocolate brown Guinness had been poured.

"Close your mouth, dear, it's very unattractive. I told you years ago that I had certain, let's call them, abilities."

"But I thought you weren't allowed to use..." Mora hadn't completed her sentence when Madeline raised her index finger while taking a large mouthful from her mug.

After swallowing and wiping the corners of her mouth she explained, "I said I couldn't use them for the benefit of those I was guarding. I'm not guarding anyone anymore. So why not help out all these lost souls in Limbo?"

Madeline could tell she had hooked Mora and that it would only be a matter of time before she was onboard.

Chapter 26

After several days of weighing all her options. Mora agreed to Madeline's plan. Her agreement came with a stipulation. She needed to find one more ingredient for her Shamus stew. The final ingredient came packaged as 100 pounds of shedding, drooling, hard headed, full of love Golden Retriever named Max.

Camille and I rescued Max from a shelter in upstate NY. I knew he was mine the moment I laid eyes on him. A big boned boy with a coat that had more waves to it than the Atlantic during hurricane season. He was in a kennel separated from the other dogs because as the matron declared, "He doesn't play well with others!"

Max was carrying a toy that resembled a basketball with dreadlocks. As he crunched down on it you could tell it was soaked in drool. It sounded as if Mr. Clean himself was wringing out a sponge. Camille just turned and looked at me and knew Max was coming home with us. Mora knew it before either of us. After a short game of pull Shamus across the yard by a leash, we loaded him into Camille's car. I drove and Camille sat with Max in the backseat. She stroked his reddish blonde coat and explained to him all the rules of the house and what was expected of him. He lay with his cinderblock sized head on her lap and fell asleep. It was probably his first sound sleep in weeks. He had been in the rescue society for quite awhile, apparently too much dog for most folks.

As he lay with his head on Camille's lap, she stroked his coat reassuring Max he was coming to a good home. It was a warm autumn day so the windows were down for the ride home. As I looked back in the mirror I saw hair flying out the windows. It looked like a dog hair blizzard behind us. Every car that passed us looked over to see what was going on. On further inspection I saw that Camille was also covered in dog hair. She quickly informed me that our first stop would be Petland Discount where a variety of brushes, combs and shampoos were bought. It was a waste of money nothing would ever fully control his shedding.

Max had lived with us for about a month and all was going well. Max took us in as one of his pack members and would always protect us from anything. The trouble was the anything. Max's enthusiasm was the same whether it was a pack of marauding pit bulls or a chipmunk.

I returned from work one evening to see Camille staring up at a tree in our backyard. There was a small green Lovebird sitting on a branch. Max was at her feet staring at it also. I joined them and suggested we bring it in the house before it became a meal for the neighborhood cats. The branch the bird was sitting on was actually a broken twig stuck between two branches. I just lifted the twig and took the bird into our basement. I stuck one end of the twig into a piece of exercise equipment we owned, yet never used. The bird just sat there, motionless, as Camille and I discussed putting up flyers, a most appropriate thing to do for a lost bird, around the neighborhood

Max sat beneath the bird just looking at it. For whatever reason, the bird made a fatal mistake. It chirped. Max took this as a sign of aggression and leapt into action. The exercise equipment was knocked over. The bird took off in flight. It headed to one of the windows above my workbench. Big mistake! Max leapt onto the bench and swatted the bird against the closed widow causing it to crack. Max snatched up the bird and leapt off the bench and walks over to us. Camille saying, "Oh, this ain't good."

I replied, "Don't worry, he's a retriever, it's a natural instinct for him to grab a bird." Then with my best hunting guide persona I reached down and commanded Max, "Drop the bird." Max looked me square in the eye and started chewing. When he was done the only part left was the beak which he spit onto the basement floor.

With his job of protecting us done, it was time for a nap and he strolled upstairs to sleep in the sunshine coming through the kitchen window. Camille looked at me like it was my fault and followed Max upstairs. I swear I could hear both of them muttering, "Drop the bird, stupid bastard!"

No animal was safe if it entered Max's backyard. Over the years I've collected a few hunting trophies. Max put me to shame. His list of kills is filled with cats, skunks, birds, raccoons, squirrels and even a possum. Yet he was an absolute angel with kids. He loved the kids next door. They would put their hands through the fence and pet him for hours. The first time I saw them do it I ran outside afraid they'd pull back bloody stumps where their arms once had been. There was never a problem. His favorite was my buddy Tommy's son, CJ. CJ was a solid kid for his age. When he was born we'd joke that when you lifted CJ to burp him it was like throwing a bundle of roofing shingles on your shoulder. CJ would run into our house full of gusto. It was boy meets dog. Then boy meets floor with a big thud. Max would have him pinned in no time flat and cover him with fur and kisses until the kid was giggling so hard he'd almost cry.

Mora knew exactly what she was doing when she picked Max. I could leave for my hunting or fishing excursions and never had to worry about Camille's safety. I could concentrate on what I was doing, therefore, never having the little slipups that usually lead to disastrous endings. Camille and Max also made me miss being home so my trips weren't as long as they used to be. The days of just leaving for a trip on the drop of a hat were also gone. With other people in my life, trips were planned and coordinated around new and different schedules.

Mora and Max also saved Camille and me from a potentially disastrous house fire. We were asleep in our bed one night when Max started whining and crying. This was a side of Max we had ever seen before. I had ordered him to get to bed several times when Camille finally asked, "Maybe he has to go out?"

I replied that I had let him out before we went to bed and he probably just hears a raccoon. Max wouldn't stop and actually increased his crying to a full blown whimper. Max was never a cry baby, so I knew something was really bothering him. I gave in and got out of bed to bring him downstairs to let him out. When I reached the bottom of the stairs and walked into the living room I was engulfed in smoke. The fire marshal's report listed a heater for a fish tank as the cause. It apparently had shorted out and caught fire. The fire moved to the curtains of the window behind the tank and was quickly spreading. I was able to pull the curtains down and dump them into the fish tank and use some water from the tank itself to douse any remaining flames. It wasn't a big fire yet, but without Max it had the potential to have killed Camille and me in our sleep. Mora stroked Max's coat lovingly. She hadn't felt any danger because I hadn't felt any. She was blind to the potential hazard but that's why she had Max on duty.

Chapter 27

Madeline was sitting out on the front porch of Twizzle's while Mora was inside destroying the place. Madeline was preventing any customers from entering. Not that they could be hurt, they were already long past their expiration dates, it was just too ugly of a scene to watch.

"What's Shamus gone and done this time, Mad's?" asked Kyle his voice thick with the accent of his New Zealand heritage. Kyle had been a resident of Limbo going on a year. In that time he'd witnessed Mora's rages a time or two but this one sounded like the best one yet.

Madeline smiled and shook her head, "Sit down this one's a winner. You heard of his friend Tommy and Big Ed?"

"Sure, sure. Shamus and Tommy help each other out fixing up each other's houses. His kid is the one Max is always slobbering on," Kyle answered. Madeline nodded in agreement.

"Isn't Big Ed the bloke he's known since they were back in knickers?"

Madeline stared at Kyle trying to navigate through Kyle's accent. It took her a moment to figure out he had Big Ed and Big Head confused. "No, Big Ed is from the dive shop that Shamus hangs out in. Big Head he's known since they were in knickers" she said trying match his accent on the word knickers.

Madeline paused for a moment and took a cleansing breathe then continued on with her tale. "Seems Shamus and the boys planned a dive trip to Freeport."

Kyle whistled and took a seat. He knew it was going to be a good tale once he heard her say dive trip.

Madeline waited for Kyle to get seated and continued.

"Mora was determined to stop this trip, and you know what a Twizzle she can be."

Kyle looked around before nodding his head in agreement.

"Shamus' buddy Big Ed is a great fellow but a little soft in the head so he became Mora's focal point. I don't know how long she was in his ear but Ed packs a spear gun in his luggage."

Kyle in amazement said "A spear gun, how'd he get a spear gun in his luggage?"

Madeline started to become perturbed by Kyle's interruptions. "It was a small pneumatic one, looks like a big pistol" Madeline finished her sentence by giving Kyle the evil eye, informing him no more interruptions would be tolerated.

"So, there they are in the security office of the airport trying to explain their way out of this while their flight is taking off. Mora's all giddy with herself thinking she's squashed the dive trip."

Kyle could not help himself and asked "Then why does it sound like a class 4 hurricane inside" nodding towards the bar.

"Glad you asked" Madeline said, while using her index finger to poke Kyle in the chest. "Shamus does some fast talking to the girl at the ticket counter and gets them all rebooked on another flight. Minus the spear gun. Instead of Freeport they're headed for Nassau, Shamus figured at least they'd be in the Bahamas.

Kyle was going to ask a question but decided to let Madeline continue.

Madeline continued "So now our little Twizzle in there" pointing her thumb in the direction of the bar. "She now goes to work on the Captain of the dive boat. She influences him and he informs the boys he ain't piloting his boat to Nassau, they need to get to Freeport. Twizzle is so happy with herself she's almost ready to dance a jig."

Kyle whistled and shook his head.

"Oh wait it gets better" Madeline was smiling so hard her cheeks hurt. "Shamus tells the guys not to worry and takes a walk around the airport and finds a pilot to fly them to Freeport" Madeline's eyes started to tear up as she started to chuckle. "Now the pilot he hires looks like he fly's for Rasta Airlines. Blacker than a coalminer's lungs and a Bob Marley hairdo. I bet all his landings were on a private airstrip if you get my drift."

Kyle answered with a bit of a chuckle "I know the type."

Madeline shot him a curious look and then continued. "Shamus asked if he has a plane big enough to haul the three of them and all their gear. The pilot says he'll find one and that they should meet him on the far side of the airstrip".

Mora's steaming mad now. She wants to get into Shamus' other buddy's head because Tommy hates flying. However there's nothing she can do. He has to get on this plane.

"The boys quickly load up the plane and Tommy is asking all sorts of questions. The only answer he gets back from the pilot is "It's all good man, but we should hurry". Big Ed pulled Shamus to the side and said "This guy doesn't look like he could afford lunch, how's he have a 4 passenger Cessna?"

"Shamus tells Ed that he didn't ask the guy for his financial statement only if he could fly them to Freeport."

"Tommy just hung his head and groaned when the pilot told them they were overloaded but it was all good. They would just fly closer to the water. Once in the plane the pilot turns to Shamus and asked him to open his door a crack. Apparently with everyone packed in like sardines the windows were steaming up."

Kyle's eyes were opened wide and he hung on every word.

Madeline shook her head, a tear of laughter rolling down her cheek. "Now they're in the air and the pilot tells Shamus he wants to check his map and asked him to take control of the stick."

Kyle couldn't contain himself "Shamus is flying the bloody plane?"

Madeline is now shaking she's giggling so hard. "Flying and diving, it's like Shamus just knows how to push Mora's buttons".

Kyle whistles and looks toward the front door, "No wonder she's busting up the place."

Now Tommy didn't hear the pilot because you can hardly hear anything with Shamus' door open. The pilot pulls out a map to confirm they're heading to the right island. Tommy lifts his head and see's what was going on. Tommy announces he has three questions,

"Why is the door open?"

"Do we have any Jack Daniels?" And the next one he specified as the most important,

"Why the hell is Shamus flying the plane?"

Shamus answered two of Tommy's questions,

"Because you guys are breathing so hard you're fogging up all the windows!"

"I'm flying because the pilot is busy reading a map."

Big Ed answered the second question by handing Tommy a small bottle of JD he kept from the flight down from NY.

Tommy just hung his head and didn't look up for the remainder of the flight.

The flight lasted 10 minutes at the most and she's been going crazy for over an hour, "I'd come back next week Kyle. Twizzle's won't be much fun until Shamus get's back from this dive trip."

Kyle entered Twizzle's again about a month or so after I had returned from the Bahamas. Mora was in a delightful mood and he asked what I had done.

"Nothing special, just being Shamus."

"Just being as irreverent as this one," Madeline answered while nodding to Mora.

"What's he done?" Kyle asked again.

Mora explains, "Tommy and his wife Suzi had bought a little place on City Island. The place was small but "T", as he's known, has hands made for working with wood. He had plans on renovating the place. Suzi decided to have Camille and Shamus over to have a toast to the new home.

Tommy was showing Shamus around the place and what he wanted to do, "It's real simple. Everything from the front wall to the back wall goes."

Shamus asked Tommy, "Well did you bring tools or should we start kicking the walls down?"

Suzi rushes in and hushes them saying, "Father Murphy's out front, get out here so he can start the blessing." The two of them walked onto the porch to meet the priest. Father Murphy is one of those true Irish priests, red cheeks and a handshake that could break stone. In America since he was in diapers and still has a brogue.

Kyle adds, "Yeah, I'm familiar with the type."

Madeline just looked at Kyle and said "You're familiar with a lot of types."

Kyle grinned and gave Madeline a wink.

Mora continued, "Well, Father Murphy starts his blessing for the house and everyone in it. Takes his plastic bottle of Holy Water and proceeds to make the sign of the cross. Shamus takes a shot of Holy Water to the eye. It's like the bottle of Holy Water had a scope on it. Anyway, a quick 'Our Father and a Hail Mary' later, Father Murphy is enjoying a glass of Champagne with everyone and toasting the house."

Tommy starts explaining his plans for the house. Now the good priest couldn't be just one of the guys, he had to be an Irish priest and say, "You know, Jesus was a carpenter."

Mora is giggling as she finishes, "Shamus turns to him and flatly states, 'Great, tell him work starts at 7:00 a.m. don't be late. He's the new guy so coffee and rolls are on him.'"

Madeline joins in, "Suzi didn't know whether to shit or go blind. She looked at Shamus as the priest was walking out the door, her eyes wide in amazement. After the good father was in his car Suzi turns to him and say's, 'What the hell is wrong with you? You can't say that to a priest!'"

Mora nearly in tears continues the story, "Shamus then says, 'Hey! he started, I felt like Moe Green getting shot in the eye. Besides what's he going to do, take back his blessing?'"

That night Tommy and Shamus grabbed some sledgehammers and breaker bars and knocked down most of the walls in the house.

The next morning Shamus arrived at their new home with coffee and a tool belt. Suzi comes out of the house and he immediately asked her, "The new kid get here yet?"

She gave Shamus a confused look and he remind her that, "Jesus was suppose to be here at 7 with coffee and rolls."

She just turned back in the house shaking her head while yelling for T, "Tommy, Shamus the heathen is here!"

Chapter 28

Madeline commented to Mora on how Shamus' hair had turned from black to silver over the years. "Maybe he's figured out who's been guarding him all these years." A smile graced her face that told Mora she was only joking with her. "Never mind him I should be grey from worrying about him all these years." "He's slowed a little bit now that he's in his mid thirties" Madeline asked. "38" Mora corrected her. "Not slowed but thanks to Camille his interests have changed. We do travel better with Camille in the picture. I like hotels and restaurants way better than those white canvas tents of his hunting camps."

Other types of trips had become part of my regular travels. Camille always kept it interesting. She was always booking trips to Aruba, Italy, or Mexico. It was due to Camille's love of travel that Mora finally got to see all the places she had wanted to. New York was easy. It was only a train ride away and we both had taken jobs in the city. Broadway plays, Radio City for the Christmas show, the Garden and Jacob Javits Center for sporting events and boat shows. The greatest thing about New York for Mora was the food. Any and every type of cuisine was available within walking distance or a short subway ride away. Madeline never checked in on Mora while we were on a subway.

Mora was always surprising Madeline with new recipes from the restaurants we'd dine in. They'd try them and then adjust them, as all cooks do, to their liking. Everything from barbeque to Dim Sum, their kitchen's cookbook was expanding weekly. So was the collection of t-shirts and other chachkas she had from our vacations. Enough so that Mora had started to embellish the bar with them. Concert shirts were framed and placed around the bar. The one from a Stevie Ray Vaughn concert was hung directly across from the bar. Every August 27th she would raise a glass to it and shake her head silently saying "What a shame". Stevie was everything she wanted in a musician. There was a shelf behind the bar which held the plastic treasures from our trips. A little Hawaiian girl in the grass skirt that would wiggle her hips side to side. An assortment of various shot glasses with names of towns imprinted on them.

It was the one from New Orleans she treasured the most. Mora wanted to hug Camille when she announced our next vacation was to New Orleans. A city built around music and food. Many of the recipes that come from the kitchen of Twizzle's are from New Orleans. The Shrimp Etouffee dish is the exact copy of the one from Mother's. Try as they might, neither Mora or Madeline could improve on the recipe and decided to leave well enough alone. Madeline added apple wood smoked bacon to her oyster poor boys to make it her own. It became a crowd favorite. Mora was devastated years later to see New Orleans flooded. Madeline reminded her of the spirit that is infused in that city and told her not to worry, "they'll rebuild."

Mora collected one item that made Madeline curious. Mora had this certain affection for the old fashioned hand crank penny presses. Those old fashioned machines where you insert a penny and a quarter then turn the handle and the penny would be pressed between some gears and be reshaped into a flat disk with the impression of whatever tourist attraction you were at. She had them from all over. The Hoover Dam, Boston, Mel Fisher's place down in the Keys, and Mystic Sea Port, to name a few. Mora had enough to redo the bar as a copper top. Everyone who entered the bar spent time looking and commenting on the coins and the places they represented. For some reason I'm also drawn to those machines, however by the time the vacation is over, those thin little coins have been lost.

Mora and Madeline opened Twizzle's and it was an instant success. Madeline had poured all her abilities into it. All visitors saw the place differently. If while on Earth your favorite place was in some ski lodge, that's how it appeared to you. To another, it resembled a Tiki Hut. The juke box also played everyone's favorite song. It always amazed Madeline that everyone's favorite song was either from their wedding or from the night they met their significant other.

Patrons would enter with a lost look on their face. Shoulders slumped as if they carried the weight of the world. They would order something warm to eat, not that they were the least bit hungry. Have a cold beer and listen to their favorite tunes. Surrounding themselves with fond memories started to loosen everyone up. Conversations were started, usually over the fact that they shared a favorite song. It wasn't long before the place had a buzz about it. Newcomers were quickly welcomed into the fold. Each told the story of their lives. Someone would inevitably say, "Oh, I ain't so sure you'll be playing a harp where you're headed!" A roar of laughter would rise from the crowd.

A customer would stop and ask Mora or Madeline if they had just called their name. "No darling, your presence is being requested by the man in charge. Best of luck to you!"

The patron would turn to leave and quickly start adjusting their appearance. Men would tuck in their shirts and button their collars. Woman would adjust their dresses and fuss with their hair. Madeline would shout out to them, "It's too late to make a good impression, honey!" but her words fell on deaf ears. All the patrons would become very quiet and together they would say their private little prayers for whoever was just called. Some were religious and some were superstitious, but no one in Limbo would dare jinx themselves by not wishing another soul good passage.

Mora was tending bar one beautiful autumn day when a feeling overcame her. This was the strongest sensation she'd ever felt. It actually caused her to grasp the bar for support.

She was at my side in an instant. At the time I had been working for a real estate company in Manhattan. They owned and operated buildings throughout Manhattan and the tri-state area. Mora was on full alert. She scanned everyone around me and saw nothing out of place.

My boss, Sebastian, had asked me to take a run downtown to our Rector Street office and reset a router that was giving them trouble. I agreed because it was a quick and easy job and the Trinity Church was next door to our location. I'm not a real religious person but the Trinity Church is this great old building with a cemetery which holds the remains of some of the earliest settlers in Manhattan. I felt something for that building. As skyscrapers chewed up lower Manhattan this old girl held her place. Since it was such a beautiful September day I figured I'd have lunch on the steps of the Trinity Church and do a bit of people watching. If people watching were a sport, than lower Manhattan would be the Mecca of that sport.

I grabbed my coat and lunch and was headed out of the office. My phone rang and one of my favorite people in the office called and asked me to take a quick look at her computer. Mora used Lorraine because she knew I could never refuse her. She just wanted me to stay in the home office until she could figure out what was wrong. The moment I saw Lorraine's number come up on the display of my phone I picked up. "What's up Darlin?" I asked.

Ever since my days as a bartender I've called every woman, "Darlin" and every guy, "Bub." I've just always had a rotten memory when it comes to names. I can hold entire conversations with people, be very engaging and never once mention their name. I remember their favorite drinks, where they live, but with names, I just draw a blank. Camille says it's because I'm just rude and don't pay attention.

Lorraine explained that her machine was not working.

"What's wrong?" I questioned her.

"Honey, it's just like my lazy ass nephew, it ain't working. Now come do that voodoo you do and make it all better!" Lorraine said in her New Jersey voice that has a wisp of southern drawl to it.

Mora picked the one and only person who could stop me from running to water if I was on fire. Over the years I have played more office pranks on Lorraine than I can count. She's a through and through Mets fan and I bleed Yankee pinstripes. Any chance I got to needle her about the Mets I would. If the Mets got swept in a series I'd have a broom perched on her desk waiting for her. She'd always take it with class.

Lorraine would tell anyone watching a game with her, "God, I hope we don't lose tonight. Shamus will have something waiting for me in the morning!"

The highlight of our rivalry was the 2000 World Series, Yankees VS Mets. While the rest of the country had no real interest Lorraine and I chewed our fingernails to the bone over bragging rights.

Lorraine is also the only one on the entire Island of Manhattan that when she found out I was a hunter, actually put in orders. "Now Shamus, you bring me back, say, six squirrels, all nice and cleaned up. I'll fry 'em up and have them ready for us the next day." The other people in the office would lose their minds when they'd find out what we were eating. Lorraine would just straight out tell them, "Now hush up. You've never tried one and don't know what you're missing," and then go right back to eating.

I repaired whatever problem Lorraine's computer was having and went back to my cubicle. I was ready to grab my coat and lunch to head downtown. The fellow who sat next to me was a true geek. His name was John Morrisey. If you cut John he wouldn't bleed. Wires and computer chips would probably fall out of him. He was always diving into dumpsters pulling out old computers and building these crazy systems. Most importantly for me that day was that John was a Ham Radio Operator. John stopped me, "Shamus I wouldn't leave just yet. Something is happening in the subways. Something big, I'm hearing codes I've never heard before."

John lives and breathes this stuff so I knew to listen to him. Then we heard the news on the radio, "A plane has hit the North Tower of the World Trade Center!" We figured it was some little Cessna. We were wrong, dead wrong. The second plane hit shortly after and America's hearts fell with both Towers.

If Mora hadn't used Lorraine to intercept me I would have been coming out of the subway station just about the time the second plane hit the South Tower. Instead of running from a cloud of toxic gas that enveloped lower Manhattan I was sitting stunned and teary eyed but safe in Midtown. Mora sat in the office with the rest of us watching the events unfold. Her hands were trembling so hard she could barely light her cigar. Madeline showed up and took the matches from her hand and lit her cigar for her.

"Twizzle," she said in a hushed voice, "Using Lorraine was a beautiful move on your part. You used friendship to prevent Shamus from being any part of that," Madeline said as she nodded towards the television set. Madeline just wrapped her arms around Mora and held her, occasionally patting her back.

A day or two later I had to travel to our downtown office to help relocate everyone from the Rector Street office. The Army had a huge presence downtown and the area I needed to be in was actually cordoned off by concertina wire. The land of the free and the home of the brave now resembled some kind of Checkpoint Charlie. Where was I North Korea, East Berlin? There were also heavily armed military personnel elsewhere. Grand Central Terminal had soldiers at every exit and bomb sniffing dogs patrolled the main concourse. The most unnerving thing was the Anti Personnel Vehicle, parked outside my building. The military can call it whatever they want but it was a tank. They softened its appearance by painting it blue. It looked as if one of the guys from the Blue Man Group was going to take it for a spin. The paint job didn't help calm anyone's nerves. It was a tank and it was parked on 42nd St. I often wondered how soon it would be before Flash Dancers or one of the other myriad of strip clubs in N.Y.C. hung one of its banners from the muzzle.

New York is probably one of the most resilient places on Earth. Not even my generation's Pearl Harbor is going to knock out the city that never sleeps. The bombing of the Towers rocked us, we took a standing 8 count, but we never hit the canvas. We buried our dead and honored our heroes. Everyone walked on eggshells for quite a while, but everyone went back to work.

Chapter 29

Mora and Madeline also returned to work. The kitchen was humming along with all the new recipes that Mora had collected from our trips. Madeline however kept a sharp eye on Mora. She just wasn't herself. The terrorist attack on NY was really starting to throw her off her game. She had watched over me going on 40 years now and had quite a bit thrown at her. Terrorist was not even on her radar. She started to over think all the possible scenarios that could befall me. The more she thought about it the more it drove her crazy. She just couldn't free her mind from the tank and the soldiers in Grand Central. In true Tinley Park fashion she "Got her Irish up." New York was deemed unsafe and I would no longer work or reside there.

Mora took a few years to get her point across. She was patient, knew I couldn't be rushed. Though I have never been near Tinley Park in my life I somehow picked up the trait of "Getting my Irish up." Try and force me to do something I don't want to do and I'll fight you tooth and nail. Mora took a much more subtle approach.

Each winter for several years Camille planned vacations to Florida for us. East Coast, West Coast, Keys it didn't matter. It would be late January or early February and we were cold, weary and suffering from cabin fever. Unless you're at a ski resort, winter's a real pain in the ass. Heavy coats, cold feet, shoveling snow and scraping ice covered windshields for three months tends to put one in a foul mood. With flights booked and Max boarded with our local vet with strict instructions that he doesn't play well with others, we would make a change in latitude for a change in attitude. Several hours later Camille and I would be on Sanibel Beach watching a sunset with some rum concoction.

Mora would wait and watch. She'd let the sun and the sand and the rum take their desired effect on us before she'd intervene. Before we would head to dinner Camille would hit the shower to knock off the sand and salt of the beach. I'd flip on the TV to check out the weather back home. Nothing makes Florida more enjoyable than knowing your buddies are freezing their butts off back home while you're rubbing aloe on a fresh sunburn. The weather report would be about some Nor'easter that just dumped a fresh foot or two of snow on the city. Scenes of abandoned city streets and plowed in cars would fill the screen. Then they'd cut to some reporter standing alone in Times Square being pummeled by windblown snow and ice. You knew the poor bastard was on the bottom of the corporate ladder and had to put in his street time or he'd have some other story to report on. He'd give his report to the anchor who would ask about the conditions outside. You just knew he wanted to scream, "It's a friggin blizzard, you jackass! How do you think the conditions are? My ass has frostbite. If the airports weren't all closed down I'd tell you to stick this job and head to Florida where it's warm and toasty!" Then a slight bit of depression would set in knowing that in a few days we'd be right back in the middle of all that nasty weather. Even worse, it would be three months before NY's weather came close to resembling what I was enjoying right at the moment.

Over dinner somehow that exact thought would always make its way into the conversation. It would begin with a long exhale from Camille. A sign that she was truly becoming relaxed and enjoying the weather. Camille's hatred for water is only surpassed by her disgust for winter. With the first snowflake of the season Camille goes into winter survival mode. The lighter meals of summer are immediately replaced by hearty soups and slow cooked stews. Basically, for the entire winter season, there is something simmering in or on her stove.

All walkways and steps are vigorously maintained to avoid any build up of snow or ice. Our winter supply of salt and sand equaled that of many small towns. Sitting by a roaring fire with a mug of hot chocolate watching the snow fall she has no problem with. Have her take one step outside and she's latched onto your arm so tight, there will be roses in full bloom before you get any feeling back into that limb.

"So why are we going back?" Camille would ask as we enjoyed dinner and watched the sun slowly melt into the Gulf of Mexico.

I don't know exactly how Mora accomplished it but this is usually when some mother porpoise and her calf would leap from the water. The first few years of coming to Florida I answered with, "It's nice for vacation but our lives are in NY; our home, our jobs and all our friends are there." After the Towers fell, my reply became, "I don't know."

Mora knew her plan was starting to come together when she heard my answer.

Madeline had been keeping a close eye on Mora lately. She knew that Mora's mind had been running wild with all sorts of scenarios since 9/11. As Madeline stepped through the kitchen door she noticed a change in Mora. Her posture was straighter, her eyes were brighter and she was actually smiling. "Twiz, you look like your old self again, what's up with Shamus?" Madeline knew if Mora was back to her old self then it had to do with something regarding me.

Beaming with pride Mora replied, "A little seed I planted several years ago is finally starting to sprout."

Madeline looked Mora square in eye and did her best Ricky Ricardo impersonation, "Lucy, what have you done?"

"I nudged Camille and Shamus into looking into possible relocation to Florida. It was all real subtle, just how you like it."

Madeline waited a minute before answering Mora. She was reflecting on what she just heard. "Ok, let me make sure I've got this straight. The guardian angel who is petrified of water, just influenced Shamus to move to a state that is surrounded by water on three sides? What's the matter? The Islands of Hawaii full?"

"No, Hawaii wasn't even in the running, too far from family and friends." Mora suddenly realized Madeline was having fun at her expense. She quickly called her a "Twizzle!"

Madeline responded, "You're moving Shamus to the sports fishing and scuba diving capital of the world! Am I going crazy or weren't you just complaining about all his... his things?" Her hands were moving as if she was conducting an orchestra.

Madeline always talked with her hands but whenever she couldn't find the right word or phrase the hand movements became exaggerated.

"I only really complained about the diving. He's done hundreds of them now and hasn't ever really been hurt. I have no control over it, but he does. He follows all the safety regulations and always dives with a buddy. Hell, he doesn't even do the deep dives anymore, just the recreational stuff nowadays. If he stays within the guidelines he won't get bent," Mora elaborated.

"Bent? Que' bent?" Madeline asked.

Mora rolled her eyes at Madeline's diving ignorance. "The bends, you know tiny bubbles in his bloodstream."

Madeline quickly responded doing a really bad impersonation of Don Ho singing "Tiny Bubbles."

"Believe me, it's a bad thing!" Mora paused, "The odds of that are astronomical, sort of like being bitten by a shark!"

"Sure if you live in Nebraska the odds are astronomical, but if you live in Florida and spend a lot of time in the water…" Madeline started to giggle at Mora's frustration. She was having fun with Mora because she knew Mora was right

"Twizzle," was all Mora could respond.

It was early fall and the last of the tomatoes were being pulled from the garden. The air was beginning to get a bite to it. Striper fishing was in full force with the migrating schools of Stripers and Blues busting through schools of balled up bait fish. The big bucks I had been keeping an eye on were starting to rub the velvet from their antlers. Camille was starting to replace flower pots filled with red and white Impatiens with Mums in festive fall orange. Corn husks were tied to the railing along the front porch. Even the red oak in the front yard was doing its part by decorating the front lawn with bright red and yellow leaves.

Camille had become a real estate agent within the past year. She had been doing more than respectfully well for a new agent. The market was in its' boom days. A house would hit the market and there would be bidding wars for it. It was not uncommon for homes which were asking ridiculous amounts to actually sell for fifty or sixty thousand more than what they were asking. Housing prices were the talk of the town. People were acting as if they were all Donald Trump, everyone was a real estate genius and everyone was rich because of their homes. We were a bit more practical than that. Mostly because of Camille's monetary sense, not mine. "Sure you can sell our house for a fortune. Whatever house you move to next is also going to cost you a fortune. Unless we move out of New York and go to Florida."

Now we are for the most part pretty practical folks. We weigh the pros and cons of any major decision. Lists are drawn up and reviewed, questions are asked by Camille until my head is ready to explode. Just buying a new car is a month long procedure. The entire conversation about uprooting our lives had no list, no charts. It was seat of your pants flying at its best.

Camille was wiping sweat from her brow from rearranging two huge terra cotta flower pots. "You know I just listed the house down the block for over $400,000."

"They'll never get it for that piece of crap! Are you kidding me?"

Without even looking up from her plantings she responded, "I'm showing it at three o'clock and it'll be sold by the end of the week." She exhaled and continued with her planting while adding "This market is out of control. It can't last forever. The bubble is going to burst one of these days."

"So let's get out before the bubble burst. We'll sell out and move to Florida."

"We'd have to find an area first. You know I'm not moving to the backwoods cracker ass cracker part of Florida with snakes and gators."

"Damn, you guessed my plan. I was going to move the girl from Harlem to a gator infested swamp!" I gave Camille my best wiseass smirk as I said it. "So we'll take a trip or two and find an area we both like."

There was no hesitation from either of us. We had no kids, so issues of schools and uprooting them from their friends wasn't a problem. There was actually a certain freedom to it once you wrapped your brain around it. We were two people who could just get up and go anywhere, anytime we wanted. Winter was just around the corner, getting out of town for the warmth of Florida sounded like a pretty good idea.

Fergy had been residing in Florida for a few years now so I called him to get a lay of the land. He told me where you wanted to be and where you definitely didn't want to be.

Trips were booked and the process began. By process of elimination the Gulf Coast was chosen. Then it was narrowed down to Tampa Bay area.

Once we set eyes on Sarasota the search was done. Sarasota is a small jewel of a town about an hour south of Tampa. It has some of the best beaches in the world. There is art and theater, great smoke houses for Southern style barbeque and a quaint but adequate airport. It just has a nice feel to it. The most striking thing about it is its cleanliness. It's a relatively new town in the sense that a building boom recently swept through the area so everything is fresh and new. NY is the greatest city in the world. Great, yes, clean no. I believe there is still some original pilgrim pollution roaming around NY. The more Mora saw of Sarasota the more at ease she felt about my safety.

We did a few more trips to Sarasota and in between trips educated ourselves via the internet. Camille was the responsible one and checked out the city council, job sites, better business, and all the usual places a mature adult would seek out. I looked into the fishing and diving sites. A few years back I had become involved in kayak fishing. It was a necessity since some bonehead in the city council decided to ban walking access to my best Striper spot. Imagine my surprise when informed by the police that the spot of land I'd been fishing from for 4 years was now off limits. Once again life handed me lemons. Once again I reached for my salt shaker and Tequila.

The following afternoon I was unloading my new Tarpon 160 from the roof of my Grand Cherokee. Sixteen feet of banana yellow kayak with rod holders and an anchor. Madeline turned to Mora and said, "I guess you really did rub off on Shamus!" gently nudging her with her elbow, "It only took him a minute or two to get his Irish up!"

Mora shot back talking through the side of her mouth never taking her eyes off me, "Yeah, you noticed that too." Mora was beaming with pride that I gave the city council the one finger salute and figured out a way around their rules. She did however not love the idea of me having a craft that would allow me more time on the water. Madeline and Mora spent several minutes inspecting my kayak for it's sea worthiness.

"It's nothing more than a piece of long, thin Tupperware. How's he not going to fall out of it when a wave hits?" Madeline's voice was ripe with concern.

Mora answered with eyes opened wide and slowly shaking her head from left to right, "I haven't the slightest idea."

Both ladies were present for the inaugural outing of my kayak. I launched from a quiet cove at Five Island Park in New Rochelle. Madeline had her shoes off and was letting the incoming waves wash over her feet. Mora was half a dozen steps behind her, the thought of water touching her skin still sent shivers down her spine. Madeline as always had packed a lunch in her ever present handbag. "Sausage and Peppers?" Madeline offered as she held an overstuffed sandwich in Mora's direction.

Mora paying only half attention to Madeline waved her off and kept her eyes on me. I simply dragged the kayak into the surf hopped on and paddled away. I gave the kayak a good test run to check its stability and tracking ability. It held a nice tight line while paddling a straight course. Its length however made tight maneuvers difficult. I was happy with her but then decided to find out where the point of no return was when leaning over the sides. I started rocking side to side making the kayak stand up on its port side and then to the starboard until it finally tipped over. This allowed me to find out two very important facts regarding the kayak. At what point does it flip over, and the second and more important one, how difficult is to reenter it while in water over your head?

"What the hell is he doing out there?" Madeline screeched.

"I don't know but it looks like he's doing it on purpose," Mora said while keeping a watchful eye on me. When she saw me flip the kayak her blood pressure spiked but she had spent enough years with me to know I was testing something and not in any real danger. "Oh I get it. He's just trying to get a feel for the boat."

"Boat? I got news for you, Twizzle, that ain't a boat! Boats have motors and steering wheels and what's that other thing? Oh yeah, they don't flip over when you lean over the side."

"That may be true, but with a kayak he'll be within sight of the shore and I can keep an eye on him. If he had a boat with engines he'd be offshore and out of sight. I'm starting to like the idea of this little yellow piece of plastic," Mora said as she leveled a plot of sand to sit on. "Now I have an appetite, pass me a sandwich!" She stretched out her hand to Madeline, who promptly corrected her, "I'm sorry, we don't use please and thank you anymore?"

Mora rephrased her request, "Please, may I have a sandwich?"

"Better," Madeline replied as she handed Mora a sausage and pepper sandwich.

"Thank you, Twizzle," Mora answered.

For the most part Mora was correct in her assumption about my kayaking. What she failed to realize was that it was intended to be a fishing vessel. The most productive times for fishing and the one with the least boat traffic were at night. I would head out after dark with several fishing buddies and hit the near shore islands for a few hours each night. As each of us grew more comfortable with our boats, our trips became more extensive. Shipping channels that during the day would be far too dangerous were void of any boat traffic during the night and became our regular stomping grounds.

Everyone started tinkering and adding items such as drift chutes or lights. Each new addition allowed us to travel farther and safer. Soon we were traversing Long Island Sound at night to fish submerged islands that only showed themselves during the right moon phase or tide. The middle of Long Island Sound is an unnerving yet magical place at night. The shoreline may be lit by the thousands of homes but out in the middle of the sound it's dark and quiet. So dark and quiet that many a fish has been spared because fishermen quickly turn into stargazers. Nothing truly connects you to ancient man like looking at a dark sky filled with stars and constellations.

While investigating fishing sites for our move to Sarasota, one immediately caught my eye. This online fishing site was dedicated to kayak fishing. www.paddle-fishing.com was quickly added to my favorites. The front page to the web site had a picture of a guy called the "Legend." In the photo he has this ear to ear grin and he has an enormous tarpon pulled halfway out of the water, all the while seated in his kayak. The best part of the picture was that it was taken in Sarasota.

I'd fished for tarpon before down in the Florida Keys and they are one of the top game fish in the world. The thought of tangling with one from a kayak had never crossed my mind. I had made a mental note to look into it once the moving and settling in process was over.

Sarasota, or should I say the west central coast of Florida, like all great fishing locales, has its folklore. Any area worth its salt has some type of renowned fish. They are the Loch Ness monsters of that locale. These animals are destined for greatness, not due to their size or actions, but it's mainly due to the fact that all fishermen are liars, braggarts, and stretch the true whenever they can. From the time a fish is caught until the time the story of the battle is told the fish has grown in size many fold.

The west central coast, an area from Punta Gorda to Tampa, has its own mystical fish. His name is Old Hitler. As the story was told to me, Old Hitler came to fame during the Second World War. At that time the Navy was testing some new type of sonar for detecting German submarines. It was installed in Charlotte Harbor.

The town of Punta Gorda lies where the harbor meets the Gulf of Mexico and is known as the Tarpon Capitol of the world. It is also the capitol for hammerhead sharks. This works out quite nicely since hammerheads feed on tarpon. They do not care if the tarpon weighs 10 pounds or 200 pounds. They just chew through tarpon like a fat kid goes through a bag of Doritos.

As hammerheads go, Old Hitler was the grandest of them all. This fish was so large that he would set off the sonar detectors. He was believed to be upwards of 20 feet long and tipped the scales at over 1,000 pounds. Even if you adjusted for a fisherman's stretching of the true, this is a big ass fish. Old Hitler, if he's still alive, would be very old. However, sharks like to do three things; swim, eat, and make little sharks so his blood line is still swimming around Sarasota somewhere.

A house was found, and an offer was submitted. The only contingency to the deal was that we had to sell our house first. We arrived home on Monday, Camille listed it on Tuesday, and had a few showings set up for the weekend. We accepted an offer the following Monday. We looked at each other with amazement and fear. Excited that we sold at the top of the market but on the other hand, wondering what the hell we'd just done. I've tried my hand at skydiving a time or two and it's the same feeling. Once you jump, you'd better enjoy the ride because you ain't getting back in the plane.

Mora watched over the entire proceedings to make sure there were no foul-ups. Next was the mandatory yard sale and finding new homes for Camille's plants. Once you realize how expensive it is to move all your belongings they lose their sentimental value real quick. If you're starting a new beginning in a new town why bring tons of old stuff with you. Sell the old to offset the price of the new. Everything was in order for the move. Items were sold, donated to Goodwill or boxed up and on a moving truck. Any personal items went with us in my Jeep. So in true Jed Clampett style, we loaded up the truck and moved to, well, Sarasota.

Mora's confidant and second pair of eyes, Max, never slept a wink the three days it took us to drive to Sarasota. He didn't understand exactly what was occurring but with all the activity going on he was on full alert. Max had a hard life as a young dog. Shipped between several owners and locked up at the rescue society for months. He'd been with Camille and me for a few years now and we were all family. He didn't care what was going on as long as he was with us. If we had called to Max and said, "Come on Max, we're going to do a Thelma and Louise and drive off a cliff together," as long as he could be with us, he'd go. Mora loved him for that reason. Max would fight to the death for either of us, no questions asked.

Chapter 30

Mora was in true Twizzle mode when we finally moved into our new home. Apparently she felt the need to even the score with me for all my years of thrills and adventures. First, she used Max as her weapon of choice. We were in the house maybe an hour or so when a neighbor's cat decided to stroll through our backyard. Max was in the screened lanai soaking up the midday sun. Apparently the cat thought that a piece of nylon screening would afford him all the protection he needed from Max. Big mistake number 1.

Max looked at the cat, then turned his head and gave me a look that said, "Excuse me while I charge through this screen and kick some cat ass." Before I could grab a hold of his collar, Max was barreling through the screen and chasing a cat that was quickly running through his 9 lives.

The cat then proceeded to scale a wooden fence that bordered our property. Now instead of going over the fence and fleeing for his life. Pussy cat thought it a good idea to perch himself on top of the fence and taunt Max.

Big mistake number 2. Max just slammed into the fence at full speed, luckily sending the cat flying into my neighbor's yard. It would have been a gruesome scene if he had landed back in our yard.

So now my dog is going crazy snarling at the fence waiting for the cat to show back up. I have a busted screen in my lanai and I haven't been in my new home an hour.

Next Mora introduced Max to the great sport of Gecko hunting. Geckos are these little lizards that are everywhere in Florida. They are not as cute as that little green one with the British accent that tries to sell you car insurance. Most are a dull brown or charcoal black. They sit in the sun all day extending a red throat patch. I'm not sure if they do it to attract a mate or to dissipate heat from their bodies. I do know they drove Max insane and no plant or bush was safe from him while charging through the yard after them.

Around 7 or 8 Geckos had fallen prey to Max the first day, so did several potted plants. The next morning Max had a black spot on his tongue that never went away. Camille and I would always refer to it as the "The Mark of the Gecko" and always said in the voice of some old gypsy fortune teller.

Madeline took notice of all this activity. "Not bad, in just 24 hours, you helped destroy a lanai screen, drove the dog crazy, gave him "The Mark of the Gecko," also using the old gypsy voice when saying it, "Broken several terra cotta planters and helped in the killing of multiple Geckos."

Mora smirked her devilish smile, "Let's not forget the cat."

"Oh yes, the cat, let's not forget using several of the cat's 9 lives," Madeline sarcastically replied while rolling her eyes.

Madeline decided to also join in on the fun. Instead of me being the focal point of her torment it would be Mora. From that day forward, Geckos where always running around the bar. They never entered Madeline's kitchen but several were always climbing on some item behind Mora's bar. They never really frightened her or got in the way but she'd have to explain why they were there to all the new patrons. It was Madeline's way of showing Mora that she was still Queen Twizzle.

"You haven't seen anything yet. I do believe Camille is going to have a very difficult time picking paint colors for the new house. I'm certain she's going to ask Shamus "This color or this color" so many times in the next few weeks his head will explode. Then there's furniture selection and curtains," Mora burst into laughter knowing all this would drive me crazy and also keep me off the water for a while.

"Ah, Twizzle, I don't want to burst your little bubble but Shamus and Camille aren't some couple fresh off the Newlywed Game. Now they might be newly engaged but they lived together for over twenty years. Hell, they can finish each other's sentences," Mora thought back to the way Millie and Red could read each other's faces while playing cards. It brought on a smile and a tear. "I don't believe they'll have as much trouble setting up a house as you think."

"You're probably right, but I'm still going to have a little fun at Shamus' expense."

Chapter 31

Within several weeks our new home was in order. We had moved down without any job prospects. We were both smart, energetic New Yorkers knowing we'd find something when the time came. Camille and I decided that we had both been working since we were in our early teens. We both wanted some down time. The decision to take a year off did not take a whole lot of arm twisting.

We quickly fell into a nice little routine. Wake up around 9:00 a.m. For two people who spent 20 years being in Manhattan by 8:00 a.m. this was a grand luxury. Eat a real breakfast not coffee and a buttered roll on the train. Then read the entire newspaper with it spread out on a table not folded in such a manner as to not intrude on your fellow train rider's personal space. This was followed by several hours of lounging on a raft in the pool in our quest of the perfect tan. A light lunch around one o'clock, followed by snacks and a frozen blender concoction at 3:00 p.m. Start the coal for the grill about 4:00 p.m. and steaks would be sizzling by 5:30 p.m. After dinner a stroll on the beach to watch the sun and all your cares melt into the Gulf of Mexico. It was a very good year. It's amazing how things like jobs can mess up a good living.

One morning while Camille slept in I broke our routine and did a beach walk at day break. This was no Robinson Crusoe jaunt down the beach. I planned ahead. Using my last bottle of Norm's Mystery mix I fixed myself a Bloody Mary in a thermos and also brought along a nice cigar for the walk. Once at the beach I poured the Mystery mix into a proper glass and lit my cigar. North was my direction of choice.

Having spent many hours in the woods in pursuit of deer I relish watching the world wake up. There's a certain order to it. Animals that live higher up in the canopy of the trees get warmed first by the sun and are awakened first. Birds and squirrels are up before everyone else. As the sun starts to warm the forest floor the more terrestrial animals start to stir. Chipmunks and woodchucks wait until the sun has fully risen before emerging from their dens.

The beach also has its order. There always seems to be one lone heron or egret working the water's edge. Normally they aren't early risers but if there has been a fisherman working the surf at night they'll keep him company either waiting for a free handout or to steal a piece of bait. Sanderling, willets and plover are the first to arrive. All are very acrobatic flyers. They arrive in tight formations and fly just above the waves. They land just above the surf line and immediately start working the sand for any morsels they can find. As the waves recede from the beach they work the area just vacated. As the surf retakes the beach they scurry up the beach careful not to get their plumage wet. They always reminded me of tourist women that run from the waves to prevent their dresses from becoming soaked. Next to arrive were the terns. They bully the smaller birds for the best pickings. After the terns you start to see brown pelicans working the water about 100 yards off the beach. Flying high then diving into the bait pods. Tossing their heads back, trying to work the food in their mandible to slide down their gullets headfirst. Last to arrive are the gulls, mostly laughing and herring gulls. They coordinate their arrivals with the schedule of the tourist. Tourist equals food and the gulls know it.

I sipped my Bloody Mary and relit my cigar as I watched the residents of the beach work the sand and preen their feathers. Any shell that caught my eye would be nudged from its sand bed by my big toe for further inspection. When one lives by the water your shell collection must be pristine.

As I looked out at the water to watch an incoming pair of brown pelicans I noticed a large swirl in the water about 75 yards off shore. All swirls in the water catch fishermen's interest; it's the nature of the beast. I spied the area for a short while then saw the silvered mirror side of a rising Tarpon. Large scales reflecting the eastern sun rising over my shoulder. Then several others revealed themselves. It was a small pod of around 10 or so. My mind instantly pulled up the picture of the "Legend" holding the giant Tarpon next to his kayak. The time was coming to meet some locals and get the scoop on Tarpon fishing from a kayak.

With our home renovations now complete and our most strenuous activity consisting of floating in a pool, Mora again was spending more time with Madeline at Twizzle's. She was starting to realize that the people who visited Twizzle's were actually helping her as much as she was helping them. Many who frequented the bar were seafaring men. There were fishermen, divers, surfers and sailors. All had their tales of adventure and narrow escapes. The one thing Mora was starting to realize was that very few had actually died because of the water. The ones who had drowned had cost themselves their own lives. Diver's who dove without the correct safety lines and became lost or entangled in a wreck. A sailor, whose leg became snared in an unsecured line and fell overboard, each was preventable. After listening to their stories she started to recall her own death. After reflecting upon her drowning and comparing it to some of the stories she'd heard from other patrons drowning was actually a peaceful sort of death.

No one remembered their births but their deaths were all very vivid to them. All except those who went to bed and just woke up dead the next morning. The common thread to those who died in car accidents was the noise and confusion. Shattering glass and twisting metal, the rolling or spinning of the vehicle. Sound of tires losing their grip on the road. Theirs was a fast death.

It was the souls who died bedridden. Forced to spend the remaining days of their lives watching the world pass them by. The thought of lying there waiting, to Mora, that seemed like the cruelest way of all. One patron, an older gentleman named Carmine, said that he wasn't sad about going slowly. Other than the bedsores, he said it wasn't so bad. It gave him time to get his affairs in order and reflect on the times he spent with his family.   Instead of dying alone in some ocean he died surrounded by his wife and grown children and their children. He had exhaled his last breathe knowing all he loved were with him in the end.

It was the ones who spent their lives on the water who would laugh at Mora's stories of trying to stop me from being on the water. "You'd be on a fool's mission, lass," a sailor named Pierre who'd crewed on a pirate ship in the Caribbean spoke up. He'd been waiting to hear his name for several centuries now.

Others, from later times chimed in. All had lived their lives on or in the water. Each spoke of the bond they had with the water. It didn't matter if the sun was shining or if the clouds masked the sky and spit cold rain on you. Each day outdoors was magical. Something new was revealed to you as long as you took the time to see it.

Each had a story to share. For one it was navigating at night by using the Southern Cross constellation to guide him. For another it was getting caught in a Category 3 hurricane while sailing back from Nassau.

A dark skinned man from the Island of Saba spoke up. His voice had a lilt to it that captured your ear's attention. "Tis a day I never forget. Now me never sail cross 'dem oceans like some of tees great sailors here," he raised his glass to toast the men gathered around him. He continued with his tale in his sing song style of speaking. He inherited this style of speaking from his mother. Who was part African, part Creole Indian with a bit of Irish, and even a little Portuguese thrown in. Many from the Islands had a very mixed heritage. Sailors call shore leave "*liberty*" for a good reason.

His name was Rubin, a conch diver of some renown on his Island. "I goes to my favorite stretch o' beach where's I know them tasty Conks be. I paddle me canoe to da right depth o' water and drop anchor. I be in the water for a short bit. I a happy man, I gots a sack o Dem sweet conks and 2 dem spiny lobsta. I surfaced for a breath of air and dump me sack in the canoe. Now whens I goes in da water the sun she shine down on me. When I comes out da sky, she change from blue to grey. But not just grey! She be all colors of grey. It be white grey, black grey, pewter like the mug in your hand, even a bright silver. It remind me of does fancy windows in the church but without the colors, if you know what I mean."

Another sailor name Liam whose home port was Killybegs in northwestern Ireland spoke up. "Aye I've seen that a time or two myself. The sky, she's warning you of a storm. She has an anger to her when she doesn't know what color to be."

"Like Mora, when Shamus has gone and done something," someone from the back of the room chimed in. This brought the group to laughter as they all agreed. Mora steeled her eyes to see who made the comment but the culprit was lost in the crowd.

Liam continued after the laughter died down. "We were a half day outside Kilronan when our helmsman noticed the sky and water become one. It was like our friend here says." Liam lifting his mug in Rubin's direction. "Both sky and water turned every shade of silver and grey there be. Not soon after the sea started to become uneasy with herself. My ship "The Nicole" a sleek Clipper of 55 feet started to take an awful pounding.

Several water spouts rose from the ocean that trip and it took all the best my crew had to deliver us to a safe port in Galway Bay. We rode out 3 days of the worst the sea could throw at us in that seaport."

Mora began to wonder if she had been wasting her time in her vigil against my time on the water. Madeline assured her that her efforts weren't in vain. "Are you insane? Shamus comes close to the edge with all his little adventures. If he didn't have you in his ear there's no telling how much trouble he'd get into." She paused for a brief moment to let her words sink in then added, "Of course it is you that put him on the path in the first place. You and all your bedtime dreams of adventure," Mora refused to get into this fight again and just let it drop.

Madeline was concerned by Mora's refusal to argue. "Twizzle, what's the matter?"

"To tell you the truth Mad, I just don't know. I get this feeling like something's not right. I go and check on Shamus and Camille and all seems right in the world. Yet I still get this weird feeling in the pit of my stomach that tells me something's wrong."

What Mora didn't realize is that the feeling in the pit of her stomach was not caused by me. It was being generated by someone she brought into my life and counted on daily. She never saw it coming and neither did Camille and I.

Chapter 32

It was another postcard day in Sarasota. Sun was shining, a warm breeze made the palm fronds sway as if they were dancing to the beat of a steel drum. Camille was at work and I had a free day. Instead of fishing I decided to spend the day with Max. I watched him as he hunted for geckos. He dove into a bush but his target of prey wasn't a gecko but another resident of our backyard, the mighty tennis ball. At any one time there are always several in different states of abuse laying around the yard. Either chewed until all bounce has been removed from them or the fuzzy coating has been peeled back to expose its rubber innards.

There is something in a Golden Retriever's DNA that they must chase a moving tennis ball. It's why they are on the banned list from Wimbledon. They can't have the Queen being knocked on her crown by a Golden Retriever leaping for a ball. It is just bad form and the English just won't have it.

Max dropped his quarry at my feet which was the sign for me to play. I gave it a good toss and Max was on it. After several tosses I gave it one last throw. Max took after it and as he passed the steps for the pool gave a mighty yelp. I shot him a concerned look because in all the years I'd known him I'd never heard him yelp. Growls and snarls I was very familiar with, yelps was a foreign language to me. Max continued on until he had the ball but now was sitting with his left front paw held up. I knew immediately something was wrong and rushed to his side. As I checked his leg he winced in pain. "Did you just break your leg?" I asked. Our vet was just around the corner so I carried him to my jeep, placed him in the back, and as I drove I called the vet from my cell phone and informed him of the situation.

Mora was sitting on the front porch of Twizzle's enjoying the flavors of a hand rolled Cuban. Suddenly a feeling of dread overwhelmed her. She was at my side before she could exhale all the smoke from her lungs.

As I arrived, the vet and his assistant were waiting with a stretcher. Max was rushed inside and the normal x-rays and blood tests were taken. Within a half hour I was brought into the doctor's office. He entered through a side door with x-ray films in hand. He spoke as he walked over to a screening board on the wall. "Just as you suspected, Max has broken his leg."

I exhaled a deep cleansing breath. A broken leg isn't so bad I thought. He flipped the switch and pressed the film into its holder. Then he spoke words that shattered my world. "It's why his leg broke that concerns us. Come look at these x-rays. See this area, that's a view of a good solid piece of bone. This area here, see how it looks like Swiss Cheese? Well, I'm afraid that's bone cancer. Now we do have a few options open to us..." I stopped him before he could finish. I immediately had my cell phone out and was calling Camille to get here fast. I didn't need to have the vet repeat everything he was going to tell me. I had a feeling this wasn't something I wanted to hear twice.

Mora was staring at the film of Max's leg. She was examining the area that the vet had pointed out to me. It didn't look good. Mora knew that she relied on Max heavily. He was her greatest ally. She never had to influence him, no whispering in his ear at night. They had a common bond, protecting Camille and I.

Camille arrived and was quickly ushered in to sit with the vet and myself. She inspected the x-rays and then we were told our options. Put him down was one. Actually it wasn't, Max would not be put down on our watch as long as he had a fighting chance. The second option was to remove the leg and have him go through chemo treatments. My brother had gone through chemo treatments a few years back and I'd sooner put a bullet in Max myself than allow him to endure that. The third option was to just remove his leg and see how he did. The doc said he'd probably last around four to six months, maybe a year with the chemo treatments. Camille and I stepped outside and through tears and choked up voices we decided to give him a fighting chance. Max went from being a four on the floor to a three speed that night.

The next morning following a sleepless night we were at the vet's to check on our boy. He lay in a metal cage, half shaved, wrapped in gauze and Ace bandages. Several pain patches were applied to his skin. The nurse in charge informed me that they were a type of time released pain medication and that Max had come out of the surgery like a champ. He was a bit groggy but had eaten and was drinking which was a very positive sign. When she said the next major hurdle was that they need to see him get up and move around on his three legs, I walked over and released the latch on the cage. I half crawled in and held him. He perked up and I could see the spark in his eye and then the sound of his tail wagging against the metal cage. It was his thank you for not giving up on him. I stood back up, walked a few feet from the cage, and yelled for Max. "Hey let's go home, buddy!" The nurse had tears welling up in her eyes and was rubbing my shoulder.

Max started to move, stoned out of his mind and missing a leg. It took a few adjustments for him to get his balance but he was determined and started to hobble out of the cage. Once free of his confinement he began to get the feel for his new way of life. Like a drunken sailor, he staggered his way over to me. Once at my side he used me for a leaning post, pressing all his weight against me. "That's a great sign," the nurse said, "He's one strong dog." She didn't know the half of it. Then she informed me that they would keep him one more night to keep an eye on him.

Madeline knew that Mora had spent the night with Max. She had that bone tired look that mothers get from sleepless nights filled with worry and dread over a sick child. Madeline smiled as she said to Mora, "Bet you never thought you'd feel that way about an animal."

"I never had a pet growing up, and I never really thought about Max. I didn't need to. I just can't explain this feeling."

"You have a common bond. That wonderful stew you've been cooking up all these years. Well, you had a," Madeline paused looking for the correct word, "Secret ingredient. Max is just the closest to Shamus so your bond to him is the strongest.

"Well I owe him and will do whatever I can for him."

Madeline stopped her, "Which is absolutely nothing!" The words smacked Mora as sharply as if Madeline had used her hand. "Max is past saving. His time on earth is almost over. He'll have a few good months but then his health will start to fail. His love for Camille and Shamus will keep him alive longer than he really would want to be."

Madeline wasn't wrong but she wasn't completely right either. Max was given four to six months. The doctor forgot to add in his heart to the equation. Max lasted 14 months. There were a few harrowing times while we dialed in his medication. For all but the last few days it was a good life for Max. At the end Max was with Camille and I. He wasn't put down in some cold sterile doctor's office. He died in my arms at home. Mora was reminded of the words of one of her patrons, Carmine. He died at home surrounded by family and was happy for it.

Max had one last act to provide Camille and I some comfort. Once he had passed, the vet and his assistant placed him on a stretcher. We were sitting in our lanai when we relieved Max of his suffering.   The shortest route to the vet's vehicle was through our side gate. This meant that they would have to exit our lanai and skirt around the pool.   As the vet was walking backwards out our lanai carrying his end of the stretcher, he was conversing with his assistant.   Camille yelled to him and he stopped. He was a half step from falling into the pool. Camille and I found great comfort in the fact that Max could still create havoc even without a heartbeat.

Mora could not help Max while he was on Earth. She made sure he always had a place at Twizzle's. He spent most of his time either on the front porch waiting and watching or with Madeline in the kitchen. He was never in Madeline's way. He would just find a comfortable spot where he could watch every move she made, as he had done for years watching Camille. Madeline even tried to lure a few of Camille's recipes out of him, but he kept all of Camille's secrets. Mora would love to sit next to him on the front porch and have a smoke and stroke his mane. New patrons would come up the stairs and lean over to pet Max. He'd wait until their hand was inches from him and let out one of his blood curdling growls. This would stop the patron cold. Mora would exhale, almost choking from laughter, shake her head and just call Max a Twizzle. Max was the first and only male to be called a Twizzle.

With Max gone there was a huge void in our home.   No longer was there the constant jingle of his tags against his collar. The sounds of nails scraping against the tile floor were absent. The worst of it all was opening the front door and not being pounced upon by a hundred pounds of drooling, shedding love. Camille and I knew the time would come to find another but it wouldn't be right away. Max left a big scar on our hearts and it would take some time to heal.

Chapter 33

I turned my attention to tarpon fishing. By chance I met the fellow known as the "Legend" at a local fishing hole. We exchanged pleasantries and I began to question him on every aspect of kayak fishing for tarpon. Dave, which is his real name, gave me the low down on gear, safety equipment and technique. He told me to meet him at daybreak on the following Saturday at Cow Creek. I don't know who actually names these places but there was neither cow nor creek anywhere in sight. I arrived just before daybreak with a true fisherman's breakfast, coffee and a glazed donut. I listened to the surf lazily rolling in onto the sand as the morning sun started to burn off the morning haze. Several other vehicles started to arrive. Dave's was one of them. He introduced me to several of the others as they were unloading their trucks and cars.

Dave had told me that the old formula of K.I.S.S. (Keep It Simple Stupid) was best for tarpon fishing A kayak, stout rod, reel with high line capacity, paddle lease, PFD: Personal Floatation Device and a drift chute was all that was needed. We would be fishing using artificial lure, no bait allowed. Dave is an old Navy man and he runs a tight ship even if that ship is a kayak. All gear stowed away neatly and in its proper place. I quickly noticed that the fellows he had introduced me to all did the same.

Everyone's gear was unloaded without haste and carried over the small sand dune and down to the surf line. Rik and Noles, the two that Dave had introduced me to earlier, were inspecting my setup. I was using my Van Stall reel, a high dollar item that I bought for myself with some bonus money a few years back. I was immediately berated for having it. Then my kayak that has always served me well was put under scrutiny for being the wrong color. "Yellow, that's the slowest color there is," mumbled Rik. Noles chimed in about the fact that I probably didn't have my hooks sharpened properly. Here I am almost 50 years old and I'm the new kid at school. My old crew were all world class ball busters so I am well callused and took it all in stride.

Mora had done something years ago to help protect me on the water. She instilled in me a steadfast work ethic regarding my outdoor activities. I have always had fun but there has always been an underlying professionalism about what I do. Be it handling firearms or fishing gear. My gear is in tiptop shape and the people I've surround myself with have always been top notch.

Bill and Emilio who taught me to dive instilled the idea of double checking my gear. John Knight was the same with his fishing tackle. John showed me more about fishing without ever giving a lesson. He's an innovator and today owns Tidaltails Lure Company. He's banned from ever opening a fishing school; if everyone had his fishing knowledge no fish would be safe.

The three men I was standing with that morning were of the same caliber. Rik runs the Paddle-fishing website where I first saw the photo of the "Legend" and his huge tarpon. Dave, well he's the "Legend" and you don't get that moniker without paying your dues. Noles, whom Dave refers to as "Kato" at certain times, builds custom fishing rods. I later purchased a pair of his creations; they are the ones I use daily. Noles even was able to take a bit of Max's hair that I had saved and incorporated it into one of my rods. Now whenever I go fishing Max is always with me.

I had my kayak ready to go but gave it another once over making sure everything was in ship shape order. I wanted no foul ups on my maiden voyage with these guys watching. Rik, the largest of the group and most personable, started giving me the lay of the land. "Just get out about 75 to 100 yards and watch to see which way they're running, North or South. Don't crowd them and cast well out in front of them." With this being my first trip it was more exploratory for me, more of a watch how it's done sort of thing.

Mora had positioned herself on the top of one of the dunes. Over the years, and with the help of the seafaring men that frequented Twizzle's, she had developed an appreciation for the beauty of the sea and its beaches. She could look at it and admire it but she was never going to put herself in a position to actually feel the water on her skin. Some wounds run too deep. Mora took a liking to the Three Musketeers standing at the water's edge with me. The fact that they were giving me a hard time from the moment they met me went a long ways with her.

They were new friends in the making. When you're a kid you bond with your friends by doing things for the first time together. David, aka Uncle Big Head, and I are forever more than friends, we're family. We shared so many experiences together as kids that we're almost the same person. Crashing bikes, our first beer together and chasing women, these shared experiences form an unbreakable bond.

The men standing at the water's edge and I will never have those experiences. We are too old for riding bikes. Everyone's married and our first beer are thirty plus years behind us. Yet we all have the sea and fishing. Each took a different road to be standing exactly at the water's edge that morning. No one used a map or GPS to get there but we all showed up at the exact same spot, on time, with coffee and with fishing gear.

Bond isn't the correct word for it; it's more of unwritten code. Tarpon fishing is in all of our blood. We spend time, money and effort in the pursuit of our passion. Tarpon are a migratory fish; they pass through our region beginning in late May and leave early September. Your best time to fish for them is from sun up until around 10:00 a.m. So between work, family and weather plus the few short hours a day you get to target them, it is a very small window of opportunity.

Now throw in the fact that some days the Tarpon don't feel like having us pull on their jaws. Oh, they're jumping out of the water everywhere; they just didn't want anything to do with us. Let's not forget the fellow in his boat that doesn't have the slightest idea of what he's doing and runs his boat right over the top of the fish, scaring them away for parts unknown. With all that against us we show up each morning with hopes of hooking a Silver King. If the guy next to you hooks a tarpon, one of us always stops fishing and shadows the person with the fish as a safety measure. I know of no other sport where guys do that for each other.

I did as I was instructed and paddled out. One eye was watching the water and the other was on the Three Musketeers. They are three individuals but when they see a pod of Tarpon rising they become a single unit. I've watched wolves staking a herd of Elk on my trips out West and these three used the same basic technique. It is all tightly choreographed, each holding their positions on the outside of the pod. A wide berth was afforded each angler.

I later learned you never want to be too close when another angler hooks up. Tarpon are famous for rocketing out of the water in a very showy display. Twisting and flipping, gills rattling. Landing back in the water with such force you would think a small car fell from the heavens. You don't want to be sitting in a tarpon's landing zone. They also have a tendency to toss the weighted lure from their iron clad jaws back at you with tremendous force.

After a few outings I was fast becoming part of that choreographed team. On, or about, the fifth day I was lucky enough to find myself in the perfect position for a cast. A pod emerged and I tossed my lure ten feet in front of the lead fish. I felt a thump on the line. It was generated by my lure bouncing off the heavily scaled body of a fish. Then I felt a much heavier thump. I set the hook, my rod bent and my reel started to scream as line was being peeled away. Rik was the closest and I turned to him for advice. "Now what do I do?" my voice screaming with excitement.

Rik was dressed to protect himself from Florida's unrelenting sun. A large brimmed hat pulled down low on his forehead, oversized polarized sunglasses, worn to dilute the glare reflected up off the water. What little real estate of his face that was left, was protected by his mustache. A mustache which is best described as either the Magnum P.I. or a 1970 porn star mustache. All I can really see of his face is the tip of his nose, cheeks and chin. I can, however, tell that he's laughing at me while advising me to "hold on tight."

Did I ever! The Silver King took a hundred yards of line in seconds. That same amount of line took me 10 minutes to retrieve. My old buddy, Mike, works construction and has a grip of stone. I work in the computer field for thirty years and have the hand strength of a pretty strong girl scout. My forearms felt like they would explode and I was worried that soon the expensive rod and reel I was holding would soon be ripped from my aching hands.

Mora stood on the sand dune cheering me on. "Come on Shamus, pump the rod! Pull back and reel down!"

Madeline decided to join the cheering section. She was wearing a spaghetti strapped sundress. Black sandals ornamented with small silver studs which reflected the morning sun. Instead of her usual black handbag she accessorized the outfit with a bag woven from coconut grass with a black border.

The smell of peppers and eggs on Focaccia bread rose from her bag. She offered some to Mora but was waved off.

"How the hell can you eat at a time like this?" Mora asked excitedly.

"What?" Madeline responded. "You can't eat and watch Shamus at the same time?"

Mora ran up the beach to keep me in front of her as the Tarpon took me on what's known as a Sarasota Sleigh Ride. A Sarasota Sleigh Ride is akin to a Nantucket Sleigh Ride. Instead of a Whaling ship being pulled by a harpooned whale, a tarpon fisherman in a kayak is towed by a fast moving tarpon. I tossed my drift chute overboard which put enough pressure on the fish to allow me to do battle. After a 20 minute fight in which I swore to quit drinking, smoking and put some serious time in at the gym, the Tarpon relinquished itself. All three of the Musketeers had shadowed me at one point or another yelling encouragement. That is if you consider Dave yelling, "Come on, you big pussy, put some muscle into it!" or Noles taking odds on whether or not I'd puke during the battle.

Rik interjected, "Oh, that's just a sucker's bet!" while laughing at me. Finally the beast was boat side and I was given instructions from all three to make sure the fish was released unharmed. A unwritten rule with these guys is that at all cost the fish must always be revived. This requires you to grasp the behemoth by its bottom jaw while someone else tows you around to allow the water to rush over its gills.

I called over to Noles, "How do you know when she's ready?"

He smirked and answered, "Oh she'll let you know."

With that the tarpon shook her head and with one swipe of her tail had released herself from my grasp and soaked me with what seemed like half the water in the Gulf of Mexico.

Dave hollered that another pod was working its way down the beach. After eyeballing me to see I wasn't dying of a heart attack, the Three Musketeers left me in search of their own Silver King. I lay in my kayak, hands still shaking so hard I couldn't light my cigar. A forest fire wouldn't be able to light my cigar after the dousing I received from the departing Tarpon. I just stayed there until the veins in my arms and head didn't resemble a road map of Kansas anymore and thought a cold beer would be perfect right about now.

Mora was jumping up and down yelling to Madeline, "Mad, did you see that?"

Madeline looked up from her sandwich just nodding in agreement and giving Mora the thumbs up sign, her mouth working on the bite she had just taken.

After swallowing Madeline wondered aloud, "For a girl who hates everything to do with water you certainly seem excited for Shamus."

Mora answered, "The guys at Twizzle's have made me realize that it's not the water that will hurt you. It's your own lack of respect for it. Shamus is surrounded by those three," she nodded in the direction of Dave, Rik and Noles, "Something tells me that he's in good company."

Mora's new found faith took a bit of a jolt as she listened in on our conversation as we all loaded up our vehicles. I had asked why everyone was crowded around me while the tarpon was boat side. Dave looked at Rik and Noles and explained; "I was steadying your kayak in case the tarpon decided to do anything crazy," then he nodded in their direction and finished, "They were keeping an eye out for the men in the grey suits." He then shared that the most dangerous part of fishing for Tarpon from a kayak, other than one landing in the boat, was a shark attack while the fish is boat side. Mora gave Dave a double take to see if he was joking or serious. It's not something that happens on any regularity but it is possible, after all we were playing in Old Hitler's playground. After that Rik would occasionally send me You Tube videos of sharks attacking tarpon. They would give me the heebie jeebies every time I watched them.

Each morning for the next several months it was the same routine. Up before the sun and load the kayak and the rest of my gear. Tell Camille I loved her and kissed her goodbye. Hit the local 7-11 for coffee and donuts and a pack of smokes. Hit the beach and watch the world wake up. The sun would rise on the four figures standing on the shoreline watching the sets of waves rolling in. Everyone making everything ship shape while watching for a tarpon to roll. One of the most important things I learned is to use a travel mug with a locking lid, not the Styrofoam cups from 7-11. Coffee and saltwater is a horrible mixture that will have you running up the beach in search of a portajohn real fast.

One morning towards the end of July, I was out on the water with Noles. He's shorter than I am and has a lower center of gravity. This affords him the ability to stand in his kayak. There was a light surface fog and Noles is standing and paddling along when I see him straining his neck looking at the water. He sits down immediately and waves me over. As I approach he signals for me to just glide over to his port side. "You see her?" he asked in a hushed voice.

"A tarpon?" I questioned while peering at the water.

"Not quite," he chuckled as he pointed his paddle in the direction of the fish he had spotted. The sun started to do its job and the fog was burning off the water. Once it did I saw the outline of the fish Noles was pointing at.

The fish was either the son or grandson of Old Hitler. He was bluish silver with a massive pectoral fin that sliced through the water with ease. His head looked to be three feet from eye to eye. He was a thing of beauty to behold. Noles and I were enthralled yet cautious to not make any movement or sound. We must have interested him also. He swam past our kayaks so close I could have touched him with my paddle. I turned to Noles and in my best Martin Brody impersonation said, "We need a bigger boat." After awhile he disappeared from sight and we decided it wouldn't be a bad idea to get off the water.

Noles said that he didn't think any tarpon would be hanging around anyway. I replied, "Would you if you were a tarpon?"

Mora spent as much time on the dunes as I spent on the water. We had both experienced wonderful sights. She giggled herself to tears one morning when a Leatherback Turtle surfaced inches from my kayak and exhaled its frothy breath on my arm. We both watched as a family of dolphins corralled a school of bait fish onto the beach. The mother dolphin was swimming in and beaching herself to grab the baitfish and toss them back to her waiting calf. She would then wiggle herself back off the sand into the water. Each time Mora returned to Twizzle's she'd tell the seafaring men what she had seen. They, in turn, would enthrall her with tales of creatures and adventures from their time on the water. Any melancholy they were feeling about being in Limbo was soon lifted.

One of the fellows instructed her to be on the beach the morning after the next full moon. "There'll be a parade like you've never seen before."

Mora followed his instructions and the morning after the next full moon she was on the beach with me well before sunup. She noticed a different set of prints in the sand. They lead from the base of the dunes to the surf. She followed them back to their origins and waited. Soon out of the sand emerged a small wiggling head. After a small struggle, a turtle the size of a half dollar started to waddle down the sand to the water. Mora thought they resembled little chicken cutlets because the coating of sand that stuck to their shells resembled breadcrumbs. Soon a small parade of miniature loggerheads were headed to the water. Only a few would actually make it. An egret that had been working the beach spied the parade and decided loggerhead for breakfast was a right proper idea. After watching the egret wolfed down two or three hatchlings she took it upon herself to become a crossing guard for the baby loggerheads.

The next day she told her story to the crowd at Twizzle's. She explained how she saved that brood of hatchlings. "Ah, Mora," interrupted the fellow who told her about the turtle parade, "You only saved them for the next predator." Mora gave him a puzzled look. He understood the look and explained that everything in the ocean love to dine on baby turtles. "Maybe one out of the hundreds of eggs that were laid live to be an adult."

Mora's concentration was broken by one of the geckos Madeline had living at Mora's bar, as it ran across her hand. "I wish the same was true for these damn lizards," she whispered to the fellow who was telling her the story. Madeline was nowhere in sight. She was busy in the kitchen yet a smile lit up her face.

Chapter 34

Anytime Mora would return Max would immediately go to her sniffing around for any scent of me. He would listen to her tales and cock his head each time she mentioned my name. After she was done he would return to his post on the front step, lay down with his head resting on his remaining front paw. A deep breath would be exhaled and his eyes would search the horizon for me. Madeline would comfort him by saying, "Someday soon, buddy." She made sure she was out of earshot of Mora when she said it.

After one of her recent trips, Mora went out and sat down next to Max. She had three fingers of Kentucky's finest in a tumbler. Her left hand found that spot just behind his ear that put him at ease whenever she scratched it. Max rested his head on Mora's lap and she looked out at the horizon. "Max, old boy," she said and then took a sip of bourbon, "We need to talk. You ain't going to like it, but," she took a long pause and another sip then continued, "They need a dog. The house just ain't the same. I also need another set of eyes on them."

Max let out a low growl, Mora let him get it out of his system and spoke again, "I said you wouldn't like it. It needs to be done. We both know that. Have no fears. No one could ever replace you." Max exhaled a deep breath and Mora knew the deal was done.

Mora stood and left to give Max his own space. She entered the kitchen and Madeline asked, "How'd he take it?"

As Mora was about to answer they heard a scream coming from the front porch. Max had bitten the old pirate, Pierre as he bent down to pet him. The old guy had been petting Max without incident since Max arrived. Max would have none of it on this day.

Mora turned back to Madeline and answered her question, "He's working through it, maybe you should keep him with you in the kitchen for awhile."

Madeline's eyes went wide. "It would be safer to close down until he feels better." They both tried to contain their laughter so Max wouldn't hear them.

Camille was sitting in the lanai with the Sunday paper when I woke up. I poured myself a cup of coffee and grabbed the comics. She let me have my first sip of wakeup juice when she said, "There a few Goldens for sale in the paper."

I replied, "Really, I've seen a few on some of the rescue sites for Florida."

We both lowered our papers and looked at each other. Max was loved beyond belief but the time was right for another dog. Camille dropped a few hints about wanting a smaller breed of dog. I thought, "Yeah right, like there's any chance of us not getting another Golden!"

A week or so later Camille saw an ad for a small female Golden.

We took a ride just to take a look at her. This was definitely no Max. A timid, underweight girl covered in flea bites. She did have the most beautiful almond shaped eyes; melt your heart kind of eyes. Her name was Luka. I didn't really love this dog at first sight but Camille felt something for her. There was no way we'd ever leave her in a home where she wasn't being cared for. Once again the sounds of nails on our tiled floor rang out. No longer would we come home to an empty house with no one to greet us. It wasn't long before Luka was my little girl.

She has this one quirk that cracks me up, she watches television. I don't mean she looks at it; I mean she's watching it. She studies every movement on the screen. I realized it when Camille and I were watching the Kentucky Derby. There was a scene where a handler was placing a horse into a paddock. Now, our TV set sits against our living room wall. On the other side of the wall is a hallway. From the angle on the television it looks to Luka like the horse walks straight through the back of the TV. She gets up and sticks her head into the hallway like she's looking for the horse. She turns around and shoots me a confused look like she's trying to say, "What happened to the horse? He was right here!"

If there is any movie with an animal in it, Luka will sit there and watch it. Any time during the show if that animal starts to run, Luka will sit up and her ears perk up. Once the animal gets to a certain distance on the screen Luka charges after it. Cleaning nose prints off the screen has become a common household chore.

Luka has another odd trait about her. She loves to sit on our couch with her ass on the arm of the couch and her head resting on the back of the couch with her paws tucked up under her chin. "Oh she reminds me of the women in my old neighborhood," Madeline said, "Always leaning out the windows keeping an eye on the neighborhood. All she needs now is a housecoat and a cigarette hanging out of her mouth!"

Chapter 35

Madeline was sitting on the front porch of Twizzle's enjoying a cup of coffee when she noticed Max wasn't in his normal spot. Each day he'd lay on the porch with his head resting on his one remaining front paw. Eyes constantly scanning the horizon for a lost loved one. This morning he was pacing back and forth. "Max, what's the matter buddy?" Madeline asked. He came and sat next to her looking up with mournful brown eyes. She looked down to hand him a piece of Cinnamon toast when she now noticed he was sporting all four legs. She set her coffee cup down and scanned the horizon herself. "Max," she said with authority to get his full attention, "This is just between us, Mora can't know about this." Max understood and went back to his usual position at the top of the steps. His head resting on his one and only front leg and exhaled hard.

It was another glorious morning in Sarasota. The thermometer was pushing 75 and the sun had yet to crest the horizon. I did a quick inventory of my gear. Both rods in the front cab of my truck. Kayak strapped down in the bed. Paddles, drift chute and spare lures all stowed away. Camille had been kissed and told she was loved, time to hit the beach. As I passed the oversized American flag on Cow Creek Road I saw it was in complete slumber. A good sign, it meant no winds, the Gulf would be calm and tarpon easy to spot. My three cohorts were already surfside watching moonlight glimmer off the surface of the Gulf like a billion diamonds. Noles had spotted one or two tails break the surface but couldn't tell if they were headed North or South. I finished hauling my equipment to the chants of, "Morning sunshine, did we sleep in a little late this morning?" I took a sip of my coffee, shivered off the morning dampness and saluted each with my middle finger.

"Little Grumpy this morning, aren't we?" Rik said as he laughed off my morning salute.

The first strands of light crested above the horizon. It backlit the few morning clouds that hung over the Gulf. The sky had that bluish purple that it can only have at sunup or sundown. The clouds looked as if Roseate Spoonbills had brushed against them during flight leaving traces of pink and rose on their surface.

The four of us paddled out together. Noles and Rik took an inside stance while Dave and I paddled out to watch the outside lane. Dave and I lit our morning cigars and sipped coffee waiting for the action to start. Mora joined us in a smoke. She was becoming more and more accustomed to our routine. She watched us like she was watching a chess match. If Rik moves here the other three will go there. She became almost complacent. She knew I was on the water with three of the best she could find. Once I was in position there was little she could do but watch from shore. Each morning she would meander down the beach scanning the shore for whatever shells the tide deposited the night before. Each morning her meandering took her a little farther, always keeping the four of us within sight.

Noles was the first to spot the rising tarpon. "Behind you at 1:00!" he yelled to Dave and me. These tarpon weren't in the mood to play. We refer to them as peek-a-boo tarpon. They pop up and show themselves but before you can make a cast in their direction they submerge and don't show themselves again. If they do show themselves they'll be 150 yards down the beach not worth expending the energy to chase them.

Rik was off to my right and I saw he was practicing the art of blind casting. It's an old tradition where a fisherman doesn't actually see anything to cast to but rather believes if he casts to a certain spot on the water a fish should be there. It paid off for Rik. Mora saw the activity from her spot down the beach. She knew it was Rik by his hat and the color of his kayak. "Hit him hard, Rik. Set that hook!" Rik must have heard her because that is exactly what he did. His rod bent, his line tightened and the drag on his reel started to scream.

Dave spied the way Rik's line was lifting from the water and warned everyone, "She's going to jump!" The tarpon must have thought he was on a movie set and Dave the director, because he came on scene right on cue. Breaking the surface of the water and delivering a flashy performance.

As the tarpon leapt from the water we could hear the sound of gills rattling from his powerful head shakes. Rik played the fish well. With each leap Rik bowed to the fish. This in turn would put less tension on the line making it less likely the tarpon would break the line. We cheered and gave instructions and soon the battle was over. Rik hoisted an 80lb class tarpon as far out of the water as possible for a quick photo. Noles kept a sharp eye out for any sharks. I attached a line from Rik's kayak to mine and towed him around until the tarpon recovered enough to be released.

With Rik's fish released and headed back on its migration, the four of us paddled back into position. A small pod rose only a few feet in front of Dave giving him no chance at them. I took a chance and casted twenty feet ahead of the pod. I started to reel up and felt no pressure on my line so I stopped to take a sip of coffee. Before I could get the travel cup to my lips my rod was almost ripped from my hands. Dropping the cup to give all my attention to the task at hand I set the hook. Unlike Rik's tarpon, the one at the end of my line decided against any showy jumps. It was going to be a bulldog of a fight. He would stay low in the water column with his head down. This was an old pro, one that wore the piercing from previous encounters with man. He knew his best bet was to stay low and try and wear through my leader.

I now was seasoned in the way of the tarpon. If he pulled left, I pulled right. I would not give an inch of ground in this fight. After a few long minutes of muscle straining pulling, I decided it was time to deploy my drift chute. This would put added strain on the tarpon and wear him down faster. After several drag screaming runs this fish wasn't tiring. Every time I gained line in he would take it back again plus some. Dave quickly scanned the horizon and commented, "That fish is acting like something is chasing it."

"Yeah, me." I replied.

Finally the tarpon started to rise in the water column. Dave and I both knew what he was trying to do. The tarpon was tired and wanted to head to the surface to take a gulp of air. Tarpon are one of the few fish that can actually breathe air through their mouths due to a special bladder that nature gave them. I had already stuck my rod tip below the surface before Dave gave me his instructions. "If he sucks air you'll be here for another 15 minutes. Stick your rod tip," Dave stopped for a moment when he saw I was already doing my part, "Good man, keep his head down. That's the way. This fish is almost beat." Dave was right. The fight was over in a few more minutes.

Dave came along my port side. Rik was 10 yards off my starboard. He was trying to snap a picture of my fish while keeping an eye on Noles. Noles was in the midst of a battle with a 40 pound fish. He was using a fly rod and the battle had just begun. Noles released Rik from his responsibilities of shadowing him since he was able to handle this fish on his own. I had just lifted the tarpon for the photo. My eyes were on Rik. Rik had one eye shut and the other was looking through the view finder. Dave was keeping a watchful eye behind us.

No one saw the large dorsal fin cutting the surface of the water in a direct line to the fish I was holding. I didn't realize what was happening when the wake the hammerhead was pushing hit the front of my kayak. I simply lost my seating. The weight of the tarpon and my now lack of balance allowed my kayak to list. When the son of Old Hitler struck the tarpon I was holding he took a third of the fish in one bite. It also tipped my kayak over. I was now in the water with a feeding hammerhead. I wasn't petrified the way I thought I would be. I was in a bad situation and the best thing to do was just get out of the water. I saw Rik and just headed for him.

Mora was now screaming and cursing like the night she fought Frank Burrows. She ran to the water's edge but the slightest touch of the warm Gulf waters stopped her dead in her tracks. "Madeline!" She cried like a hurt child calling its mother.

Madeline was behind her, "Mora!" she called forcing Mora to look from the scene on the water. She clasped her face with both hands and said, "Look at me. It's done."

Rik had dropped his camera once he realized what was happening. Each of us has always known about the possibilities. Each has played the scenario in our minds but there is no practicing for this. Noles broke his fish off when he heard the screams. He paddled with every ounce of strength he had but it was too far away. Dave had lost the nails off three fingers from where he was holding my kayak steady for the photo. When the shark struck, Dave had his eyes glued on the water behind us and never saw the attack. I was already in the water before Dave could even turn his head around. I tried to put as much distance between myself and the rest of the tarpon carcass that was turning the water around me into a blood soup. I had just rolled onto my left side and had given the first kick of my legs to get to Rik. The vibrations I gave off were like ringing a dinner bell to Old Hitler's kid.

Old Hitler's son never broke the surface of the water this time. Dave and Rik were trying to get to me all the while scanning the surface for signs of a fin. Rik arrived first and I had just placed my hand on the bow of his kayak when my right leg felt as if it was hit by lightning. The water around me turned darker with my blood. My ears were filled with the sound of Rik screaming, "Give me your fucking hand!" The sting of salt water overwhelmed me as I started to slip below the surface of the water.

Mora's bond with me was now broken. A new bond had taken its place. We would forever have the bond of dying by slipping away beneath the surface of the water. There is a certain peace to it. Once the body gives up the struggle for air and relaxes. You become aware that the water in your ear canals is amplifying all the sound around you. For me, the blood in the water created a veil muting the morning sun. The silhouette of Rik's kayak started to fade the deeper I sank. The warmth of the Gulf water caressed me like the warmth of a mother holding its child.

A mother's touch keeping you warm and safe until you fall fast asleep.

Chapter 36

Mora was inconsolable. She was an unholy terror around Twizzle's. She was in a foul mood drinking Bourbon and burning through cigars. Even the geckos knew to stay out of sight. Her only comfort was Max. They would sit on the front porch and stare off into the horizon. The Three Musketeers showed up at Camille's job to tell her the news. They had now become three of the riders of the Apocalypse, for Camille. None of them could actually say the words and Camille didn't have to hear them to know what was wrong. Camille was also inconsolable but had Luka to hold during the worst times. The Coast Guard recovered what was left of me. A cremation was the only proper thing to do. Camille held on to the ashes for a few months until the thought of what would be the right thing to do had come to her. Max's ashes and mine were combined. She handwrote a note to all I had shared adventures with. A bottle of bourbon was sent along with the note and my ashes.

On June 16th in the fading light of dusk, please raise a glass and scatter Shamus and Max anywhere you shared an adventure.

My parents, as well as David and Joan, flew to Sarasota to attend a ceremony with my paddling buddies. The Three Musketeers paddled out to the spot where I was taken and scattered what little was left of me. Some in our fishing community wanted to do nothing more than collect revenge on Old Hitler's son. Rik was the voice of reason, "Why? We play in his world fully knowing the risk. That shark did nothing more than he was born to do. Shamus was fully aware of the risk and showed up every morning during tarpon season."

Dave Loos, with whom I hunted Elk in Hells Canyon, went one step beyond. He had hand loaded the ashes into a 12 gauge shell and blasted me out of his favorite side by side. My old friend, Mike, scattered some around my tree stand in the woods behind his home. He traveled back to New London and released a handful on the water where we dove in our youth. Fergy traveled to Islamorada and he and Captain Paul released me overboard under the bridge where I nearly wrecked his boat decades earlier. Paul joked that he'd probably never be able to catch another fish from this bridge ever again. Martin put me to rest at Lucky's stand.

Uncle Big Head regaled everyone with a story about how he and I were laid low by a simple crab in Martha's Vineyard. He cleared his throat and took a moment to collect himself. "Here we are, both over six feet tall, and a combined weight of over 400 pounds. We have masks, fins and snorkels. This Jackenhiemer," he lifted the box that used to contain my ashes, "talks me into going with him. Chasing this one crab around the ocean floor until it turned around with both claws extended," David took on the persona of the crab using his best Edward G. Robinson impersonation, "Come on, I'll mess the both of you up." David explained that we were both chased from the water by a 4 ounce crab.

Camille and Joan burst into tears and laughter and everyone else joined them. A bonfire was lit and everyone told stories and made a toast. My father walked along the shoreline and stared out at the site where the attack occurred. He soon found himself in the presence of the Three Musketeers. Artie picked up a handful of wave worn pebbles and started skipping them into the water. The others standing beside him joined in. He tried to thank them for their efforts but the words were lost. They, in turn, tried to think of something to say that would alleviate his sorrow. No words were said, none were needed. Each knew what the other was feeling. They all continued skipping stones into the tranquil Gulf of Mexico, until the darkness forced them back to the light of the fire.

As the fire finally subsided, everyone left for home, warmed by the fire and friendship. The next day everyone continued on with life. The three remaining Musketeers still fish for tarpon at Cow Creek but with a renewed respect for nature and her wonders.

Madeline had given Mora her distance for awhile. Finally she could take no more. She had poured two tumblers of Bourbon and walked out onto the porch. She perched herself down so close to Mora that she was practically sitting in her lap. She handed one of the tumblers to Mora. "Twizzle," she said as she held her glass high to toast Mora, "I need you to write me down that stew recipe of yours. It seems to have worked out rather well."

Mora turned with tear reddened eyes and with a choked voice cried out, "No I didn't! I failed! Shamus is dead."

"Don't be a stupid Twizzle. Of course he was going to die. Everyone dies. There is no escaping it. He's dead but he's not gone." Mora was confused and Madeline could see it in her face.

Madeline exhaled heavily then took a sip from her tumbler, "You watched over Shamus for what, 50 something years?" Mora sniffled and just shook her head affirmatively. "Now he did have his faults but with you as his guardian, what do you expect?" Madeline chuckled a bit and nudged Mora's elbow with her own. It reminded Mora of the way Millie did the same thing when they first met. She couldn't control her tears. "Let's take a look at things. Shamus was no saint, that's for sure. So I don't believe he got a free pass to Heaven. He's also not the worst thing that ever walked the Earth so I'm fairly certain he's not burning at the moment." Mora's head flew up, "Oh good, you've finally caught on!" Madeline said with an air of superiority.

"He's here?" Mora asked, her voice almost squealing. Max's ear lifted and he looked at Mora with confusion in his eyes.

"Sort of, it's hard to explain. When you arrived here it wasn't on an express train," Madeline could never lose the fact that she was a New Yorker in her heart of hearts. Madeline nodded to Max, "I am pretty sure Max will let you know when he arrives."

Mora went back to work but she always had an eye fixed on Max. It didn't escape her eye that Max was now walking on all four legs more often lately. She'd look at Madeline for answers, "Some day," was the only answer she ever received.

Chapter 37

The waves rolled me up on the shores of Limbo, lost and confused. All I knew to do is what nature taught me over 50 years on Earth. I was an outdoorsman. I walked the beach, searching for signs. After a while I spotted tracks in the sand. I'd tracked animals most of my life but these made no sense to me. At times I saw three prints and at others four. All I knew to do was keep on the trail.

Mora was in her usual position sitting next to Max on the porch of Twizzle's. Max was enjoying being rubbed behind his ear when suddenly a scent struck his nose. Max sat up, then sprinted away from Mora. She wanted to follow but Madeline stopped her, "He'll be here soon enough. Give Max his time."

Max charged down the beach on all four legs. He left a trail of fur behind him in the air. I spotted movement on the beach in front of me. At first I was scared and wanted to flee, but a feeling of calm overtook me. In a flash Max barreled into me covering me with kisses. We rolled in the sand for what seemed like hours. Max was also picking up the scent of Camille off of me. His nose was sniffing every inch of me enjoying the smells of home. I was covered in dog drool and hair and it was the best I'd felt in a very long time. After Max had received his immediate fill of hugs and kisses he started to run back down the beach. He'd go about 50 yards and then run back to me, placing his full weight against my leg the way he did shortly after having his leg removed. Then he'd take off again. I caught on that I should trust my friend and follow.

After one of the happiest walks of my life we arrived at a shack on the beach. It just had a certain familiar feel to it. It was Norm's and the Aft all rolled into one, and yet it was neither. Max ran up the stairs like he owned the place. At the top of the weather worn steps stood two women. One black haired lady with a white apron over her black dress and one blonde dressed in dungarees, flip flops and a Fore "N" Aft shirt. I followed Max up the stairs. The moment I touched the top stair the blonde engulfed me in a hug. Her arms where wrapped around my neck so tight I felt I was being strangled by a Boa Constrictor. She was crying and covering my shoulder in tears and snot. Between Mora and Max my shirt was in tatters. Her voice was muffled from her burying her head in my shoulder and her hysterical crying. I looked to the woman with the apron but I could tell she was on the verge of tears herself. She tried to say something but instead turned sharply and scurried into the building.

Once I was past the initial shock of being mauled by the blonde I began to get a feeling of familiarity. I held her away at arm's length studying her face. The only thing I recognized was the shirt. It was actually a collector's item back in the day, a "We Rocked Your Mothers" shirt. I was so confused I couldn't place this woman yet there was something about her. I felt like I should know her.

The woman in the black dress reemerged in the doorway. "Shamus, my name is Madeline and this slobbering Twizzle is Mora. I think you should come inside; we need to have a little talk. Once we were inside, Madeline hung a sign on the door stating the place was "Closed for the holiday." I sat at a table by the bar, Max was by my side. This place had a strangely familiar feel to it. There were concert shirts from the Stones' tours, Stevie Ray Vaughan and ZZ Top in frames hung about the walls. I nodded to them and said I went to those shows. "I know," they said in unison.

I gave them a double take. Madeline said, "Pour yourself a beer, you're gonna need it."

I figured, "What the hell," and walked over to the bar. I know I'm dead if my boy Max is sitting with me. I just can't figure out who these two are. As I grabbed the beer tap I look down at the coppertop bar. Each one of the coins pressed into the bar top represents a place I'd visited. I'd even forgotten about a place or two but it was all coming back to me after seeing the coins. Mora stood up and just blurted out, "Shamus, I'm your guardian angel."

I took a moment to digest what she had just said. Lifted the beer stein to my lips and took a swallow. Memories of my last hours on Earth flooded back into my mind. "Well then you're fired! What, were you drinking on the job? Hell I was eaten by a shark! The thought of, I don't know, keeping me on dry land, never occurred to you?" Mora gave me a look that said if I wasn't already dead she'd kill me.

"Keep you on dry land? I've been trying to do that your entire life, you idiot!" Mora then turned to Madeline, "Dry land, now he wants to be on dry land. It would have been easier to keep a fish on dry land compared to you!" Madeline just sat there laughing until tears rolled down her cheeks. Her laughter became so infectious Mora and I joined in.

Madeline suggested we all sit down and eat. I hadn't felt hungry. The moment Madeline suggest food I started to smell linguine and clam sauce and said "I could eat."

"Oh yeah, he's one of ours for sure!" Madeline chuckled then stood and headed for the kitchen.

Before the swinging door stopped she was back through them with a huge bowl of pasta and plates for all of us, including Max. I reached over and grabbed him by his jowls and gave him a loving shake. "Still a big grubber, huh boy?" Through the course of the meal Madeline explained things to me. These women knew intimate details about events I'd forgotten about. Madeline did most of the talking. Mora was quiet and just kept looking at me and rubbing my forearm. It was like she was touching me to see if I was real.

When we emptied the bowl of linguine and all the dishes had been cleared from the table the stories of Shamus continued. I kept asking questions to see if I could catch them on some detail. I finally asked, "What song did Camille walk down the aisle to at our wedding?" Max just started barking like crazy then. I thought it was because I mentioned Camille.

Madeline turned to him and said, "Great idea."

I turned to Mora about to ask if Madeline knew what Max was saying.

Mora rolled her eyes and said, "Don't ask, I can't explain it, she just does things."

Madeline walked over to the jukebox and pressed some buttons.

My ears picked up the haunting sounds of violins playing the first notes from Etta James' "At Last." Madeline suggested Mora and I dance to it. It's a great song, but it belongs to Camille and me.

Madeline reminded me about "Death do us part," and even Max chimed in with a bark or two. "Believe me, it's OK," Madeline explained.

As Mora and I danced to "At Last," memories of my life and times started to fill my mind. I didn't really feel my dancing partner and the music sounded very far away. My memories were as clear to me as the moment I had lived them. Every sound, smell and taste was vivid. There was one thing different in every memory. The woman I was now dancing with was in every scene. Always somewhere in the background, but she could be seen. Good memories or bad, she was there. I started to realize we were holding each other very tight. After the music stopped Mora held on. I let go of her and cupped her face in my hands and said, "Thank you, I had a great time," I wasn't just talking about the dance and the tears on her cheeks told me she knew it.

We all walked back to the bar. I looked at Madeline and said, "There were so many times in my life people would say I was crazy. But I was never scared or crazy. Don't get me wrong, I had plenty of butterflies in my stomach. Folks would question me about my skydiving, kayaking and hunting or scuba diving."

Madeline shot me a look and said under her breathe, "Let's not bring up the scuba right now."

"It was great a great life. Camping, hunting and fishing. The places I've seen. My wife, family and friends," Max nudged against my leg, "Pets, too," I included.

"Kind of like a big happy stew," Mora said while giving Madeline a smug look.

Madeline just exhaled deeply and called Mora a "Twizzle".

Chapter 38

The room was getting small with Mora holding on to one side of me and Max pressed up on the other. I excused myself and took a walk on the beach. I was able to leave Mora back at Twizzle's with Madeline's help but Max wouldn't listen and was right by my side. Madeline explained to Mora that she needed to give me some space.

"I can't explain it I just have this need to hold on to him." Mora said fighting to find the words that fit her feelings.

"Your bond to him was broken the moment he died. You feel the loss of his presence."

"Is this how you felt the night you lost Vinny and me?" Mora questioned.

"It is how every guardian has felt at the end of their duty. It is the reason why I have a bond with Max. He lost Shamus and Camille the day they relieved his suffering," Madeline stopped, unable to speak with her heart in her throat.

I sat on the sand with Max forcing his head under my arm so it would drape over his back, "You know, Luka does the same thing" Max answered with a low growl. I thought about Camille and Luka and was crushed by the feeling of loss. Max knew what to do. He just leaned all his weight against me. I could smell Camille's perfume on his fur and the feeling subsided. Anytime I ever started to feel that sense of loss he would lean against me. I stayed on the shoreline for quite some time before I decided to head back.

Entering Twizzle's I was again overwhelmed by the sight of my life covering the walls and the shelves behind the bar. It was if Ralph Edwards had stalked you your entire life. I helped myself to a Romeo and Julieta from a humidor on a glass shelf behind the bar. "Oh no, I'm not putting up with two cigar smokers in here. Take that outside right now Shamus!"

As I was being ushered out the door I hit Madeline with classic bar line, "I've been thrown out of better establishments than this!" When I returned, I noticed that the "*Closed for the Holiday*" sign was down.

Twizzle's was open for business. Mora was bursting at the seams to show me off to all her new friends. The joint was jumping, people were lined up three deep at the bar. I know the party was for me but it's very strange to be at a party were everyone knows all about you yet you don't know anyone. I did relax after a while and soon realized that most of the folks at Twizzle's were seafaring folk. Everyone was toasting me and slapping me on the back. All except this old man dressed in pirate garb. I turned and whispered into Mora's ear, "What's the story with the old guy dressed like a pirate? Why is he staring at us like that?"

"Oh, he and Max had a small misunderstanding a while back and he's keeping his distance."

"Max didn't eat his parrot, did he?"

Mora stopped for a moment then started laughing, "The Love Bird incident all over again? No, nothing at all like that. He was just in a sour mood the day you..." Mora quickly paused not wanting to mention Camille's name. She knew the wound was too fresh, "You brought Luka home. Old Pierre, there, was just in the wrong place at the wrong time."

I looked down at Max. He looked up and just smiled.

At first I was at a major disadvantage trying to swap stories. I'd listen to their tales but if I started one of my own they already knew it from Mora. I did find a few faults in Mora's telling of certain stories. Once I told my side of the story everyone was laughing and making good natured fun of Mora. She was in bliss and had finally had that feeling of family that she'd known from Gunning's. Madeline stood in the doorway of the kitchen and just smiled while watching Mora.

Chapter 39

The next day I was sitting on the top step with my two shadows flanking me. Mora and I were sharing a cigar and coffee. Not a word was said. Words weren't needed between us. Her guardian bond may have been broken but we shared a life. We had memories and words really weren't needed. Mora turned her head back towards the front door and said, "What?" She turned her attention back to Max and I but then suddenly spun around said, "What do you need, Madeline?"

Madeline was wiping her hands upon her apron when she pushed open the screen door from the kitchen onto the porch, "What do you need, Twizzle?"

"I don't need anything, you called me."

"I didn't call you," she stopped before finishing her sentence. Her face was blank.

"Mora, you heard your name called?"

"Yeah, didn't you just call me?" Mora suddenly realized who was calling. Her name was being read aloud from the book of souls and it was her time to leave Limbo.

I looked at Madeline like a confused foreigner. She said, "Say your goodbyes Shamus, Mora's been called home." Clarity entered my mind and I knew she was leaving forever.

As I was standing to speak, a big Indian motorcycle came roaring up to the steps. Before the rider could unsaddle himself, Madeline rushed to Mora and hugged her hard. Mora was crying but Madeline held herself together. Madeline knew everything had its time and place. This was the place and it was Mora's time. There's no fighting it. Time was short and I had to say goodbye. The only thing that came to me was to cup her face and kiss her. I whispered, "Thank You."

Max's tail was beating against the railing so hard I thought he'd knock it free from the stairs. Mora's tears rained on Max's head as she bent over to kiss him goodbye, "Watch out for them," she told Max as she nodded in Madeline's and my direction.

The rider of the Indian removed his helmet and spoke, "Mora, it's time."

When Mora heard his voice she spun around and looked down at him from the porch. Her eyes opened wide and she screamed, "Connor!" her feet never touched the last few steps as she leapt into his arms. Connor kissed her and said, "You've owed me that kiss for a very long time."

Mora ran back up the stairs for one last kiss from each of us. She looked at me and asked what I would do next. "That's easy," I patted Max's head, "We'll, wait for Camille besides I think a bartending gig just opened up."

Madeline thought to herself, "Shamus and Camille, huh? I might have use for a couple like that." Max growled, Madeline looked him in the eye and said, "Like I could have those two and not you."

Then she returned to her kitchen not wanting to see Mora ride away.

Connor yelled up to Mora, "Mora, we got to go! Millie says the pasta's getting funny!" Connor had no idea what Millie meant but Mora turned and ran down the steps to the big Indian. Connor kick started the bike and the pipes roared. Connor and Mora rode away from Twizzle's with Mora's arms wrapped around his waist, her head on his shoulder, her blonde hair blowing in the wind and tears of joy and sorrow running down her face. Max ran after them but I knew he'd never catch them, so I turned to go back into Twizzle's, where I'd wait for him and Camille.

The End

ABOUT THE AUTHOR

The author lives in Sarasota, Florida with his wife Camille and their Golden Retriever, Luka. He spends most of his free time in the pursuit of Tarpon, Snook and Redfish, when he's not hunting.

Made in the USA
Charleston, SC
01 December 2011